THE BAYOU BULLETIN

Philip Delacroix Faces Murder Charge!

Longtime senator Philip Delacroix will face murder charges in relation to a crime committed in this area more than sixty years ago. As a result of a recent statement by local herbalist Desiree Boudreaux, the senator has been placed at the scene of the murder of Camille Gravier, who, some thought, had lost her life in a drowning mishap on Delacroix property. But now Ms. Boudreaux has come forward with the admission that she actually witnessed the crime! Defense attorneys for Senator Delacroix have been quick to dismiss Ms. Boudreaux's claim as a bid for revenge for the wrongs she believes have been perpetrated on her family by the Delacroix.

Byron Calhoun, who heads up the prosecution team, is confident that Ms. Boudreaux's testimony, along with that of her grandson, former police detective Jackson Boudreaux, will see justice served at long last.

The jury that heard testimony during the original trial held in this case in 1938 found Rafael Perdido, a drifter who worked cutting timber for the Delacroix family, guilty of the crime. Mr. Perdido was remanded to the Louisiana State Penitentiary in Angola, where he was killed by a fellow inmate while awaiting an appeal.

Penny Richards is acknowledged
as the author of this work.

ISBN 0-373-82572-2

DESIRES AND DECEPTIONS

DELTA JUSTICE

Desires and Deceptions

PENNY RICHARDS

Harlequin Books

TORONTO • NEW YORK • LONDON
AMSTERDAM • PARIS • SYDNEY • HAMBURG
STOCKHOLM • ATHENS • TOKYO • MILAN
MADRID • WARSAW • BUDAPEST • AUCKLAND

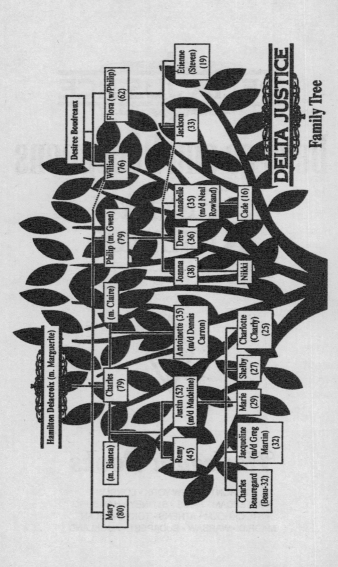

DELTA JUSTICE

Family Tree

Hamilton Delacroix (m. Marguerite)

Mary (80) — (m. Bianca)

Charles (79) — (m. Claire)

Desiree Boudreaux

William (76)

Flora (w/Philip) (62)

Philip (m. Gwen) (79)

Étienne (Steven) (19)

Jackson (33)

Remy (45)

Justin (52) (m/d Madeline)

Antoinette (35) (m/d Dennis Carron)

Joanna (38)

Drew (36)

Annabelle (35) (m/d Neal Rowland)

Cade (16)

Nikki

Charles Beauregard (Beau-32)

Jacqueline (m/d Greg Martin) (32)

Marie (29)

Shelby (27)

Charlotte (Charty) (25)

CAST OF CHARACTERS

Philip Delacroix—twin brother of Charles and a longtime senator, whose relentless desire for power leads to the lies, manipulations and deceptions that finally catch up with him.

Mary Delacroix—the Delacroix family matriarch. Her desire to keep her family intact prompted her to give up everything dear and abandon the man she loved.

William Delacroix—a retired priest and the youngest Delacroix brother, whose youthful desires led to his own sinful secret.

Rafael Perdido—Mary Delacroix's one true love. An "expendable" drifter, Rafe came to Bayou Beltane sixty years ago and wound up going to prison and ultimately his death for a murder he didn't commit. His only desire was to make Mary Delacroix happy.

Desiree Boudreaux—an herbalist whose life is bound to the Delacroix in many ways, ways no one suspects. A powerful man's desire left her no recourse but to deceive.

Flora Boudreaux—Jackson's mother and Philip's former mistress. Philip's desire for revenge sends Flora toppling over the edge of sanity. Her desire? To take Philip with her.

Dear Reader,

Writing in a continuity series is always challenging. Even with a reference "bible," you never know what twists and turns the stories by your fellow collaborators may take. What a pleasant surprise—and sometimes a pain—when it's something you hadn't expected! For an old warhorse writer like me, it's a challenge to come into the fray with certain characters' backgrounds and personalities already carved in stone and seeing what I can do with what's gone before. Maybe that's why I like to create continuity stories—and I must like to, since this is my third series.

With the added dimension of a sixty-year-old murder case threading through all twelve books in the series, a new bit of information, a new character, a new development keeps the action spiraling up toward the resolution.

I wanted to write the last book because I wanted to tell Mary and Rafe's love story, and because, mystery buff that I am, I wanted to write the murder scene. As usual, things happened that I had no idea would happen. People and situations weren't always who or what I thought they were. Questions to other writers led to new and better solutions—or in this case, resolutions. At times, the things the characters did and said surprised even me. As we say in Louisiana, that's the *lagniappe*—something extra—of writing that makes the hair-pulling and nail-biting worth the effort. Or maybe that's the real meaning of "poetic justice."

I hope you've enjoyed the Delta Justice series and that you are pleased and surprised by some of the twists and turns this final story takes.

Happy reading!

Penny Richards

This book is dedicated to Marsha Zinberg.
Thanks for offering me the challenges of working on a
continuity series and for giving me the latitude to write the
books I want to write, and for being such a pleasure to work
with. And for Sandy—my partner in crime (or is that
justice?), sounding board and sometimes armchair shrink.
I just love workin' with your cowboy heroes!

Thanks to Brenda, Susan, both Margarets and everyone else
involved for all their hard work on the series.

Finally, my deepest gratitude to all the Delta Justice authors,
who were so willing to help me work out the kinks—
talented, wonderful ladies ALL!

PROLOGUE

June 1938

"FORGIVE ME, FATHER, for I have sinned." The words, spoken in a hushed voice, echoed off the walls of the cramped confessional.

In the course of fifty years, the priest had grown indifferent to admissions of petty failings, though he was still sick at heart at hearing more serious disclosures of wickedness and immorality. He drowsed now, while the sinner—a parishioner whose voice he knew well—told the familiar and tedious tale of youthful covetousness, debauchery and fornication.

The word *killed* banished the priest's lethargy.

His forehead puckered in a frown as he sat straighter, listening, torn between horror, despair and the desire to clamp his hands over his ears and shut out the sound of the voice.

Long after the transgressor left, spirit cleansed, sins absolved, penance pronounced, the priest sat slumped against the confessional wall. Though he was far from perfect to begin with, he found his mind saturated with painful secrets of others' trespasses, his soul burdened with sins he had not committed. Now this! This tale of murder was too much to bear, even with God's help. The human part of him whispered that he should go to the police and see justice done. The priestly part reminded him that the confessional was sacrosanct.

The old man pushed himself to his feet, longing for a glass of sherry, wishing—as he often did of late—that he'd gone into teaching instead of the priesthood. It was time to retire. He'd given God the best years of his life. Perhaps, if he was lucky, the Almighty would grant him a few more, a thank-you for a lifetime of dedicated service. Time he could spend trying to forget the offenses he'd heard and reclaim a measure of peace.

CHAPTER ONE

ON THE MORNING BEFORE his twin brother, Philip, was to be tried for the murder of Camille Gravier, an event that had taken place some sixty years before, Charles Delacroix sat in his bedroom at Riverwood, awaiting the appearance of two sons, four of his five grandchildren, his brother William and his sister, Mary. Some in-laws would be there, too. Everyone was coming for a family breakfast except Antoinette, who was dealing with a troubled pregnancy and didn't feel up to making the trip from New Orleans. Charles had unburdened himself to her on the phone the night before.

He'd summoned his loved ones because the powerful and legendary Delacroix dynasty was falling apart. Like a tract house built with inferior materials, the Delacroix legacy was based on self-delusions, desires and deceptions. Tomorrow, events would begin unfolding that would send what remained of that house of cards tumbling. In retrospect, Charles was surprised it had stood so long.

During the past few months, the family had learned that nothing in the past had happened as they'd believed and no one was what he or she seemed, including Charles himself. Even Mary, that paragon of virtue and integrity, had lived a lie for more than half her life.

When Mary had collapsed during that first trial, sixty years ago, Charles and his brothers had been told it was due to the stress of losing her best friend. To help her get over her grief, she would be going to Europe for an extended vacation.

A lie. Mary had gone no farther than a convent at Baton Rouge, where she'd given birth to a daughter, the child of Rafael Perdido, the man convicted of the crime. Mary and Charles's father, Hamilton Delacroix, and Judge Neville Alvarez had arranged for Mary's child to be adopted by the judge's mistress's sister. For all these years, no one else had suspected a thing.

Not once in all these years had Mary admitted to her affair. Not when she'd told him of seeing Rafe and Camille together in Bayou Beltane; not when the police had asked what Rafe was doing on Delacroix property the night of the murder. What hurt wasn't that Mary was as human as the rest of them, but that she hadn't trusted any of them with her secret—not even William.

Ah, William. Another lie. Another deception. William the Good wasn't a Delacroix at all. The brother Charles loved and admired, who with his patience and wisdom had helped the family through many ups and downs of life, was actually Desiree Boudreaux's son, half brother to that icon of wickedness, Flora. Since being told the truth some weeks ago, William refused to speak to anyone about his feelings on the matter. Still, he seemed to have taken the news with his customary equanimity, at least on the surface. A priest, William was perhaps best equipped to deal with blows such as the ones they'd all received lately.

Then there was Philip's unshakable story that he'd been with his buddies gigging frogs while Camille was being drowned by Rafe Perdido, a story Charles had never been convinced was the truth and which Desiree Boudreaux had recently confirmed was a lie.

Which, Charles thought, brought the whole sordid tale full circle with the matter of his own subterfuge. When he had taken the stand those many years ago, Charles hadn't told the whole truth about what transpired the night of the murder. He had lived the bulk of his life wondering if an innocent man had been sent to prison, where he died in a fight, because of his own fear of being implicated in Camille's death.

He raked a trembling hand through his thinning hair. Everything his family had ever believed him to be—decent, honorable, trustworthy—would soon be made a lie. The only thing he could do was tell the truth before they heard it dragged out of him on the witness stand. The pedestal they'd placed him on would be shattered, but he might find it easier to face himself in the mirror each morning.

HALF AN HOUR LATER, Charles's gaze moved from one troubled face to the other. They were all gathered around the polished walnut table that graced Riverwood's dining room, waiting and wondering what was so important that they'd been called to meet on a weekday morning.

"What's this all about, Dad?" fifty-three-year-old Justin asked.

Charles looked at his older son with love and admiration. A federal judge, Justin was everything he believed Charles to be. If there were any skeletons in Justin Delacroix's closet, they were Halloween decorations left over from his five children's childhood days.

Feeling the full weight of his eighty years, Charles straightened his shoulders and cleared his throat. "It's about the trial." He was dismayed to hear the quaver in his voice.

"What about it?" This question came from Charles's younger son, Remy, another man of character and honor.

Charles cleared his throat again. "Since Desiree Boudreaux came forward after the election last November with her accusations against your uncle Philip, I know you've all been wondering what really happened the night Camille Gravier was murdered. You know what kind of man your uncle Philip is—driven, ambitious...."

Charles's voice trailed away. There was more he could say about Philip, but he was, after all, his twin brother. "I also know that despite Desiree's story about what happened that night, you find it hard to believe your uncle capable of murder, and—"

"Sorry, Granddad," Justin's daughter Shelby interrupted, "I know he's your brother, but to be honest, it doesn't sound so far-fetched to me."

Justin silenced his outspoken daughter with a quelling look.

"In a way, that's why I asked you to come," Charles said.

"*You* think Uncle Philip really is guilty?" Beau, Justin's only son, asked.

"I'm not saying that," Charles prevaricated. "I'm saying that Byron Calhoun didn't become the best prosecutor in the state by letting small things get by him. He'll pull out all the stops and dig up every bit of evidence he can. This trial won't be the travesty of justice the first one was."

Looking insulted that anything his family was connected with could be less than honorable, Justin demanded, "What do you mean, travesty of justice?"

"First," Charles said, ticking off points on his fingers, "the shoddy reporting in the *Beltane Bugle* pretty well summed up the biased attitude of the entire community toward Rafe Perdido. Everyone considered him a no-account drifter, no one of importance. That would never happen today, or Perdido would be screaming about his civil rights being violated."

"True," Justin agreed.

"Second, my father should never have been allowed to defend Perdido, no matter what Mary wanted."

"Why?" Shelby's sister Marie asked, sweeping back her dramatic dark curls with one hand. She'd driven all the way out from New Orleans to attend the breakfast gathering, leaving an assistant to open her shop.

"Conflict of interest," Charly answered promptly. Justin's youngest daughter, now a private investigator, had briefly been a cop. "Two of Great-grandfather Hamilton's children were at—or near—the scene."

"Right, Charly," Justin agreed. He rubbed his chin thoughtfully. "The fact that he was allowed to defend Rafe is a testimony to the trusting nature of Bayou Beltane's populace, and as well as evidence of Delacroix power."

Charles's smile was more grim than amused. "Exactly. Add to that the notes about Judge Alvarez's rulings Shelby found in my father's files, the fact that this was the only murder trial my father ever lost, and the things Alvarez's mistress wrote in her diary, and it's clear that there was a miscarriage of justice."

Justin blew out a troubled breath. "I've been over every scrap of information I can dig up about the trial, and you're right. Something just doesn't add up about this whole thing, and maybe Philip is the missing quotient."

"Wait a minute!" Justin's oldest daughter, Jax, said. Elegant as always, she held her tiny daughter, sound asleep, in her arms. "We girls have already had this discussion, Granddad. You're implying Rafael Perdido might have been innocent, but if that's true, and if Desiree is lying about Uncle Philip, doesn't that make you the guilty party?"

Charles drew in a steadying breath and plunged on before he lost his courage. "I didn't kill Camille, but I'm not without guilt in the matter. I called you all here because I want to—what is it you say nowadays?—come clean.''

''Come clean? Good grief, Dad, what do you mean?'' Justin asked, clearly horrified at the idea of his father being involved in a murder—no matter how small that involvement might be.

''I don't want to believe the worst about my brother.'' Charles's pain was clear to everyone in the room. ''But I never was convinced Philip was where he said he was the night of the murder. When I took the stand, however, I didn't say anything to anyone about my doubts. I don't want to believe Philip is guilty, but if he is, my silence might have cost a man his life.''

''Why didn't you believe him?'' Justin asked.

''Just a feeling,'' Charles said, being deliberately evasive.

''Why didn't you say something?''

Charles sighed. ''It's no real excuse, but I was twenty years old and scared. Camille and I had argued. Like everyone else in Bayou Beltane, I found it easier to let Rafe Perdido take the blame than to take the chance my brother would be sent to prison.''

Shelby shook her head. ''Why do I get the feeling there's something else you aren't telling us?''

Charles favored his strong-willed granddaughter with a wry smile and uttered a small prayer for strength to say what needed to be said. ''Very astute of you, Shelby. There is more.''

Charles let his gaze move from one face to the other. ''Word is out that Desiree claims Camille said she was pregnant. I knew that at the time of the first trial.''

''So?'' Marie said.

''So when my father asked why Camille and I were at the lake, I told him we were there spooning. I didn't say anything about her telling me she was pregnant or that the baby she carried could have been mine.''

DRAWN BY MEMORIES that would not be denied, Mary Delacroix stepped onto the footbridge that spanned the bayou separating the main house from the more modest dwelling she'd lived in for so long and shared with William ever since his retirement. Not trusting her trembling legs, she clung to the handrail. Louisiana had been blessed with an inordinate amount of rain the past few weeks, and the murky waters gurgled past, sweeping along twigs and debris in their eagerness to get to the sea.

Across the bridge, Mary left the azalea-bordered path leading to Riverwood, Charles's house, and started toward the huge magnolia tree that grew at the back. She picked her way carefully. Slipping on the wet grass or tripping over a root might send her tumbling and shatter bones grown brittle with age.

She would celebrate her eighty-second birthday come the twenty-sixth of July, yet Mary remembered clearly the sultry summer days of her childhood, when she and her family had divided their time between Belle Terre, where her brother Philip now lived, and this place.

Her childhood had been a time of innocence, blessed as she'd been with a doting father and a loving mother. Mary recalled long, lazy days redolent with the aroma of fresh-cut grass and the spicy scent of roses, days alive with the drone of bees, the murmur of the bayou. Even now she seemed to hear girlish shrieks and giggles from her and Camille, mingling with her brothers' raucous laughter as they'd played childhood games beneath the great magnolia's outstretched arms.

When she'd grown older, the shady site had become her sanctuary. There, a young woman burdened with plainness, plus a load of responsibilities that had fallen on her narrow shoulders when her mother died, could hide away with a book and forget—at least for a while—that even though her family was one of the wealthiest and most powerful in the state, she had slim matrimonial prospects.

Not until Rafe had come along.

Mary's heart, still fragile from the severe attack she'd suffered in November—her second—ached now with the pain of remembrances. She ducked and pushed through an opening in the stiff, waxy foliage. A twig caught at her hair, painfully tugging a drift of snowy white from its pins. She stood beneath the protective limbs and turned her face upward, as she had so often in the past. Sunlight filtered through the dense leaves of the old tree, spattering the fallen leaves and decaying seed pods underfoot with splashes of golden light. Rafe had been the sunshine in her life, a much needed brilliance snuffed out before it reached its brightest glow.

Ignoring the protests of her arthritic joints, Mary sat down at the base of the tree, leaned against its massive trunk and drew her knees against her chest, the way she had as a young girl. Rumored to be the oldest of its kind in the state, the tree was so huge it took four adults holding hands to encircle its trunk. Someone at some time had trimmed away the lower limbs. Now the sprawling branches above her head dipped toward the ground, as if they'd grown too heavy to bear their own weight, and then climbed upward again. Many an unsuspecting viewer thought the single magnolia was a cluster of trees.

It was strange how the eye sometimes registered objects as being entirely different from what they were. Stranger still how the mind could distort impressions and facts and convince a person of something he or she knew to be impossible. Could sift through supposed truths and base decisions on apparent logic, disregarding the whisperings of the heart.

The Delacroix family was like the great magnolia: it appeared to be something it wasn't. Mary realized that. Like her brother Charles, she couldn't deny it any longer. None of them could. That luxury had been snatched away back in November, when Desiree Boudreaux had gone to the authorities with her version of what had happened in the woods the night Camille Gravier was killed. Deep in her heart, Mary knew that even if Desiree hadn't come forward, fate—or perhaps God—had decided it was time to end it, time to bring all the Delacroix secrets to light. Charles had started with his confession earlier that morning.

Who would have thought that the files dealing with Mary's father's last case could stir up such a need to ferret out the truth in her niece Shelby? Or that yellowing letters hidden behind a mirror in Texas, and a young man's promise of vengeance, could set a series of events in motion that would shake the very foundations of a family? Who would have believed that lovers' pillow talk, transcribed in an old diary, held information that could hurt so many people after so many years, or that it would come to light simply because a young woman was hungry for information about the parentage of her adopted aunt? Who could have grasped that these unrelated, seemingly innocent events were connected to the horror of one fateful night?

Whether the happenings were a series of bizarre coincidences or God's plan for retribution was of little significance. Tomorrow Philip would go on trial for the murder of Camille Gravier. Philip—successful corporate attorney and long-time state senator. The brother who, as a child, Mary had felt was not so bad as he was misunderstood.

It had been more than four months since Katherine Beaufort and Philip's son, Drew, had translated the diary that once belonged to Neville Alvarez's mistress. Neville Alvarez was the judge who had presided over Mary's father's last trial, the only murder trial Hamilton Delacroix had ever lost. The same trial where Rafael Perdido, Mary's first and only love, had been sentenced to death for Camille's murder.

Patrice Forêt's diary seemed to incriminate Philip, but there had been no concrete proof of his guilt, not even with Jackson Boudreaux's admission that it was Philip who had ordered him to search Katherine's apartment to find and bring back the damning journal. Though everyone, including police chief Jake Trahan, believed Philip had been involved in Camille's death, there had been nothing concrete to link him to the murder.

Then Desiree Boudreaux had had a vision, apparently—one that motivated her to come forward to tell what she'd seen that night in the woods. It was the right thing to do, she said, something she should have done long ago. It was time for justice—if there was such a thing anymore—to be exacted.

Mary's heart clenched in pain. She tensed, waiting for the ache to grow and spread, to wipe out the hurtful memories of lies and betrayal as well as what was left of her mortal life. Instead, the pain eased, and she was left with nothing but the anguish of the past.

Though their reasons were different, she and her brothers had shoved memories of that night into the deepest, most inaccessible corner of their minds. Unfortunately, doing so didn't mean the past was truly buried, any more than the single magnolia looking like a cluster of trees made it so. The choices they'd made back then had affected all their lives, and now the truth would come out for the whole world to see. Not even Delacroix power and wealth could stop it this time.

Mary let her head fall forward onto her updrawn knees. It was time to face the past and lay it to rest. Time to own up to her own weaknesses and mistakes. Time to take out

every remembrance of her twenty-second summer and look
at it once more before she finally joined Rafe in the land
of endless days....

March 1938

IT WAS SPRING, and everything was burgeoning, from the
plants pushing through the rich ground to the Thoroughbred mare her father had purchased in the fall. Three young
rabbits had scampered about the lawn this morning, inves-
tigating their big, new world while Mary and her father
laughed at their antics. Several days earlier, five baby rob-
ins had hatched in the nest built in the gardenia bush outside her bedroom window. Mary had spent hours watching
heads that seemed too large for their featherless bodies bob
on frail necks as they opened their beaks wide and
screamed for food.

Unlike at Belle Terre, the big house, there was no per-
manent help at Riverwood, only a woman who cleaned
two days a week. The situation suited Mary just fine. She
loved taking care of her father and brothers, especially at
the smaller, more informal place they often used during
the hotter months. More, she felt it was her duty since their
mother had died.

Even though she had work to do, she found herself vulnerable to the siren song of the season, catching herself
daydreaming or sighing for no reason. After lunch, she had
washed, dried and put away the dishes, then baked a pie
that was now cooling on the counter. Knowing Mary's
brother William was home from seminary for the weekend
and was partial to fresh catfish, Desiree Boudreaux had
brought a mess for their evening meal. William had
cleaned them, and they now lay in the coolness of the
icebox, awaiting a coat of cornmeal and a pan of hot
grease.

Secure in the knowledge that the evening meal was well underway, Mary had succumbed to the lure of the outdoors and brought her novel outside in the hope that she could forget the dull routine of her own life while vicariously enjoying Scarlett's scandals.

Now the dull thud of an ax on wood shattered Mary's concentration, which was poor at best. The man her father had hired to cut up a dead oak that had fallen across the path at the side of the house must have arrived. With a sigh, she closed her book and laid it in her lap, knowing it would be impossible to keep her mind on the story. She had spring fever, no doubt about it. The trials of Rhett and Scarlett only sharpened her sense of loneliness.

Mary got to her feet and shook out the quilt she'd spread beneath the magnolia. Draping it over her arm and clutching the book to her breasts, she stepped from under the tree.

The man her father had hired stood with his back to her, shirtless. His shoulders were broad and tapered to a narrow waist. As she watched, he lifted the ax above his head and swung it downward. It sliced through the air, propelled by muscles that corded and rippled beneath tanned skin sheathed with a sheen of perspiration that glistened in the sun.

Mary clutched the quilt tighter in an effort to slow the sudden rapid beating of her heart. Her breasts felt heavy and tingled in a most curious way. The thunk of the blade against the wood roused her from her trance.

Lust, she realized with a sudden rush of shame that sent a hot blush to her cheeks. She was lusting after a man whose face she hadn't even seen. But if there was a God, and Mary believed deeply that there was, the stranger's face could only be one of manly beauty.

Contain yourself, Mare. It isn't as if you've never seen a man without his shirt before.

Indeed she had, but only her brothers, and they didn't count. The ax swung downward again and again. Wood chips flew. Mary watched, mesmerized by the fascinating display of muscle and sinew and masculine grace. The young man's dark hair looked in dire need of a pair of scissors. She was shocked to realize she longed to touch the damp strands that clung like wet commas to his nape, to trail her fingertips down the line of his spine to the hollow half hidden by the loose waist of his denim trousers.

After a while, he buried the blade in the freshly cut groove. It was only when he reached for the faded chambray shirt draped over a nearby bush and wiped his perspiring face that Mary realized she was staring and had been for some time. She half turned, intent on slipping away unnoticed, but the movement must have caught his peripheral vision, and he spun around on the toe of one scuffed work boot.

She gasped. She'd been right: in a purely masculine way, he was beautiful. Rough fingers had been combed through his sweat-dampened hair, scraping it back to reveal the lines of a finely sculpted face. His jaw was strong, his nose bold and aquiline, his eyebrows twin slashes of dark brown over deep-set eyes of an indeterminate color. Quite simply, he was the most gorgeous man she had ever seen.

Mary's second reaction, which she barely managed to stifle, was the age-old and purely feminine urge to pat her wayward hair into place. She found herself wishing she'd changed her dress when she'd finished cooking and cleaning. Wished her hair wasn't so curly and untamed. Wished her eyes weren't set so far apart and her nose wasn't so big. Wished she were as pretty as her friend Camille. But she wasn't and would never be.

Without warning, the young man smiled and started for-

ward. Mary was stunned, not only at the way the sudden
flash of white teeth in his olive-skinned face made her
heart beat faster, but at his lack of self-consciousness. Any
man of breeding would have donned his shirt before approaching a female. He stopped a few feet from her.

It gave Mary a ridiculous feeling of pleasure to note that
as tall as she was, he was taller.

"Hello. I'm Rafe Perdido. And you are...?" He let the
question trail away, let his bold gaze rake over her from
her head to the tips of her worn shoes.

His voice was low, husky, as warm as the gleam in his
eyes. For a moment Mary's mind was a complete blank.
"M-Mary," she said at last.

"M-Mary," he repeated solemnly. He nodded. Grinned.
"Unusual, but it fits." With three brothers, Mary knew
teasing when she heard it.

He gestured toward the quilt and book. "Slacking off?"

"What?" she asked.

"It looks as if you've been hiding out to keep from
doing your chores." He made a tsking sound. "What will
Mr. Delacroix say?"

Suddenly, Mary realized Rafe Perdido thought she was
one of the servants. She swallowed a sharp reply, uncertain
whether to be embarrassed or offended. Then it occurred
to her that this man—this *handsome* man—was talking to
her as if she were his equal. More important, he acted as
if he enjoyed talking to her. There was no harm in teasing
him back a bit, was there?

"As long as Mr. Delacroix's dinner is on time and the
house is clean, he doesn't care what I do with my spare
time," she said truthfully. Never mind that Mary, who
knew how her mother had liked things done, oversaw the
care and maintenance of Riverwood, and Gracie, who'd
come to work for her father soon after Marguerite Delacroix died, did most of the actual cleaning.

"You like working for him, then?"

Mary lifted one shoulder in a careless shrug. "As well as anyone, I suppose. What about you?" she asked, hoping to shift the conversation to a safer topic and learn more about the man standing in front of her. "Do you like working for him?"

"He only hired me this morning. Ask me again in a week or so." He smiled again. "May I ask a favor, M-Mary?"

"Anything."

His eyes twinkled with mischief. "Mary, Mary, quite contrary! I do believe you're making a pass at me."

Only then did Mary realize how provocative her answer had been. Another of those bothersome blushes bloomed across her cheeks. She couldn't have replied if her life depended on it. She knew he was only teasing again, but she'd never been teased by a man before. She'd never had more than a casual date, and those few had been with young men who were clearly more interested in finding themselves a rich wife than in Mary Delacroix, the woman.

"It is an interesting offer, though," he said, the contemplative sound of his voice filling the silence spinning out between them. "I might just hold you to it in the future. Right now, all I need is something to drink."

Silently, Mary cursed herself for ten kinds of fool. She was behaving like a gauche, naive simpleton! Which, of course, she was. She struggled to gain control of herself.

"Water or lemonade? We have an icebox, so either will be good and cold."

"Lemonade sounds good."

"It is good," Mary said, knowing she made the best lemonade around. "I squeezed it fresh this morning." She gave him a quick smile. "I'll be back in a minute."

Pivoting on her toe, she turned and crossed the lawn with a lightness in her step that hadn't been there earlier.

Inside the shady kitchen, she dumped the quilt and her
book onto the oak table and hurried to the foyer to peer
into the cloudy mirror above the hall tree. She hardly recognized the woman staring back at her. Her oval face was
flushed with color. Excitement danced in her dark eyes.
Though there had been little enough to bring her joy as
she'd grown older, her mouth now wore the barest hint of
a smile, a smile she knew could grow ridiculously wide
with the least provocation.

She laid her palm against her hot cheek. Why, she
looked almost pretty! It occurred to her that, like the flowers springing up all around, she was blooming. All it had
taken was a little attention from Rafe Perdido.

Rafe! He was outside baking in the warm spring sunshine, waiting for her to bring him something to drink,
while she stood admiring herself in the mirror. What a dolt
she was!

Murmuring words she'd heard her brothers use, words
entirely unfit for the lady of the house, Mary scurried back
to the kitchen and drew the pitcher of lemonade from the
dark confines of the icebox. She retrieved a glass from the
cabinet over the porcelain sink her father had had installed
the year before and took the ice pick from the drawer. The
iceman had made a delivery earlier that morning, so there
was plenty of ice. She would chip some from the new
block to put in Rafe's drink. She knew from experience it
would be deliciously cold, immensely satisfying.

On an impulse, she took down an inlaid mahogany tray,
spread it with a new dish towel she'd made from a flower-
patterned flour sack, and set the glass of lemonade on it.
Then she cut a slice of the coconut pie she'd baked especially for her father and put it on a gold-rimmed plate,
rounding out her offering with a fork and a freshly ironed
napkin. Satisfied that she'd done all she could to impress

Rafe Perdido, she picked up the tray and, pushing the screen door open with her hip, carried it outside.

"Pie, too?" he said, surprise in his dark eyes.

"It's coconut. I hope you like it."

"I've never had coconut," he confessed, taking the tray and setting it on the fallen tree. "It's too rich for my pocketbook." He wasn't self-conscious about the admission, just stating a fact. Mary watched his throat work as he took a long pull of the drink, then he lowered the glass. Smiled. "Very good lemonade."

"Thank you." To cover her confusion, she asked, "Did you just get into town?"

"You're welcome," he said, ignoring the question. "You're blushing. Again. Don't you ever talk to members of the opposite sex, M-Mary?"

Once again, Mary's color deepened. "Of course I do," she said tartly. "I have three brothers and a father. It's just that...living so far from town, I don't see many people outside the family."

Rafe nodded and picked up their conversation where he'd dropped it a moment earlier. "Actually, I've been around since fall."

When he didn't offer any more information, Mary asked, "Doing what?"

"This and that. I worked the cane fields down by Thibodaux and then filed a few horses' teeth at some of the Thoroughbred farms here and there." His lips curved sardonically. "I guess you could say I'm a jack-of-all-trades."

"What made you come to Bayou Beltane?" Mary asked.

Rafe shrugged. "Just drifting. I was ready for some different scenery. I like music, but I don't like the city. Bayou Beltane isn't too far from New Orleans." He cut into the pie, popped a bite into his mouth.

New Orleans. Mary loved New Orleans but didn't often get to go there. She wondered where Rafe went to listen to music.

"I don't know," he was saying thoughtfully. "Lately, I've been thinking maybe it's time to settle in one place and try to make something of myself."

The possibility of his staying in Bayou Beltane filled Mary with a quiet pleasure. "How did you meet Fa...uh, Mr. Delacroix?"

"Some other guys and I have been cutting that stand of hardwood timber over near Belle Terre. He came looking for someone to come cut up this fallen tree, and I volunteered." Rafe held a forkful of pie aloft. "Coconut pie is wonderful. Thanks for letting me sample your wares."

The words were innocent enough, but something about the way his gaze moved over her made Mary feel as if he'd made a personal—even improper—comment.

"Belle Terre is something, isn't it?" he said, shattering the sudden tension.

"It's a fine house," she agreed. "And very old."

"How old?"

"It was built before the Civil War by George Preston, a rich Yankee who came to New Orleans for a visit and fell in love with our Southern culture. He moved his family down, lock, stock and shingle."

"He was a lawyer?"

"Yes. Preston's son followed in his father's footsteps and became an attorney, too. When Mr. Delacroix was fourteen, he went to work for George Preston II, who had this house built. Mr. Delacroix had a taste for the law, and an aptitude as well. The younger Preston realized his potential, took him under his wing and financed his education."

"That was decent of him."

Mary nodded. "Evidently he was a fine, upstanding gentleman."

"How did Mr. Delacroix come to own the place?"

"When he passed the bar, he became a junior partner at Preston, Preston and Alvarez. The elder Mr. Preston retired. Mr. Alvarez became a judge."

"Neville Alvarez?" Rafe asked, a sharpness in his voice Mary hadn't heard before.

"Yes."

"He's a tough old bird," Rafe said. "From what I hear."

Judge Alvarez and his wife were friends of Mary's father, and she'd known them all her life. She felt obliged to set Rafe straight on the other man's character. "Mr. Delacroix says he's a hard judge, but just. And he knows the law."

"I didn't mean to ruffle your feathers," Rafe said. "Finish telling me about how Mr. Delacroix came to own both plantations."

Mary nodded. "After he became a partner, Mr. Delacroix helped build Preston and Delacroix into the best law firm in the state. He was building his own fortune, as well. George Preston II died fairly young, with no heirs. Both places came up for sale, and Hamilton Delacroix bought them."

Rafe polished off the last of the pie while Mary told her story. When she finished, he whistled. "So Hamilton Delacroix wasn't always rich?"

"No. He grew up a sharecropper's son. But he had a good mind, high standards, determination and goals."

"Why does he need two houses? Why not sell one of them?"

Mary thought about that for a moment. "I think he kept Belle Terre because owning it was a way to tell the world he had truly arrived. And Mrs. Delacroix always loved that house.''

Rafe's eyebrows lifted in question. ''Loved?''

''She died ten years ago.'' Mary rushed ahead with her story, afraid that lingering over memories of her mother would bring tears that in the midst of her deceit, she couldn't defend to Rafael Perdido.

''He kept Riverwood—this place—because it *isn't* so grand. He likes to spend weekends and vacations here with his children.''

Rafe's gaze shifted from her to travel over the rambling lines of the house. ''I'm going to live in a place like this someday.'' There was a strange mixture of determination and aggressiveness in his voice.

''I'm sure you will,'' Mary told him, saying a little prayer that he'd get his wish.

His smile was back, as dazzling in its whiteness as the house. ''In the meantime, I'd better get back to work or I won't even have a job sawing timber.''

''There's nothing wrong with sawing timber or cutting cane,'' Mary hastened to say. ''My father says all work is honorable if it's honest.''

Rafe regarded her thoughtfully for a moment, swirling the last of the lemonade in the glass. ''Your father sounds like a fine person.''

''He is.'' Afraid he'd ask her more about her family, Mary reached past him and picked up the tray.

Taking the hint, Rafe finished his drink and set the glass on the tray. ''Thank you, Mary. It was a genuine pleasure meeting you.''

There was no laughter in his eyes now. Just a gentleness that filled her heart with alien feelings. ''You're welcome,'' she murmured.

Mary carried the tray inside and filled a half-gallon canning jar with cool water, which she took out to where Rafe was working. She set it beside his shirt, which he'd thrown on the ground.

Back inside, she busied herself with preparations for supper for her father and brothers. Outside the open kitchen window, the rhythmic whack of the ax on wood became the backdrop for sweet fantasies spinning through her mind....

CHAPTER TWO

HOLDING TIGHTLY to the handle of the car seat where prematurely born, five-week-old Mary Lorelei Weston lay sucking on a pacifier and sleeping peacefully, Shelby Delacroix knocked on the door of the house her uncle William and aunt Mary shared. Her cousin Joanna, who'd driven up from New Orleans, stood beside her, looking down at her sleeping daughter, a weary smile of pure love on her face.

Shelby grinned at her. "It'll take Uncle William a while to get here," she warned. "His arthritis has been acting up lately."

Joanna shifted the bag of fresh doughnuts she carried from one hand to the other. "Lori's fine. It's plenty warm."

The door opened to reveal a tall, spare man of seventy-six with a thatch of thinning gray hair that stood on end.

"Hello, Uncle William," Shelby and Joanna chimed in unison.

"Why, if it isn't the two prettiest girls in St. Tammany Parish," William said, giving them each a hug and stepping aside for them to enter the living room.

"Better make that the three prettiest girls," Shelby said, setting the carrier on the floral sofa. "Joanna's brought Lorelei to visit you and Aunt Mary."

William smiled down at the baby, dressed in pink and

lace, and sporting a bow in her unexpectedly thick, dark hair. "She's a beauty, all right. Like her mama."

Joanna smiled. "Thank you, Uncle William. I don't feel so beautiful. I feel a bit frazzled. Not to mention tired to the bone."

William's eyes twinkled. "A condition that goes with motherhood, I understand."

"Where's Aunt Mary?" Shelby asked.

"I don't know," William said. "I just woke up from my nap a little while ago, and I couldn't find her anywhere. Maybe you could check on her whereabouts for me." His bushy eyebrows drew together in a frown. "I'm worried about her."

William didn't have to tell them his worry for his sister had increased since Philip's indictment, and since word had gotten out among the family about her bearing Rafe Perdido's baby.

"We're all worried about her," Joanna said. "And you and Uncle Charles, too." She gave Shelby an anxious look. "Why don't you look around outside for her, Shel? I'll make some coffee." Joanna smiled at her uncle. "I brought you some of those raspberry-filled doughnuts you like."

"You're a thoughtful girl, Joanna," he said. Then he turned to Shelby. "My arthritis is kicking up today. Do you mind looking for Mary?"

"Of course not." Shelby headed for the door.

"Look under the magnolia tree," William suggested. "It was always a favorite spot of hers, and lately she's taken to hiding out there again."

"I'm on my way," Shelby said. She closed the door behind her and started down the path to the footbridge.

Joanna was right. The whole family was worried about Mary. Since Philip's arrest for the murder of Camille Gravier, and the family finding out Mary had given birth to a child fathered by the man who'd died in prison for that murder, their gracious, elderly aunt seemed to be fading before their very eyes.

None of Shelby's sisters quite understood why their great-aunt was so upset. In modern times, having a baby out of wedlock and even giving that baby up for adoption wasn't such a big thing. Justin had reminded his daughters that social mores had been far different sixty years ago. Pregnancy outside of marriage brought terrible shame to a family.

Unlike her sisters, Shelby still lived at Riverwood, and she was closer to her great-aunt than the others were. She knew Mary better. She knew beyond a shadow of a doubt that Mary Delacroix had loved Rafael Perdido with all her heart and that she'd never forgotten him. If she hadn't loved him, she wouldn't have gone against her staunch Catholic beliefs and borne his child. If she'd been able to forget him, she would have married someone else.

She couldn't forget Rafe, and you can't forget Travis. Not in a few months. Not in a thousand years.

She pushed aside thoughts of the handsome Texan—a distant relative of Camille Gravier's—who had come to town, stolen Shelby's heart and hightailed it back to his native state when things between them didn't work out to his satisfaction.

"Don't think about Travis," she said out loud.

Now wasn't the time for that. As her grandfather had pointed out at breakfast, the trial was scheduled to start tomorrow, and no one knew how it would affect the Delacroix family. They'd all stood by Uncle William when they'd learned he was Desiree Boudreaux's son—not a Delacroix by birth—and they needed to support one another through the upcoming trial. That was one of the reasons Shelby had suggested she and Joanna come and visit their aunt and uncle. Working together as attorneys at Delacroix and Associates, Charles's law firm, Shelby and Joanna had become particularly close. Just because Joanna's father was a jerk, a cheat and possibly a murderer was no reason Shelby should snub a colleague she respected highly, a cousin she happened to love very much.

Not only did she and Joanna love each other, they both loved their great-aunt. Shelby sighed. This had to be as hard on Mary as the first trial, yet she was her usual caring self, no doubt suffering in her own quiet way.

Old newspaper clippings Shelby had seen stated that Mary had fainted at the first trial. This time her aunt wouldn't be called to the stand to relate what she'd seen the night Camille Gravier's life ended. Because of Mary's recent heart attacks, arrangements had been made to take her deposition at home.

Shelby approached the giant magnolia tree, as great a favorite of hers as it was of her aunt's. She pushed through the break in the branches and found Mary there, her knees drawn up like a child, her white head resting against the massive trunk of the tree, her eyes closed. It might have been a trick of the light, but Shelby thought she saw the glitter of moisture clinging to her great-aunt's pale eyelashes.

"There you are!" she said, injecting an upbeat note into her voice. "I've been looking all over for you. Joanna brought little Mary Lorelei for a visit."

Mary's eyes fluttered open. They held a faraway, almost dreamy quality.

"What are you doing out here, anyway?" Shelby asked. "You'll catch your death sitting on the damp ground."

"I'm ready to go, Shelby," Mary said.

The sincerity of the statement shook Shelby. "Well, I'm not ready for you to leave me, so you'd better start taking better care of yourself."

"Bossy child," Mary said, a reluctant smile claiming

her lips as she let Shelby help her to her feet. The elderly woman staggered a bit, and Shelby slipped an arm around her waist.

Mary squeezed her niece's hand. "Thank you, my dear."

"Joanna's making coffee," Shelby said cheerfully as, arm in arm, they made their way to the path. "She brought some of those wonderful raspberry-filled doughnuts you and Uncle William like."

Mary, who still seemed almost lost in thought, didn't answer. When they reached the bridge, she turned to Shelby and asked, "Have you heard from your young man lately?"

Shelby's breath caught in surprise. "No," she admitted. She hadn't heard from Travis since they'd called off their engagement and he'd gone back to Texas. Evidently he subscribed more to the out-of-sight, out-of-mind school of thought than that of absence makes the heart grow fonder.

"You really loved him, didn't you?" Mary asked.

"Yes," Shelby said. "I really did."

"Then why did you let him go?"

"I didn't have a choice, Aunt Mary. There was a lot going on back then. He came here looking for revenge against us Delacroix, and after we got that all settled between us, he accused me of putting my family before him. Now it appears Uncle Philip may have killed Travis's great-aunt...." Shelby's voice trailed away and she shook her head.

Mary waved her hand dismissively as they started across the bridge. "Whatever happens, *you* didn't kill Camille, so all that is workable. But Travis is right about the other. You do put this family ahead of your own feelings and wants. You always have."

"Gee," Shelby said, squeezing her aunt's fragile waist. "I wonder who taught me that?"

Mary laughed and Shelby had a brief glimpse of what her great-aunt must have been like as a young girl. Suddenly, she stopped and faced Shelby, taking her hands in a tight grip.

"Don't do what I did, Shelby. Life is too short, too uncertain. None of us is guaranteed tomorrow, and sometimes we never find another love. Don't let this family—don't let *anything* come between you and the man you love. When this is over, go to him. Go!"

Stunned by the vehemence in Mary's voice, Shelby could only nod.

"Promise me?"

Seeing the intensity in her aunt's eyes, Shelby nodded again. "Yes. I promise."

The almost fanatical light in Mary's eyes faded, and she smiled and touched Shelby's cheek with gentle fingers. In silent, mutual agreement, they started toward the house again.

Inside the door, they were greeted by the scent of chicory-laced coffee, plus the sounds of a baby's wail and Joanna's somewhat desperate attempt to quiet her daughter, all coming from the vicinity of the kitchen. Shelby knew that becoming a mother again after seventeen years was hard on Joanna. And, she thought with a frown, facing the fact that one's father might be a murderer would put anyone's nerves on edge.

As Shelby ushered her aunt into the cheerful blue-and-white kitchen, the crying came to an abrupt halt. They found Joanna ensconced in a rocking chair, her infant daughter nursing hungrily in her arms.

"Starving, huh?" Shelby asked, peering over Joanna's shoulder at the top of the baby's head, just about all that was visible over the flannel receiving blanket.

"She's like her daddy. When either of them wants something, they don't stop till they get it." A smile curved

Joanna's lips and crinkled the corners of her eyes, but Shelby saw worry and pain hiding beneath the veneer of happiness.

"That isn't exactly a trait the Westons have a monopoly on," Shelby reminded her. "We Delacroix are known for our tenacity, too."

"Good point."

Shelby rounded the table and went to the cabinet, taking down four cups and saucers.

"I'll get that," Mary said. "After all, I am the hostess."

"Don't be silly." Shelby opened the bag of raspberry doughnuts and began arranging them on a rose-patterned plate. "Let me spoil you for a change."

Mary favored her with an indulgent smile. "All right. I will." She pulled out a carved oak chair next to Joanna's and reached out to touch Lori's plump hand. There was no hiding or denying the sorrow residing in her eyes. "She's beautiful, Joanna. You must cherish every moment you have with her."

Briefly, Joanna's gaze met Shelby's. They both knew Mary's thoughts were on the daughter she'd given up sixty years before.

"I will," Joanna said as serious as her aunt.

The coffeepot sputtered as the fragrant brew finished perking, and Shelby filled the cups.

"Where were you?" William asked his sister as he shuffled into the kitchen. Shelby placed coffee and pastry before him as he slowly took a seat at the table.

"Thinking."

"About what?"

Mary wrapped her blue-veined hands around her cup and shook her head in disbelief. "You know, William," she said gently, "you're the only person I know who can have his life fall apart around him and still keep his equanimity."

"The Lord works in mysterious ways," William quoted.

Joanna's gorgeous face took on a haunted, incredulous look. "Since I moved back here, my daughter has been on trial for murder, my relationship with my father has deteriorated, and now he's been indicted for killing some woman. How can I believe this is God's plan, that something good will come from it all?"

"Something good has come from it," William said. "You're holding at least part of that something good in your arms. If you hadn't wanted the best lawyer in the South to defend Nikki, you'd never have met Logan and fallen in love, never had Lori."

A look of shame flitted across Joanna's face. "You're right, Uncle William—as usual."

"We have little control over what happens in our lives," William said. "We can only trust in God and deal with what unfolds as best we can. If we're lucky, we learn and grow from it."

"What about you, Uncle William?" Shelby asked in her usual blunt way. "How are you dealing with finding out Desiree is your mother and that she gave you up in exchange for a parcel of swampland? You haven't said a word to anyone since you found out your own life is a lie."

"Just because my parents aren't who I thought they were doesn't make my life a lie, Shelby."

She gave him an exasperated smile. "You know what I mean. You can't be as impervious to all this as you seem to be."

"Yes," William said, "I do know what you mean. And yes, the news has affected me greatly. How I feel is thankful."

"Thankful?" Shelby asked incredulously. "Why?"

"Because I had a wonderful upbringing, wonderful parents—'' he smiled at Mary ''—a generous and loving sister and two brothers whom I love very much.''

Tears glittered in Joanna's eyes. ''I don't know how you can say that. Even I know my father isn't a particularly nice person.'' She shifted Lori in her arms, so abruptly the sleepy baby murmured a protest.

''That doesn't stop you from loving him, does it?'' William pressed.

''No,'' Joanna said in a harsh whisper, but she didn't look any too pleased about the confession. ''But it makes me sick to think that he may have...'' Her voice trailed away and she straightened in the rocker. ''I'm going to put the baby on your bed, okay, Aunt Mary?''

She nodded, and Joanna left the room. ''Philip was always difficult,'' Mary noted, stirring a spoonful of sugar into her coffee. She took a sip, added another smidgen of sugar. ''I never understood how two people who are virtually identical on the outside could have such a totally different outlook on life. But I'm like William. Philip is my brother, and I love him.''

''Even if he's guilty of killing Camille Gravier and his silence cost the life of the man you loved?'' Shelby pressed.

Mary's face turned pasty. Her spoon clattered against the side of the cup. Contrition washed through Shelby. Until recently, she'd kept the information gleaned from digging into the past a secret from her aunt to spare her any heartache, but ever since Mary had suffered a heart attack on learning the identity of the child she'd borne Rafe Perdido sixty years ago, she'd insisted on hearing everything. There'd been too many hurtful secrets, she said. Too many mistakes swept under the rug instead of being dealt with.

''Right or wrong, what's done is done,'' Mary said now. Her voice was as unsteady as her hand. ''William's right.

Love isn't like a water tap. Even though we might like to, we can't turn it off and on at will just because people hurt or disappoint us.''

William nodded his agreement.

Shelby blew out an irritated breath. "You know, it's sheer hell for us poor mortals, who experience awful emotions like hate and envy and the lust for revenge, to live among you saints. What about Desiree, Uncle William? Aren't you angry that she gave you away? That she's pointing the finger at the man who was raised as your brother?''

"I'm sure she had her reasons for letting Hamilton and Marguerite adopt me, just as I'm sure she has a reason for coming forward with information about Camille's murder after so long.''

"Do you think Desiree is lying?" Shelby asked. "Maybe she just has it in for Uncle Philip, since he's supposedly responsible for kidnapping Flora.''

According to Jackson Boudreaux, Flora's son, who was singing for the prosecution like a tweety bird in exchange for immunity, Philip had blamed Flora not only for his losing the election in November, but also for causing him extreme mental anguish. In retaliation, he'd had her kidnapped and locked in a vault in the Delacroix family cemetery at Belle Terre. The forced incarceration had shattered Flora's already deteriorating mental state, and Desiree had had her only daughter committed to a nearby mental hospital.

"I have no way of knowing if she's lying or not, but if she is, God will take care of it. It's not my place to judge her.''

"Don't give me all that pious priest stuff," Shelby said, growing more agitated by the moment. "How do you *feel* about her?''

"Honestly?''

"Yes, honestly." Her eyes begged for understanding. "Please."

"I feel sorry for Desiree," William said. "She hasn't had an easy life. So many people have looked down on her and ridiculed her. One of her grandsons—Steven—is dead. The other—Jackson—was arrested for breaking and entering. Who knows what other charges they'll bring against him? He'll probably spend time in prison."

"Jackson cut a deal with the D.A.," Shelby said. "He got his sorry butt out of a sling by agreeing to testify against Uncle Philip."

"People like Jackson usually find a way out of their problems," William said philosophically. "Then there's the fact that Flora is in a mental institution—allegedly Philip's doing." He picked up his cup. "As I said, I feel sorry for Desiree."

Joanna came back into the room carrying the baby, now wide awake. "She woke up when I tried to put her down."

"Brat," Shelby said fondly, with a loving smile at Joanna.

"I couldn't believe it when Jake Trahan told me Flora was probably the one who sent us the wedding gift that exploded," Joanna said, taking her chair again.

Mary pushed aside her half-eaten pastry. "As malicious as I've known Flora to be in the past, that's hard for me to believe, too."

"It makes sense in a twisted sort of way," William said. "After all, she blamed Nikki for Steven's death. Perhaps Flora wanted to make you suffer as she had."

"If I'm hearing you right, you think Desiree went to Jake with her story about what happened at Moon Lake the night Camille Gravier was killed because she feels we Delacroix have destroyed her family."

"About what *allegedly* happened," Joanna corrected her. "My father is innocent until proven guilty."

"You're right," Shelby said, yet even as she spoke, a mental image of her great-uncle holding a struggling woman under the water flashed through her mind. Again she thought how easy it was to imagine him doing it.

She forced her attention back to her cousin. Joanna gazed down at Lori, as if the features of the bright-eyed infant might give her a clue into the hearts and minds of man. Then her troubled gaze met Shelby's. "How can a mother and daughter be so different?"

Shelby shook her head. "I don't know. The same way two brothers can, I suppose."

FEELING AN OVERWHELMING need to talk to his brother, who was out on bail, Charles made the short drive to Belle Terre. As he pulled into the long drive, he realized it would be the first time he'd been to the house in nearly sixty years.

Always looking to the future, Hamilton Delacroix had named his good friend Neville Alvarez executor of his will in the event that he passed on before his children were of age. Hamilton's property was to be divided equally among his children, since he had no living spouse. William, who would take a vow of poverty, was exempt, which left Mary, Charles and Philip to inherit.

After Camille's death, Rafe Perdido's trial and the death of their father, Charles and Philip had, by unspoken agreement, gone their separate ways. Guilt lay heavily on Charles's shoulders. Guilt and a deep-rooted suspicion he was afraid to look at too carefully. He didn't know why Philip had turned on him. Anger, because he'd had the audacity to try and win Camille, Charles supposed. Whatever the reasons, the friction between them was so great that even the vastness of Belle Terre hadn't been big enough for them both. Unable to live in such a strained environment, Charles moved his things to Riverwood, the smaller house, but the larger of the two tracts of land.

This separate living arrangement worked well for them until they finished law school and legally divided Hamilton's estate in a manner the three children felt was equitable—Mary and Charles taking Riverwood; Philip taking Belle Terre. Philip bought out his siblings' interest in the law firm, and Charles started his own practice. Mary built her own house across the bayou, and when William retired, he moved in with her.

Now Charles got out of the car and went up the broad steps. He rang the doorbell and then stood with his hands clasped loosely in front of him, waiting patiently. After a few moments, the door swung open. Clovis, whose father had worked for Charles's father back before any of them were born, stood there, looking courtly in his black butler's uniform, which accentuated his tall gauntness.

"Mr. Charles," he said with some surprise and a slight smile of greeting.

Charles felt the reception was genuine, even though there was no discernible emotion in the old retainer's eyes—one as black as the pits of hell, the other as hazy as the surface of the bayou at daybreak. Rumor had it that the injury to Clovis's eye had happened when he was a young man fighting over a woman. That had been a long, long time ago. Clovis was older than Charles and Philip.

Smiling, Charles extended his hand. "Hello, Clovis. May I come in?"

Instead of shaking his hand, Clovis stepped aside deferentially. "Certainly, Mr. Charles."

Charles thrust his hands into the pockets of his trousers and entered the foyer. It was the first time he'd been inside the house in more than half a century, the first time since he and Philip had split up their father's property and his law practice. Charles wasn't prepared for the barrage of childhood memories that swept over him, or the crushing sorrow those memories engendered.

He pictured his mother coming down the stairs in a floral wrapper. Imagined he heard Mary's shrieks as he and Philip chased her down the long hall. Visualized a pecan wood fire burning in the fireplace that dominated the large foyer, pine boughs and bright red pyracantha berries draped along the bannister at Christmas...

"How have you been, Mr. Charles?"

The sudden question jolted him from his thoughts. He pushed away his sorrow with an effort and turned to the old servant. "I'm splendid, Clovis. And you?"

"Fine, Mr. Charles. Just fine. What brings you to Belle Terre after all this time?"

"I've come to see my brother. Is he here?"

"Yes, sir. He's in the library." Clovis turned. "I'll tell him you're here."

Charles reached out and touched the older man's arm. "Thank you, Clovis, but I know the way."

"WHAT ARE YOU DOING HERE?" Philip asked when he answered the knock on the library door and saw his twin standing there. Philip hoped his gruffness masked his surprise.

Charles's smile was tentative. "You're my brother. Under the circumstances, I thought it might be a good idea if we buried the hatchet. Preferably not in each other's backs. May I come in?"

Philip's face turned red, but he allowed Charles entrance. "What circumstances?"

"Since it was Camille Gravier—in life—who came between us, it seemed appropriate that perhaps, in a roundabout way, this new trial could bring us back together."

"Desiree Boudreaux is a liar." Philip's voice was cold, flat.

"I'm sure the truth will out," Charles said after a moment. He stretched forward his hand in an offering of peace. "Whatever this trial brings, I wanted to let you know I'm behind you."

"You always were a bleeding heart, Charles," Philip said, ignoring his brother's proffered hand. "Worse even than William, I think. But then, that's not so surprising, since Brother William isn't a Delacroix at all."

Sadly, Charles realized that William had been more a brother to him than Philip had. Even more lamentable was the fact that though Philip's back was to the wall, he showed no sign of remorse for anything he might have done in the past, no softening of heart, no concern for what this was doing to other members of the family.

Realizing his quest for a reconciliation was futile, that Philip probably despised him for even making the gesture, Charles let his hand fall to his side. "He may not have been born into our family, but as far as I'm concerned, he's my brother, the same as you."

Charles started to leave, but turned at the door, an apologetic smile on his face. "By the way, Philip, I forget where you said you were that night."

"Getting senile, Chas?" Philip taunted. "I told you. Gigging for frogs in the Bayou with some friends." The alibi tripped from his lips with the ease of a politician's promise.

Charles nodded. "Right. Were you in a boat or along the bank?"

The look in Philip's eyes said he realized Charles was looking for some bit of information. Philip flashed his most engaging smile. "Come on, brother. You know as well as I do there are gators in the bayou. We were in a boat."

Charles smiled back, but his smile was melancholy, defeated. He nodded. "Good luck tomorrow, Philip."

Charles reached for the doorknob, but it turned beneath

his hand, the door swinging open almost magically. Clovis stood there, his face impassive, the droop of his eyelid hiding the expression in his one good eye. Charles wondered if he'd been standing there all along, listening. He'd always heard the servants knew everything that went on in a household. He didn't doubt it.

"Thank you, Clovis," Charles said. "I'll see myself out."

"Good day to you, Mr. Charles."

Charles let himself out the leaded glass door and started for his car, his heart heavy. After he and Mary had given their statements to the police the night Camille was killed, Charles had shucked off his wet pants on the back porch where the wringer washing machine stood. When he'd thrown his trousers in, he'd seen the pants Philip had been wearing when he'd left the house. The same terrifying question tumbled through Charles's troubled mind now as had back then. If, as Philip claimed, he had been frog gigging from a boat, how had his pants gotten wet?

PHILIP PUSHED ASIDE the drift of lace at the window and, through a blur, watched his brother get into his car. As Charles drove around the driveway of crushed white shells, a sharp pang pierced Philip's heart. Automatically, he pressed a hand to his chest, but the spasm passed, leaving only a dull throb to remind him he was still alive.

No thanks to Flora Boudreaux.

Only when Philip had had one of his flunkies bring Flora to Belle Terre—Jackson had refused the directive—and forced her to spend the night in the family crypt, did he learn why his former lover was so set on destroying him: because of Jackson. Jackson was his son, and Philip had already done the young man a lot of favors because of that fact, as well as paying his mother for decades. It wasn't enough for Flora, who wanted nothing less than a public acknowledgment of paternity and a change in Philip's will assuring that Jackson was bequeathed enough cash to secure his future.

As if he'd ever give the whoring, gambling, weak-hearted excuse of a man anything, Philip thought in disgust. He stomped to the bar and poured himself a shot of whiskey. To hell with doctor's orders. If it weren't for Jackson letting Flora out of the crypt, Philip wouldn't be in this mess.

He threw back the drink and shuddered at its potency. Thank God Desiree had seen the sense in getting her daughter some help, even though the old woman did intend to see him dead. Flora was locked up, where she could do no more harm. A few more weeks of finding various and sundry voodoo items when he least expected them would have sent Philip to the grave. A wry smile twisted his lips. Of course, there was always the consideration that if Flora's voodoo had killed him, he'd have been spared the humiliation of this confounded trial.

The trial. Charles had come to him today to make their peace before the trial. Philip had refused, unwilling to bend even the slightest bit. Through the years he'd learned that softness was equated with weakness, and even within his family, he was afraid that any sign of weakness would send his whole world crumbling.

Remembering the sadness on Charles's face when he'd refused to shake his hand brought another of those strange pains to Philip's heart. He poured himself another drink. Well, it was too late to turn back the clock. As he tossed down the whiskey, he realized something else, something he might have known but would have never admitted before: he missed his brother. Had missed him every day since they'd agreed to split up the property and go their separate ways.

AFTER JOANNA AND THE BABY left, Shelby crossed the bridge to the big house and tried to immerse herself in a custody case she was handling. After more than an hour, she gave it up as a lost cause. Her mind was too filled with thoughts of the upcoming trial and its far-reaching effects on her family to leave room for much else. When something else did manage to derail those thoughts, it was the memory of her aunt telling her that Travis had been right, that Shelby did put her family first.

For the first time, she admitted it was true. No wonder Travis had dumped her and headed back to Comfort, Texas. No doubt there were lots of pretty, denim-clad dollies who wanted nothing more from life than to give comfort to a big, good-looking cowboy with a slow drawl and slower hands....

She shivered as a memory of Travis making love to her slipped past the barriers she'd erected, destroying her fragile, hard-won facade of indifference.

"You're a fool, Shelby Delacroix," she said aloud, brushing away a stray tear. "Aunt Mary is right. Nothing and no one should come between two people who love each other."

Just saying it made her feel better. She vowed then and there that as soon as her uncle's trial was over, she'd hop the first plane to Texas, drive right up to Travis's front door and tell him she'd been an idiot to let what they had slip away.

What if he doesn't care anymore? What if he's found someone else?

The thought made Shelby's stomach churn sickly. As Uncle William was always telling her, there was enough evil in the day you were living, without having to worry about what might happen tomorrow. Good advice if you could take it, she thought as the phone rang. Since she seemed to be alone in the house, she picked up the receiver.

"Riverwood."

"Shelby? This is Annabelle."

Shelby hadn't seen much of Annabelle since her cousin had opened up a bed-and-breakfast in one of the town's nicest old homes—and gotten married to Jake Trahan, Bayou Beltane's police chief, once her high school sweetheart. Shelby was surprised but pleased she had called, busy as she was—especially since her father was going on trial the following day. "Hi, Annabelle. How are you?"

"Holding up," Annabelle said, but Shelby heard the weariness in her voice.

"How's Drew?" Shelby asked. Until a few months ago, Annabelle's brother had been on the same course of destruction as his father, but the arrival of Katherine Beaufort had changed the direction of his life. The subsequent unraveling of the sixty-year secret and their unexpected romance had wrought changes in Drew that were nothing short of miraculous.

"He's like a different man since he met Katherine," Annabelle said, the words echoing Shelby's thoughts.

"I'm glad. I always knew there was a lot of good inside him if he'd just stop looking to your dad as a role model." Shelby gave an embarrassed laugh. "Sorry, I don't mean to kick a man when he's down."

"It's okay," Annabelle assured her. "I know my father's faults better than you."

Silence filled the phone line, and finally, Annabelle cleared her throat, leaving Shelby with the distinct impression that she wanted to say something but was unsure how to proceed.

"What's wrong?"

"Nothing."

"Don't give me that. Whatever it is, spit it out."

"It's Travis."

"Travis?" Shelby echoed. "What about Travis?"

"He's here."

"Here?" Shelby heard the incredulous squeak in her voice. "In Bayou Beltane?"

"Here," Annabelle said. "In town. More specifically, here at the bed-and-breakfast. He's rented a room for the duration of the trial. I thought you'd want to know."

CHAPTER THREE

LONG AFTER HIS NIECES left, long after Mary had gone to bed and the last light at Riverwood winked out, William sat on the back *galerie* of the house he shared with his sister. His mind was so filled with the conversation he'd had with Mary, Shelby and Joanna that he was hardly aware of the frogs and crickets singing a Cajun springtime ballad.

There was, he thought, something to be said for learned behavior. Contrary to the things he'd told them and the way he'd behaved, William wasn't feeling particularly priestly. To the best of his knowledge, the facts surrounding his birth were known only to his immediate family. He wanted it kept that way.

He didn't want to be Desiree Boudreaux's son.

There had been times since he'd learned he wasn't truly a Delacroix that he had been tempted to have Remy take him to Desiree's place and demand to know how she could have given him up in exchange for a piece of land. Times when he knew Flora had committed some heinous act and he'd prayed that it was a mistake, that he and the woman who shared Desiree as a mother weren't related at all. Times he'd rather have been dead than have anyone know the same blood flowed in his veins.

He'd grown used to being a Delacroix, and no amount of prayer had squelched the sinful feeling of pride he felt knowing he was part of one of the most powerful families in the state.

Pride goeth before a fall.

Yes, but pride was the least of his sins. Despite what Shelby thought, he was as mortal as the next person. As a young man, he'd lusted and satisfied that lust, just as his brothers had. He'd coveted their popularity, their looks. Sometimes hated them for their ability to fit so easily into a crowd, to joke and laugh. Despite his belief that he was a Delacroix, he'd never felt he fit in. He'd often thought that feeling of not belonging was one of the reasons he'd decided to become a priest.

In some ways life became easier when he went to the seminary. He no longer had to compare himself to Charles and Philip on a daily basis. And when those hateful, sinful feelings crept into his soul and his heart, he'd covered them with his priestly garments and a demeanor of dedication.

If his life was a lie, as Shelby suggested, his own duplicity was the greatest falsehood of all, for like Charles and Philip, he, too, had slept with Camille Gravier.

A captive of the pleasures of the flesh, he'd been willing to desert his God and his calling to the priesthood if she'd only said the word. But she hadn't asked anything of him except the use of his body, and when he'd told her he loved her and that he'd leave the seminary if she would become his wife, she had laughed until tears ran down her face. He was, she said, nothing but a pleasant diversion.

For the sixty years since the Jezebel's death, William had alternated between hating her and hating himself for wanting her.

April 1938

IT WAS A PERFECT late-spring afternoon. The sun blazed in an azure sky, so bright it hurt the eyes. A thunderstorm had swept through the parish the night before, ushering in high winds and hail and leaving behind an unexpected drop in temperature. So far, the humidity hadn't reasserted itself.

William, who'd crossed to his and his siblings' favorite place on the far side of Moon Lake—ostensibly to fish, but really just to have some time by himself—shucked off his shirt and wadded it into a makeshift pillow. His cane pole was stuck in the soft earth of the bank. The red-and-white bobber bounced over ripples created by the soft breath of the wind.

The idyllic spot was on a small cove of the large lake. It was all but hidden from Belle Terre by a stand of cypress trees. The sloping bank was grassy, dotted with willows. Beyond them, a mixture of oak and pine and tangled undergrowth hid the outlet to the bayou, the dense swamp where Desiree Boudreaux and her strange young daughter, Flora, lived.

William found the cove a great place to be quiet and think. Mary liked to sit on the huge oak a storm had toppled into the lake, and dangle her feet in the water while she fished. Philip and Charles liked to bring their girlfriends there to neck.

Thoughts of necking made William shift uncomfortably. For better or worse, he would be home a lot this summer. On one hand, he was glad to be with his family again. On the other, separating himself from the strictures of seminary life might make it easier for the sinful feelings taunting him of late to take hold of his mind.

When he'd first decided to become a priest, his enthusiasm and zeal for molding himself into what God wanted him to be had gone a long way toward keeping his thoughts and words pure. He still had no problem controlling his tongue, but his thoughts…well, those were something else. Ever since he'd come home for the Easter holidays and chanced upon Camille Gravier kissing his brother Philip in this very spot, William had found himself obsessed with thoughts of his brother's girlfriend.

Camille's mother had worked for the Delacroix most of his life, and William knew Camille as well as he did his siblings. But he had never felt anything but friendship, and more often irritation, toward the girl.

Though she was Mary's best friend, he often thought the friendship was one-sided. Yet as strange as their companionship was, he was the first to say it seemed to work. Having inherited her father's height and strong nose, quiet, introverted Mary was far from beautiful. In contrast, flirty, vivacious Camille was gorgeous with her flaming auburn hair and emerald green eyes. While Mary often voiced her desire to be more like her friend, there was no discernible envy in her voice. In fact, William often thought her attitude toward Camille bordered on worship.

To her credit, William had never known Camille to flaunt her beauty in Mary's face. As they'd grown older, she'd done her best to help his sister make the most of her own modest attributes. Still, nothing Camille did could change Mary's feelings about herself, or William's conviction that Camille suffered Mary Delacroix because being best friends with her was her ticket into Bayou Beltane's society—not because there was any deep feeling there. William had suspected at an early age that social acceptance and moving up in the world were very important to Camille Gravier.

If you feel that way, if you think she's so shallow, a user, why do you feel like punching Philip when you see them together?

Because William was jealous, that's why. Because he wanted her himself. Wanted to feel her arms around his neck. Wanted to have her full, ripe lips press against his the way they had against Philip's. And may God forgive him, he wanted to feel those full, lush breasts against his chest.

William had prayed about his unwanted feelings, had asked God to deliver him from such sordid desires, to no avail. So far, *le bon Dieu* either hadn't heard his prayer or had answered no, for despite the frequency and fervor of William's petition, his feelings for Camille grew.

Lately, he had begun to question his decision to become a priest. As a Delacroix, he was accustomed to having almost anything he wanted. Maybe he wasn't cut out for a life of deprivation and denial. Was his calling genuine? Was he worthy of it?

He'd also considered the possibility that Camille was a trial, that God was testing him. Most likely she was a temptation sent by the devil. Or perhaps, as had happened to the apostle Paul, William's longing for this woman was his cross to bear, his thorn in the flesh. If so, he'd just have to deny those feelings until they went away.

Which shouldn't be hard, considering she has eyes only for Philip.

The reminder brought a dejected sigh. At seventeen, William was wise enough to realize Camille would never see him as anything but a friend, and the sooner he convinced himself of that, the sooner he could work through his own feelings. Still, being home, seeing her daily, would be a supreme test of his faith.

But he wouldn't think about that just now. For the moment he was content to be alone, unencumbered by lessons or unwanted emotions.

He settled down onto the blanket of lush grass that grew to the water's edge. It was nice to breathe air that didn't feel as if it needed to be wrung out, William thought, dragging in a deep breath filled with the scents of jessamine and rain-soaked earth. A squirrel chattered in a nearby tree. A hawk screamed. From far across the lake, a horse whinnied. William closed his eyes and spread his arms wide, embracing the quiet and sacrificing the strength and perfection of his young body on the altar of Ra....

SOMETHING TICKLED. He brushed a languid hand over his bare chest. Even half asleep, he was acutely aware of the feel of his wiry chest hair against his palm. He felt the tickling sensation again, brushed at it again. This time his hand encountered something smooth. His fingers closed over it—a hand, he realized—and his eyes flew open.

William was shocked to see Camille smiling down at him. "It's hard to catch fish when you're asleep," she said, her green eyes alight with mischief. "But flies, now, those are a different thing."

He was too stunned by her presence to be concerned that he'd been sleeping with his mouth open. "What are you doing here?" he asked, letting go of her hand.

Instead of moving it, she let it rest lightly on his stomach. An unfamiliar heat began to grow inside him. "I came to see Philip, but Mama said he and Charles have gone into New Orleans with your father. Mary was nowhere to be found, and Mama said you'd gone fishing, so I thought I'd join you."

As she talked, her fingers skimmed idly over his chest, toying with the pelt of dark hair growing there.

"Don't." He was surprised at the harshness in his voice.

Her eyes widened in turn. Her hand stilled. "Don't what?"

"Don't touch me."

For a moment her eyes narrowed thoughtfully, then she smiled, a slow, taunting smile. "What's the matter, William?" she cooed. "Am I a temptation to your immortal soul?"

The question was so close to his earlier thoughts that he was momentarily taken aback. But there was no sense lying about it and adding to his list of transgressions. "Yes," he told her. "You are definitely a temptation."

Her eyes grew wide and guileless. "I had no idea you felt that way toward me—since you're going to be a priest and all."

"Priests are men, Camille," he reminded her. "And you shouldn't be flirting with me."

"Why not?"

"Because after what I saw here a few days ago, it's obvious you're my brother's girl."

Her silvery laughter drifted through the balmy air and settled over him like a soft caress. "What you saw was just a kiss, William. What makes you think I'm Philip's girl?"

Her casual attitude caught him off guard and offered him tentative hope. Still, he wouldn't be convinced so easily. "Maybe you aren't," he conceded with a contemplative look. "I've seen you flirting with Charles, too."

She dismissed Charles with a wave of her hand. "Charles isn't my type."

"What is your type?"

"A man who knows who he is, what he wants. Someone like Philip." Her sultry gaze drifted from William's face to his bare chest and down the length of his legs, encased in tan twill trousers. "Someone like you."

William couldn't have denied the thrill that coursed through him even if he'd known doing so would cost him his soul. Through little fault of theirs, he'd played second fiddle to his older brothers all his life. Now the most beautiful girl in the parish was actually saying she found him interesting.

She smiled. "Funny. I never noticed before what a handsome man you've become, William. You have become a man, haven't you?"

Even in his innocence, William knew what she was alluding to. He felt his face flame, but again, he answered honestly. "Not in the way you mean, no."

She looked into his eyes for long moments, then favored him with another of those dazzling smiles. "That's sweet," she said in a soft voice.

"What about you?" he asked boldly. "Are you a woman?"

Laughing, Camille doubled up a small fist and hit his shoulder. William caught her wrist in a loose grip. "William Delacroix!" she said in a breathless voice. "I do believe you're flirting with me."

Flirting. The thought pleased him. "Is that what we're doing?"

"You know it is, you naughty boy," she told him, her eyes twinkling with unholy glee. She uncurled her fingers and let her palm rest against his shoulder. Her touch seared flesh already hot from the sun. She rubbed the pads of her fingers over his skin.

"Why, what would your teachers at the seminary say if they knew you were talking to a girl about..." Her voice trailed away and she looked around, as if she were about to impart a secret and was afraid someone would overhear. "Sex." Her voice was barely more than a whisper.

"I'd have to do penance."

"Penance. Hmm. Would that bother you?"

The seminary and the idea of penance seemed as far away as the sun blazing down on them. The only thing that mattered at the moment was Camille's nearness and the contradictory way her nearness made him feel.

Hot and cold at once. Nervous but cocky. Vulnerable. Secure in his masculinity. All soft and yielding inside. All hard and wanting below. "At the moment, I'd have to say no," he said, surprising them both with his answer.

She moved her hand from his shoulder to the grass beside it. The simple action brought her breast into contact with his chest. It felt firm in its cotton binding. The heat inside him burned hotter.

"You've never had a woman." It was a statement.

"No."

"Would you like to?"

His heart began a thunderous pounding. "Are you offering?"

"What if I said yes?"

William knew he should tell her that it would be wrong, that it was a sin. Instead, he said, "What about Philip? I don't think he's the kind who likes to share."

Her lips parted in an expression of incredulity. "I've never—you know—done it with Philip."

"No?"

"No." Her gaze met his with a candor he couldn't resist. "Why would I give myself to Philip when he won't even be seen with me in public?"

"He won't?" William asked, astounded. "Why?"

"Evidently dating someone whose mother works as a domestic is below Philip's standards." Her lips twisted in a wry semblance of a smile. "To put it bluntly, I'm not good enough for your brother."

William frowned. "You're good enough for me," he said. "I'd be proud to be seen in public with you."

A smile bloomed across her features. "Really?"

"Really."

The smile widened. "Well, I'm not going to do it with you, either!" she told him, and to William's surprise, she sprang up and ran toward the path that circled the perimeter of the lake. Without thinking, he jumped up and followed her, catching her by the shoulder and spinning her around to the accompaniment of her startled shriek.

The green eyes looking up at him glittered with excitement, danced with deviltry.

"You were teasing me."

"Of course I was," she said, her eyes wide and innocent. "What kind of girl do you think I am, William Delacroix?"

"A beautiful one," he said, amazed at how easily the words tripped from his lips and how Camille's eyes darkened when he spoke them.

Before he had a chance to think about right or wrong, acceptance or rejection, he dipped his head and touched his lips to hers. She didn't pull away, but didn't respond. Finally, he stepped back. His lips tingled from the touch of hers. Pleasure battled guilt. "I'm sorry."

"For what?" she said, smiling up at him. "It was only a kiss."

"Kisses lead to other things."

"You wish!" she said, and spinning, raced down the path.

That was the beginning. Like the small perch fighting futilely at the end of his forgotten fishing line, William was good and hooked. They met in secret whenever he could get home for the weekend. William knew she was still seeing his brother, at least casually, but found his jealousy took second place to his hunger for her. For the first time in his life, William felt ten feet tall—his brothers' equal. For the first time, he knew what it felt like to be a Delacroix. He buried his guilt beneath memories of his time with Camille, the vow of chastity he was to take all but forgotten.

Then, when his affair with Camille had passed its five-week anniversary, he came home and heard Philip cursing the fact that he'd ever given Camille a moment of his time.

"What's the matter?" William asked.

"Camille is what's the matter. She's been hinting around about getting married."

Hearing that Camille had lied about her relationship with his brother, that she was actually pursuing marriage to him, was like having the wind knocked out of William. He sank onto the side of Philip's bed, stunned to silence. Thankfully, his brother was too angry to notice.

"I told her Father expected me to marry someone with a little better pedigree," Philip said, pacing the room, his face twisted with rage. He spun on his heel and pinned William with a disbelieving look. "Do you know what she had the audacity to do?"

William shook his head. His voice was hushed, trembling. "No."

"She broke off with me." Philip swore. "She's nothing but a grasping, social-climbing bitch, and I'm better off without her."

Though he was still in shock, that bit of news perked William up a bit. If it was marriage to a Delacroix Camille wanted, he'd be glad to accommodate her. Philip's next statement knocked that idea from his mind.

"Not only did she jilt me, the hussy's taken up with Charles."

"Charles?" William echoed, his head spinning in disbelief.

"Yes, Charles! He's squiring her all over town. When I asked my goody-two-shoes brother how he could do such a thing to me, he had the gall to tell me it was over, so why shouldn't he take her around, show her off? Then he gave me that condescending grin of his and said at least he's not ashamed of her the way I am. He's *proud* of her."

The wave of pain that hit William was like a fist to the gut. A feeling of betrayal supplanted the happiness he'd felt during the past weeks. Once again, he'd come in second place to one of his brothers. He had to talk to Camille. Soon. He stood to go.

"Where are you going?" Philip asked.

"Out," William said, not bothering with an explanation.

It was later that evening when he finally managed to get Camille alone at their spot on Moon Lake.

"How could you?" he demanded, more hurt by her betrayal than angry.

"How could I what?"

"Lie to me. You said there was nothing serious between you and Philip, but he says you wanted to get married, and when he said no, you broke off with him and took up with Charles. How do you explain that?"

Camille put her hands on her hips. "Why do I have to explain it to you? I don't see any brand that says I belong to you."

The blow to his confidence actually caused William to stagger back a step. "But what about me? What about us?"

Camille reached up and touched his cheek with her fingertips. "It's been wonderful, William," she told him in soft voice, "but Charles loves me."

"I love you, too."

Annoyance flashed in her eyes. "I don't doubt that, William, but we have no future. You're going to be a priest and...and Charles has mentioned marriage. I'm not getting any younger."

William stared at her, a hopeless, helpless feeling washing over him in great waves. "What if I told you I've been thinking about my decision to become a priest, that I'm not so sure I'm cut out for it, that I'd rather be married to you?"

She began to laugh then, a sound that held a bit of desperation, a hint of hysteria.

Hurt beyond belief by her callous cruelty but unable to deny his love for her, he took her shoulders and shook her hard. She sobered in an instant. She'd laughed so hard there were tears in her eyes.

"I love you, Camille. Say the word, and I'll give it all up."

She heaved a great sigh. It might have been his imagination, but he thought there was sorrow in her eyes. "You'd give up the church for me?"

"Yes."

"I can't let you do that, William," she said in a firm voice. "You'd wake up one day and realize what you'd done, and you'd hate me. I'm sorry if my behavior seems selfish to you."

It did seem selfish of her. And cruel and cold. "I thought Charles wasn't exciting enough for you," William said, reminding her of what she'd told him.

Her shoulders moved in a delicate shrug. "A girl has to think of her future," she had told him. Then, to William's astonishment, she'd turned and walked away. One last vestige of pride was the only thing that kept him from calling her back. After many sleepless nights and unmanly tears, he'd seen their summer affair for what it was: the summer he truly became a man. The summer he lost his innocence. The summer he almost lost his soul. He'd been caught in the devil's snare as surely as God made little green apples.

Now, SIXTY YEARS LATER, as the nighttime sounds rose and fell around him, William realized he'd been outsmarted from the first. He'd believed Camille's interest in him was as genuine as his for her. He'd been wrong. The only honest thing about Camille Gravier had been her dedication to getting what she wanted. Any interest she'd had in any of them was only to further her self-centered goals.

She had been as cunning as a fox, as changeable as a chameleon. The fact that she'd also been beautiful and could be charming were just two more items in her bag of tricks. She'd played him like a master fiddler, promising what he wanted with a look, a stolen kiss, a furtive touch.

By the time they'd finally made love—when Camille finally managed to seduce him away from his God—William had been head over heels in love with her. The fact that she'd used him was something he'd never quite gotten over. When she died, he'd cried, uncertain if his tears were those of sorrow or a twisted kind of relief.

"William?"

The cool breath of the evening carried Mary's voice to him over the sounds of the serenading wildlife. "Yes?"

"What are you doing out here?"

"Thinking about...things."

"Philip?"

"Partly."

"It's an unholy mess, isn't it?" Mary asked. Wearing a thin cotton robe, she came out onto the porch and sat beside him. The glider squeaked as it resumed its rhythm.

"Do you think she's out there conducting some sort of voodoo ritual to send Philip over the edge?"

"Desiree?"

"Yes."

"I don't think Desiree is the vengeful kind, William, despite the fact that she's come forward about Philip."

William turned to Mary, his face a study of confusion in the moonlit darkness. "Then tell me. What kind is she? What kind of woman gives up her child?"

Mary sucked in a wounded gasp, and William realized that he'd thrust a knife into his sister's tender heart. He reached out and took her cold hand in his. "I'm sorry. I didn't mean to imply—"

"It's all right," Mary interrupted, giving him a forgiving smile. "There's no use pretending that any of what happened didn't. No use trying to hide from it." She gave his hand an encouraging squeeze. "What do you say, William? Shall we finally talk about it?"

"I don't know that I can." How could he tell anyone about his secret summer trysts with Camille? Mary would think less of him. The whole family would.

"Holding in your feelings about Desiree isn't healthy. It would be better for you to get it off your chest."

So she only wanted to talk about his parentage. Perhaps he could talk about that. God knew he needed to.

"Tell me how you feel." Mary glanced at the three-quarter moon, sighed and looked back at him. "You tell me how you feel about Desiree and I'll tell you why I gave up Rafe's child. You of all people should know that confession is good for the soul."

He nodded but didn't speak.

"You wonder how she could have done it," Mary said. "Think about how things were back then, William. Times were different. Most folks—including Desiree—were poor. She was young then, too. She couldn't have been more than seventeen. Her mama had died, and her daddy deserted them long before that. She was working for Mama and Papa, scratching out a living as best she could. When she found out she was expecting, it must have been a very frightening thing...being alone with no one to turn to. It *is* a very frightening thing."

William made no comment, and Mary continued, "By giving you to Mama and Papa, Desiree was making your future secure, something she couldn't do alone and unmarried. I don't think she did it for the land. I see it as an act of love."

William mulled over Mary's words.

"Actually," she said, "it reminds me of the story of Moses. Like his mother, Desiree did what she thought was best for you, and she was close by, so she could watch you grow up." The moonlight and Mary's smile made her look young again. "No matter who your parents were, you're my brother, William. You always have been and always will be."

As much as he might hate to admit it, Mary's premise made sense. Times had been different back then. Very different. Understanding the reasons Desiree might have done what she had made forgiveness more possible.

"Thank you, Mary," William said, his voice husky with unshed tears. "You've always been such a source of strength to me."

"And you to me," she told him.

They sat swinging in the glider for several moments. Finally, William said, "Your turn."

"What?"

"You didn't think I'd forget you were going to tell me about your and Rafe's baby, did you? Confession is good for the soul, remember?"

"Touché," Mary said. She didn't speak again for long seconds. William wasn't sure if she was searching for the right thing to say or if she was caught up in her memories.

"I loved him," she said at last. "He made me feel pretty and wanted, and needed. I think I was good for him, too. He acted so cocky and arrogant, but inside he wasn't sure of himself at all. I think—I hope—I gave him a belief that he could do whatever he wanted, to be whatever he chose to be."

"I'm sure you did."

"He loved me, too." Even after so long, there was fierce defiance in her voice, a tone that challenged anyone to imply otherwise.

"Ah, someone told you he didn't," William surmised. "And that someone must have been Camille."

Mary slanted him a questioning look.

"It must have been Camille, since no one else knew you were seeing him, and you told her everything."

"Yes," Mary said. "It was Camille. I saw them together one evening when I'd gone to town to pick up the ironing from Mrs. O'Grady. They were standing outside Beauchamps Grocery. They were kissing. They saw me drive by. Rafe looked sick. He tried to explain, but I wouldn't listen. Camille came over later and told me he'd made a play for her. She said he was no good, a fortune hunter whose only interest in me was to land himself a rich wife."

"Then why was he after her?"

"For a casual fling, she said. She told me she knew I'd be driving by to get Papa's shirts, so she arranged for me to see them, so I'd believe her. She said she did it for my own good."

"And you did believe her," William said heavily.

"Yes. At least at first. I broke off with him for a couple of weeks."

"When was this?"

"Shortly before Camille's death. You were at seminary, and Philip was going around like a bear with a sore paw. Charles was courting Camille—I remember that much because I didn't waste any time telling him what I'd seen. I figured he had a right to know, and I wanted to hurt Camille. Charles was furious, as I recall."

It was, William thought bitterly, classic Camille. Stretch the truth. Bend it. Take a circumstance, any circumstance, and twist it into whatever suits the moment's need. It didn't matter who got hurt as long as Camille's best interests were served.

"You changed your mind later," he prompted.

"Yes. Rafe tried several times to see me. I wouldn't meet him. Finally, the night of the murder, I agreed to let him come over. By then I suspected I was carrying his child. I didn't know what to do, but making up seemed like a good place to start. I told him to come to the house because Papa had a late meeting in town."

Restless from the relentless rush of memories, Mary pushed herself up from the glider and went to grip the porch railing. "He came and told me that contrary to what Camille had said, she was the one after him. He told me she'd tried to get him to sleep with her on more than one occasion. He swore he never had."

"Did you believe him?" William directed the question to her back.

"I didn't know what to believe," Mary said. "I told him I needed time to think. He said he'd take a walk, smoke a cigarette. He left me on the front porch of Belle Terre and headed toward the lake.

"Charles and Camille still weren't back together, but she'd talked him into going out with her so she could try to convince him that what I saw was Rafe's fault." Mary sighed. "Charles was so hurt when I told him. You don't know how many times I've thought that if only I'd kept my mouth shut, she'd still be alive."

"Stop it!" William commanded softly. "You can't blame yourself."

"No?"

"No. Did you know Charles and Camille were at the lake?"

Mary shook her head. "She told me they were going to the movies. You remember what Charles said when he testified."

"Actually, I was at seminary, remember? I couldn't get away for the trial."

"That's right," Mary said. "He said they'd gone down to the swimming hole to talk after they got back from the movie. I always figured she wanted to get him someplace private where she could seduce him. They used to meet there and kiss."

"Really?" William said in a bland tone. His mind roiled

with memories of making love with Camille on a blanket spread on the soft grass at the water's edge.

Mary turned and faced her brother. "You can't imagine how badly I wanted to believe what Rafe told me."

"Oh, I think I can," William said, recalling his own willingness to believe whatever fabrication Camille offered.

"I cried and paced the porch and prayed, and then, when he'd been gone ten minutes or so, I heard this horrible screaming. I knew it was Camille. My first thought was that she'd seen a water moccasin...maybe been bitten by one. I took off running to the lake. The moon was nearly full. When I got to the lake, I found Rafe in the water with Camille. He was drenched. He was holding her shoulders, I think. Charles rushed up from the opposite direction about the same time I got there. When he realized she was dead, he started screaming that Rafe had killed her."

"What did Rafe say?"

"That he didn't do it. That he was only trying to get her out of the water. I was so scared I was shaking." Mary shivered now, as if the memory of that night chilled her to the bone. "He dragged Camille's body to shore, and then he looked at me and said that surely I knew him better than to think he could kill someone."

"What did you do?"

"I remember looking from him to Charles and thinking that if Rafe hadn't done it, Charles had. Who should I believe? My brother or my lover?"

"And in the end, blood was thicker than water."

"Yes," Mary said hopelessly. "Charles stayed with Camille, and Rafe followed me to call the sheriff. I was numb. I couldn't talk to him. When I couldn't say I believed him, he took off. They picked him up at his rooming house. He was packing his clothes. The sheriff took that as an admission of guilt. I testified for the prosecution, but

Papa took Rafe's defense because I begged him to. You know the rest.''

"Even though Rafe denied he'd done it, he was found guilty, went to Angola Prison and was killed before Papa could mount an appeal.''

Both siblings were silent for a moment, remembering their father's fatal heart attack soon afterward.

"Yes. I never really believed Rafe did it, William,'' Mary said at last. ''I knew Charles hadn't, but I couldn't see Rafe doing anything so terrible. He was too gentle. There was talk about a hobo skulking around town, but one was never found, and it was so easy to pin the crime on Rafe. After all, he was no one of consequence.''

"We humans always seem to take the easy way out, don't we?'' William stated. ''What about the baby? You were supposed to be telling me about why you gave up the baby.''

"Oh, yes.''

"Did you tell Rafe you were expecting?''

"No. I didn't think he needed that worry.''

"Probably not.''

"I didn't know how to tell Papa. I knew he'd have a fit, so I put it off. When I fainted during the trial, I had no choice but to tell him. He was more disappointed in me than angry, I think. I'll never forget the look on his face.''

"So you decided to give the child up for adoption?''

"No. Papa made me give it up. He called Judge Alvarez and told him to find a suitable family. Then he sent me to a convent in Baton Rouge and told everyone I'd gone to Europe to recover from the terrible mental anguish of my best friend dying.''

"I still can't believe none of us knew about you and Rafe. All these years...''

"Yes, well...''

"I do understand what you were saying earlier, though," William said after a while. "There are lots of reasons a woman gives up a child, and without knowing the circumstances, one shouldn't judge too harshly."

CHAPTER FOUR

THE FIRST DAY OF PHILIP'S trial dawned hotter than the furnace of hell. It was one of those south Louisiana spring days that reminded residents what was in store for them come July and August. "Real fitting," joked many of the locals with a smile, since they figured old Philip stood a greater chance of spending eternity in Hades than inside the pearly gates.

The defense had tried to get a change of venue, but the judge had decided that few people would have preconceived notions about the murder since it happened so long ago. Shelby watched the gathering of the media vultures from the window of her office at Delacroix and Associates, the family law firm. Traffic was so congested on the street in front of the courthouse that folks out doing their everyday errands were forced to a snail's pace. Every parking spot on the street was taken, every parking lot in the small town filled to capacity.

A few enterprising citizens whose homes were within walking distance of the courthouse showed surprising entrepreneurial spirit by turning their yards into parking lots for a small fee. Others offered soft drinks out of ice-filled coolers to thirsty passersby.

The media was well represented, Shelby noted. Various radio stations had sent delegates, as had several newspapers, the *Times-Picayune* among them. According to Rick Roswell, down at the café, journalists from as far away as

Monroe and Shreveport stood with pens and pads at the ready.

Shelby spotted Gator Guzman among the correspondents; she'd recognize that smarmy smile anywhere. She shuddered to think what his take on the trial would be.

She was surprised at the amount of television coverage as well, with the three big networks out in force. Cameras were set up; microphones were clutched in sweaty hands, ready at an instant's notice to be thrust into the face of anyone worthy of commenting intelligently—or semiintelligently—on the players at the center of this circus. Meanwhile, carefully made-up faces familiar to the residents of Bayou Beltane melted beneath the scorching sunlight. Crisp linen and starched shirts withered even though the day was still young.

Just before nine, at Justin's suggestion, he, Charles, Remy and Shelby headed for the courtroom, the only representatives of their side of the family to make an appearance that day. Shelby's sisters all claimed to have businesses to run, babies to feed, other things to do, and Beau was delivering some Thoroughbreds to a new client in Texas. The truth was, it would be tough to run the media gauntlet and keep a cool facade while Delacroix laundry was aired before the world. It was no secret that many people would be privately thrilled at the possibility of seeing the mighty family brought to its knees.

But that hadn't happened yet, Shelby thought as her great-uncle Philip was led into the courtroom. He took his place next to his legal counsel, his usual condescending air firmly in place. Shelby had to admire his ability to project such outward contempt for what had to be a very difficult time of his life.

Legal pad in her lap, pen in hand, Shelby sat near the back of the courtroom between her uncle and her father.

She watched the spectators enter the room, speaking to some, waving at others across the way.

She was shocked when Travis sauntered by, even though she knew he was in town for the trial. She only saw his back, but knew it was Travis because no other man in Bayou Beltane had shoulders so wide or filled out a pair of Wranglers so well. No one else had that particular hue of blond hair. He turned to take a seat near the front, revealing his rugged profile with the strong, masculine nose and full bottom lip. Shelby's heart began to pound and her palms grew sweaty. He hadn't seen her, thank God!

Assaulted by a sudden barrage of memories she'd tried for months to keep at bay, Shelby spent the few remaining moments before Judge Ramsey entered the courtroom praying that Travis wouldn't turn around and attempting without much success to slow her ragged heartbeats. When a masculine hand reached out and covered hers, clenched tightly in her lap, she glanced to her left and encountered Remy's understanding look. Her uncle gave her an encouraging wink. She squeezed his fingers and forced herself to focus on the prosecutor's opening statement.

Byron Calhoun sauntered over to the rail separating him from the group of people selected to decide Philip Delacroix's fate. "Ladies and gentlemen of the jury, it is a matter of record that on June 8, 1938, Camille Gravier was found drowned on the east side of Moon Lake, land that has belonged to the Delacroix family for more than eighty years. It is also a matter of record that Rafael Perdido, who offered no reason why he was on private property that night, was found guilty of the crime, that he was sentenced to death and remanded to the Louisiana State Penitentiary, better known as Angola Prison, until his sentence could be carried out. Mr. Perdido's attorney, Mr. Hamilton Delacroix, wasn't happy with the verdict and filed for an appeal, but while waiting for the slow wheels of justice to turn, Mr. Perdido was killed by an inmate.''

Shelby let her gaze roam over the faces of the jury members while the D.A. paced back and forth, telling them that even though Perdido offered no logical reason for being on private property that night, he had maintained his innocence throughout the course of the trial.

''From what we can glean about his past—which, unfortunately, is mostly unflattering, prejudicial commentary by various area newspapers—it appears that Rafael Perdido was many things. He was a drifter who came to town when the cane-cutting season was over and took a job cutting timber for Mr. Hamilton Delacroix. Newspaper accounts indicate Rafael Perdido liked hanging out in bars and pool halls and was a hard drinker who enjoyed a good time. He was arrested once for drunk driving in New Orleans.'' The D.A. paused, rubbed a hand down his chin and gave the jurors a rueful smile. ''Sort of sounds like my youngest son.''

As he'd hoped, the comment brought smiles and nods of understanding. ''Rafe Perdido was painted as—'' the prosecutor sketched quotations marks in the air ''—'mean-tempered, a shiftless drifter who was out for himself.' Apparently, he was also quite handsome and was considered something of a ladies' man. He even told some of his friends on the job that he wanted to settle down—preferably with a rich wife.'' The prosecutor smiled. ''As I recall, that was a goal of my own when I was that age and struggling through law school.''

A titter of laughter rippled through the courtroom. When the noise abated, the D.A. continued. ''On the surface, he sounds pretty unsavory, doesn't he? Or at best, shallow and immature. Yet during Hamilton Delacroix's quest for the truth, as was noted in recently discovered files, he found out his client was a good and conscientious worker.

No one in the bars and pool halls he supposedly habituated ever knew of him drinking overly much or losing his temper except once, when a drunk became offensive to his wife. He coldcocked the man, put him in his car and had the wife drive him home.''

Calhoun let the jury think about what he'd just said while he walked to his table and picked up a set of papers. ''I suggest to you that Rafael Perdido wasn't perfect, but neither was he a killer. The state will prove that he was simply a man with the odds stacked against him, a poor man who got caught up in something a lot bigger than he was. We will prove, beyond a shadow of a doubt, that the only murder case Hamilton Delacroix ever lost as a defense attorney should have been yet another victory, albeit a bitter one. We will prove that Judge Neville Alvarez made the decisions he did because he was being blackmailed by the real murderer.''

A gasp of shock reverberated throughout the courtroom. Calhoun held the jury's full attention as he said, ''We will prove that Rafael Perdido was an innocent man and that his incarceration and subsequent death was a gross miscarriage of justice. And, finally, ladies and gentlemen of the jury, we will prove that Senator Philip Delacroix, a man who has spent the past sixty years free, savoring the good things of life, did in fact drag Camille Gravier into Moon Lake and hold her under the murky water until she was dead.''

The whole courtroom was in thrall. Byron Calhoun had managed to cast a totally unexpected slant on the drama. More important, there'd been no hesitation in his delivery, no faltering in his declaration that he would prove Philip Delacroix guilty.

Philip's attorney, James Killian, a hotshot from Shreveport, yelped about lies, secondhand information, blackmail and revenge, doing his best to reduce the prosecution's case to nothing but the bitter ventings of Flora Boudreaux, a rejected mistress, and the vicious retaliation of Desiree Boudreaux, an old woman with an ax to grind. Still, it seemed to Shelby that he was relying more on bluster than fact. It was a long morning, and she was glad when Judge Ramsey recessed for lunch.

Charles drove back to Riverwood to rest a bit before court reconvened at two o'clock. Shelby and the rest of the family headed for the Catfish Shack, which, surprisingly, was one of Justin's favorite lunch places. They dined alfresco at one of the half-dozen picnic tables, spreading out their meal in the shade cast by a brightly hued umbrella.

While munching on creamy coleslaw, curly fries and crisp-fried fillets of Opelousas catfish caught in the cold deep water of the Atchafalaya River, Shelby, Remy and Justin discussed their impressions of how the morning had gone.

"Byron Calhoun was great," Shelby said, popping a bite of fish into her mouth.

"Yeah," Remy said. "I always knew he was a good prosecutor, but he really pulled out all the stops in his opening."

"You're right," Justin said. "He knows how to play the jury and get in touch with the common man. By the time he was finished, he had every one of them thinking that what happened to Rafael Perdido could have happened to him or her."

"What about the defense?" Shelby asked.

"Bluster and bull hockey," Remy said, squirting a stream of ketchup onto his fries. "In my opinion, Uncle Philip is in a heap of trouble."

"Remy's right," Justin agreed. "Killian was grandstanding."

"What do you think Granddad is feeling?" Shelby asked.

The expression that flitted across her father's face was one of unbearable sorrow. "He may be eighty years old, but he's still sharp as a tack. I think he'd agree with our assessment, which means he knows Philip doesn't stand a snowball's chance in hell of beating this."

"This has really taken a toll on Dad," Remy said.

"The past year or so has taken its toll on all of us," Justin said. "I know God doesn't put any more on us than we can bear, but right now I'm ready to yell uncle. If I thought I could negotiate a plea bargain with God, I'd give it a try."

He smiled, and Shelby thought what a fine-looking man her father still was.

"Having your mother come back into my life is the only thing that's made getting up every morning bearable."

Shelby smiled fondly. The whole family was more than thrilled that after a ten-year divorce Madeline and Justin had realized they still loved each other and managed to work out the problems that had driven them apart.

From beside her, Remy muttered a mild curse.

"What?" Shelby asked.

"Don't look now, but your old flame just pulled up in a brand-new pickup truck."

Shelby's gaze followed the direction of Remy's thumb. Sure enough, there was Travis climbing out of a fancy new Ford. He was halfway to the window to place his order when he saw the Delacroix trio. He stopped in his tracks, his gaze unerringly finding Shelby's.

He looked tired, she thought, and as sad as her grandfather Charles. Had those lines in his forehead and in his cheeks been so deep when he left? Was she responsible for that emptiness she saw reflected in his eyes?

Her heart thudded heavily, painfully. Shelby wanted

nothing more than to jump up from the table, go to him and tell him she was sorry…for everything. She started to push to her feet, but the icy coldness that replaced the surprise on his rugged face froze her in her place. She watched in numb disbelief as he turned on one booted foot and started back to his truck, cutting her off as effectively as his return to Texas had cut her out of his life.

When Travis pulled out of the parking lot, spewing gravel, spitting dust and leaving Shelby fighting the tears pooling in her eyes, Remy called him a couple of choice names, a colorful commentary on Travis's lineage. Justin, who had never handled a woman's tears well, even his daughters', just sat there looking helpless.

Knowing he was hurting for her, Shelby gave her father's hand an awkward pat. "I think I'll go on back to the courthouse," she said.

"But you haven't finished eating," Justin protested.

"I just lost my appetite," Shelby told him, gathering up her partially eaten meal and dumping it into a trash bin. "You two take your time. I'll walk."

A big mistake, she thought a few minutes later. Not only was the heat stifling, she was waylaid by no less than six media representatives, all wanting to know how she felt about her great-uncle's chances. Somehow she managed to get by them all with little more than the customary "no comment." She spent the remainder of the recess holed up in an empty office, sipping a cup of tea and nursing a heart left bruised and battered by the painful blow of Travis's rejection.

By two o'clock she had her emotions firmly in control, but it was only when the prosecution called Desiree to the witness stand that Shelby managed to rout Travis fully from her mind.

There was a definite stir in the courtroom as the venerable old woman made her way to the stand. Shelby shot a look at her uncle Philip. His profile, exactly like that of her grandfather's, was all that was visible from where she sat, but she saw his lips tighten and watched as he reached up almost nervously to straighten his signature bow tie.

Contrarily, the old quadroon was the epitome of composure, carrying herself with an undeniably regal bearing despite her ninety-four years. She seemed calm, confident and in surprisingly good health—unlike Philip, whose complexion the past few months had taken on a pasty look.

After being sworn in and stating her name, address and what she did for a living—drawing a few titters from the visitors' gallery when she answered, "Herbalist and healer"—Desiree started answering the D.A.'s questions. He asked her if she knew any of the Delacroix family and what her relationship had been with them in the past and more recently.

After establishing that she'd known Philip all his life, Byron Calhoun proffered some papers to Desiree and said, "Do you recognize this document, Miss Boudreaux?"

Desiree looked over the papers, taking her time. "I do."

"Can you tell the court what it is?"

"It's a statement I gave to Chief Trahan on November 28 of last year."

"Have you had an opportunity to refresh your recollection of those events?"

"Objection!" the defense council called out.

"Overruled."

"Would it be fair to say that your statement is a true and accurate account of what you saw on the night of June 8, 1938?"

"Yes."

"Your Honor, let the record show that Miss Boudreaux's statement wasn't given contemporaneously to the incident," Calhoun said.

The judge nodded.

"You saw what happened that night," the D.A. continued. It was a statement, not a question.

"Yes," Desiree replied with a nod.

"What did you see?"

She looked directly into Philip's eyes. "I saw Mr. Philip Delacroix kill Camille Gravier."

At the bold announcement, the courtroom erupted in a cacophony of shocked babble. Shelby exchanged surprised looks with her father and Remy. Apparently, the prosecution's strategy was to bring out the trump card at the outset, use the remainder of its witnesses to corroborate Desiree's story and hope the power of the testimony destroyed whatever defense Philip might have mustered. Judge Ramsey banged his gavel and called for order.

When silence finally reigned once more, the prosecutor said, "Miss Boudreaux, will you tell the court what you—a woman of approximately thirty years of age—at the time—were doing alone in the woods behind Hamilton Delacroix's home."

"I live in the swamp smack-dab in the middle of Delacroix property. I was going to meet my man, and had to pass across Delacroix land to do so," Desiree said without hesitation. Despite her age, her voice was strong.

"Your man? Your husband?"

She laughed, a deep, husky laugh. "I never been married, me. I was meeting my beau on the Bayou Beltane bridge. To get there, I had to pass right by the trystin' place."

"Trysting place?"

Desiree nodded. "That's what I called the place where the Delacroix children liked to gather. When they were kids they swam and fished there. Mos'ly as they grew older they used it for spoonin' and such." Her smile was filled with reminiscence. "Used it for that a few times myself. That's why I call it the trystin' place."

Again there were scattered titters of amusement from various spectators. The prosecutor smiled.

"Miss Boudreaux, I realize a lot of time has passed, and that through the years we forget little details of the things we've seen and experienced, but I'd like you to tell the court in your own words what you recall seeing that night at Moon Lake."

"I forget a lot of things," Desiree said, fixing Philip with a steady gaze, "but I haven't forgot a thing about that night." She shifted her attention to the D.A and began to speak....

June 1938

THE NIGHTTIME SKY was nearly cloudless. The moon was bright, a few days shy of being full. Desiree would have preferred to take the pirogue to meet Reggie at the Delacroix bridge, but the moon's brightness made crossing the lake chancy. It was the weekend, and she knew from past experience that some of the Delacroix offspring would be courting in the back gardens and might see her as she paddled across their private lake. They were good folks but they didn't take kindly to trespassers.

Though the brightness of the night made her rendezvous more difficult in one way, she was grateful for the moonlight as she hiked the soft fabric of her calf-length dress up over her knees and picked her way carefully through the woods. She was as familiar with her surroundings as any of the other woodland creatures born and raised there, but it had rained earlier, and her cautious progress was prompted by the need to protect her new red satin slippers. She'd bought them at the mercantile that very morning, especially for her weekly excursion into Covington for a night of dancing at the Blue Moon Saloon.

She should hurry. She was running late, and Reggie

would be getting impatient. He didn't like meeting her at
the bridge, which meant he had to cut his lights when he
turned onto the lane to the Delacroix house, and drive over
the rough logging road without any illumination. He sure
didn't like trespassing—especially on Delacroix land—but
since she didn't have a car, it was the quickest way to
meet.

Desiree smiled in the darkness. He'd forget about Delacroix anger and his own irritation when he saw how pretty
she looked. She conjured up an image of her newest par-
amour, a handsome Redbone, a man of mixed blood, from
up around Florien way. He'd like the shoes, she thought.
He'd like her fancy new underwear even more. Thinking
about Reggie stripping her from her silky, store-bought
undergarments at the evening's end made her breasts tin-
gle. A pleased smile flitted across her face, like the wisp
of cloud that darted across the face of the moon. That
Reggie! He was all man and then some. Just the way she
liked them.

Through the trees, she saw the mirrorlike surface of the
lake shimmering in the moonlight, creamy ripples undulating in the soft southerly breeze. Her footsteps soon
found the path that fringed the lake's edge, and she headed
northeast toward the bridge.

Whoever blazed the track had chosen ease of passage
instead of a straight line. Bordered by the water on one
side and the forest and swamp on the other, the trail wan-
dered willy-nilly, sometimes coming within feet of the
lakeshore, other places veering through a maze of trees.

She hoped none of the Delacroix were at the trysting
place. She didn't have time to go out around the area tonight, and besides, she might snag her dress or ruin her
new shoes if she strayed off the path.

Desiree drew in a deep draught of the moisture-laden
air, filling her lungs and her senses with the fragrance of

honeysuckle, rain-soaked earth and the fecund scent of de-
composing leaves. An owl hooted, asking, "Who cooks
for you-all?" Bullfrogs croaked out a rich bass accompaniment to the croaking frogs and chirping crickets. This
was Desiree's special place in the universe, the spot the
good Lord meant her to inhabit. The bright lights of the
city were fine on occasion, but she far preferred the glitter
of fireflies to the glow of neon lights.

Suddenly she heard the sound of voices, followed by a
rustle to her right. Turning, she saw the flash of a white
tail as a doe bounded to safety through the tangle of brush
and vines. The nearer she got to the trysting place, the
louder the voices grew. She recognized the lilting, pleading
cadence of Camille Gravier's voice. This wasn't the first
time Desiree had heard her use that light, flirty tone to try
and get her way.

Desiree paused, peeking from behind the trunk of a
mighty oak. Camille was with one of the Delacroix
twins—which one was anybody's guess. She'd messed
around with Philip for a long while—in secret—then taken
up with Charles as bold as you please. Desiree had seen
Camille with one or the other of them on more than one
occasion, doing things that would send Hamilton Delacroix
to an early grave if he but knew about them.

Camille had even used her wiles to seduce William.
Thank the good Lord, she'd soon tired of him and taken
up with Charles. As much as it had hurt Desiree to see the
boy fall from grace, she'd understood how hard it had been
for him not to. Camille could be powerfully persuasive
when she set her conniving little mind to it.

It was a wonder how Camille kept all her menfolk
straight. Desiree liked men as much as the next woman.
Liked them a lot, in fact. Liked the way their hands and
mouths and hard, stroking manhood made her feel. But
while it was true that variety was the spice of life, one at

a time was plenty. Right now that one was Reggie—if she could ever get to him!

She sighed and lifted a dismayed look to the heavens, as if to ask the Almighty why he was testing her so. Then she instinctively left the path, carefully working her way deeper into the shadows of the pines and giving the swimming area a wide berth so there was no chance of Camille and her beau seeing her.

As Desiree grew closer to the couple, the clear night air carried their voices distinctly. She paused, taking in the scene before her. Barefoot, the man faced the lake, his hands thrust into the pockets of his denim trousers, which had been rolled haphazardly above his ankles.

"Rafe Perdido means nothing to me, Charles," Camille said, putting her hand on his shoulder, which was covered in a short-sleeved, light-colored shirt.

"Then why were you kissing him on the street?" Charles asked, turning to look at her. Even from her hiding place, his torment was clear to Desiree.

"*He* kissed *me*," Camille said. She shrugged and wrung water from the hem of her skirt. "I admit I flirted with him, but only because I knew Mary would be coming by on her way to pick up your daddy's shirts from Mrs. O'Grady. Mary has a crush on him and I wanted her to see me with him. It was the only way I could think of to prove to her that Rafe Perdido is no good."

"Mary is interested in Perdido?" Charles asked. "How did she meet him?"

"He came over a while back to cut up that fallen oak tree... I wouldn't worry about anything coming of it, Charles. Mary might have her heart set on him, but she isn't Rafe's type." Camille touched his arm. "I don't want to lose you just because I was trying to help Mary come to her senses. Please believe that."

With ears acutely attuned to her surroundings, Desiree

heard the faint sounds of furtive movement. She went stock-still. The hair on the back of her neck stood up and goose bumps covered her arms. She had a sixth sense about certain things, and something was warning her that danger was near. Danger and evil. For the first time in her life, Desiree's beloved swamp prompted an undeniable feeling of fear. Should she make herself known? Warn Charles and Camille?

Don't be silly, Desiree. You're just jumpy because you're running late and you know Reggie will be peeved. Satisfied that she'd put a finger on the source of her unease, she lowered herself to a crouched position and forced herself to complete stillness. She held her breath, waiting....

"I want to believe you," Charles was saying. He bent to unroll his pants legs and cursed mildly when he realized they'd gotten wet in spite of his efforts to roll them out of the way. He leaned against the fallen tree and began to pull on his socks.

Camille moved closer to him. "Stop worrying about your stupid pants being wet and talk to me," she said in a huffy tone. "This is important."

Charles looked up from his task. "I'm aware of that, Camille."

With a little cry, Camille hurled herself at him, flung her arms around his neck and kissed him. His arms went around her, almost reluctantly, it seemed to Desiree. Since the couple was occupied and less likely to hear her should she make any noise, Desiree took a stealthy step through the brush, eager to escape and anxious to feel the safety of Reggie's arms around her. A twig snapped close by.

"Did you hear something?" Camille asked, pulling free of Charles and turning abruptly toward where Desiree hid, frozen behind some scrub pines.

"Probably a deer," Charles said, sliding his feet into his shoes.

The tension seeped from Camille's body, but she crossed her arms and hugged herself as if to ward off a sudden chill. "Probably."

"Come here," Charles demanded, drawing her close again.

She allowed him to pull her nearer. "Do you love me, Charles?"

"You know I do."

"Enough to risk your father's wrath and marry me?"

Charles laughed. "Of course I'm going to marry you. As soon as I finish law school."

"Law school!"

"I need to finish school, so I can take proper care of you and a family," Charles said in his most reasonable tone.

"But I can't wait."

"What do you mean?"

"I mean, Charles," she said in a voice that quavered with tears, "that I'm expecting a baby."

Charles released her and stepped away. "A baby! B—but we only, uh, did it a couple of times."

Once was all it took, Desiree thought, her anxiety vanishing at Camille's announcement.

"That's all it takes, Charles, if the time is right." Camille stepped nearer and put her hand on his chest. "That's why I wouldn't do it anymore. It was too much of a risk." Her bitter little laugh drifted over the night air. "It seems my concern came a bit too late."

"But a baby! I don't know what to say."

Camille again crossed her arms over her breasts. "Well, I'm so sorry this upsets you!"

"It doesn't upset me," he said, striving for logic. "It just changes things."

"You don't care about me and the baby!" she retorted, turning her back on him.

"Of course I do." Charles seemed to realize he'd disappointed her in some way. "Don't turn away from me, Camille, please."

A whispered rustle a few yards away held Desiree immobile, her hands clenched together to still their trembling.

Charles reached for Camille. "Sweetheart, please," he said in a cajoling voice. "You have to understand that this has caught me by surprise, that's all."

She whirled around to face him. "What's the matter, Charles? Aren't I good enough to marry? Philip wouldn't even be seen with me in public. Would you be ashamed to have a millworker's daughter for your wife?"

"Of course not!" he said staunchly. "Just settle down. Give me a few minutes to think things through and decide the best way to tell my father, all right?"

She pulled free of his grasp and sank onto the fallen tree that lay half in the water. Her voice was heavy with tears. "There's only one way to say it, Charles. 'Camille is pregnant and we're getting married.'" She buried her face in her hands. "Oh! Just go away and leave me alone."

Apparently uncertain what he should do or say, and undone by her feminine tears, Charles left her sitting there and headed down the same trail Desiree had just traveled.

From her hiding place, she straightened. Now perhaps she could slip away unnoticed. She heard another twig crack, this time from behind her, and bit back a gasp of surprise. There was definitely something—or someone—out there! Whatever it was had circled around her, going in the direction where Charles had just disappeared. Desiree drew in a deep, calming breath and decided there was nothing to do but stay put until all chance of being discovered was past. Reggie would be furious!

She counted slowly to three hundred, then, hoping a full

five minutes had passed, raised her skirt and began to ease through the tangled undergrowth. She took a half-dozen stealthy steps, pausing after each one to see if Camille was aware of her progress. Suddenly a flash of movement to Desiree's left froze her in place. With her heart beating a frightened cadence, she turned her head cautiously in that direction.

A man was moving along the trail, his light-colored shirt visible through the trees. Steady purpose marked each step. *Charles.* Desiree went limp with relief. She passed a trembling hand down her side.

Hearing the approaching footsteps, Camille jumped up from the log and turned. "Charles!" She clasped her hands against her breasts and waited for him to join her at the water's edge. "I knew you'd come back! I knew you weren't like Philip. I knew you wouldn't let fear of your family keep you from doing the right thing for us and our baby."

Desiree smiled in the darkness. Little did Camille know that no matter what Charles had decided, things were likely to get plumb ugly when he broke the news to his daddy.

The young man drew to a halt in front of Camille and took her shoulders in his hands. She gave a little cry of pain, and once more, Desiree became motionless.

"What do you mean, *baby?*" he said, giving her a hard shake.

"Philip!" Camille cried, her shock clear.

Philip! Holy mother of God! Desiree realized it was Philip she'd heard in the woods. A jealous Philip had followed his brother and Camille to the swimming hole and heard about the baby.

Philip reached up and grasped Camille's throat. She whimpered in pain but made no attempt to free herself.

"Is there a baby," he asked, "or is this just another one of your schemes to get your own way?"

She knocked his hand away. "Oh, there's a baby, all right." Her voice held a sharpness completely foreign to the soft, wheedling tone she'd used with Charles.

"Why didn't you tell me?"

"Why should I?" she countered.

"Is it mine?"

"What difference does it make if it's yours or not? Would my being pregnant make you marry me?"

"Of course not. You're not fit to be a Delacroix."

She laughed, a sound completely without mirth. "Then it really doesn't matter whose baby it is, does it?"

"It matters because you slept with my brother." He ground out the accusation.

"You know, Philip, a dog-in-the-manger attitude is very unattractive. Even on you." She laughed again, a hushed, mocking sound. "Yes, I slept with Charles. I've slept with a *lot* of men."

"Including Rafael Perdido?"

"What do you think?"

"Whore!" he spat.

"Bastard!"

Neither Camille nor Desiree was prepared for the open-handed slap Philip aimed at Camille's cheek. The blow sent her reeling sideways, while the smacking sound of flesh meeting flesh echoed through the night. Camille managed to regain her balance. Holding a hand to her cheek, she backed toward the water, putting herself beyond Philip's reach.

Desiree was torn between going to help Camille and hightailing it out of the woods. She started to move and thought better of it. No, she wouldn't get involved. This was a rich man's problem. A white man's problem. If she tried to intervene, Philip Delacroix and his daddy could make it bad for her—and possibly even for William. Besides, Desiree knew that whatever Camille Gravier's faults were, she had a lot of grit.

Philip lunged toward Camille, eliciting a small shriek. She stumbled backward, slipped in the mud and fell to her knees in ankle-deep water. Philip reached for her, snagging one arm. She struggled to free herself, but he manacled her wrists with his hands, dragging her to him, twisting her arms behind her back and kissing her with bruising force.

When he released her lips, they were both breathing as if they'd just sprinted up a hill.

"Charles loves me," Camille panted, her breasts heaving. "He thinks my baby and I are worthy of the Delacroix name, and he's going to marry me and see that we have it."

"Shut up," Philip said.

"What's the matter, Philip? Don't you want me for a sister-in-law?"

"I said shut up."

"I won't shut up!" She jerked one wrist free. "Charles is better than you are, Philip. In every way. He's smarter, kinder, and he's a lot better than you'll ever be at knowing how to please—"

Philip struck her again, a backhanded blow that toppled her into deeper water. Camille's scream ripped through the darkness of the night.

He waded thigh-deep into the lake, reached down and grabbed her shoulder to haul her upward. The fabric of her blouse gave way, severing the sleeve from the bodice. She screamed again.

Philip put his hands around her throat. "Shut your filthy mouth!" he commanded, shaking her as a terrier would a rat. Camille made a gagging sound and flailed at him. She lost her footing again and slipped fully beneath the water.

"Shut up," Philip said, his hands still fixed on her neck. "Shut up, Camille."

Desiree saw Camille's pale hands emerge from the darkness of the water to claw at the fingers around her throat. "You won't marry Charles, damn it," Philip said, his voice hard and flat. "You won't, do you hear me?"

Horrified, Desiree could do nothing but stare transfixed at the scene unfolding before her. She wasn't aware of how much time passed, but Camille's struggles grew slower, weaker. Again her arms rose out of the water, as if reaching for the sky...first one, then the other. Then nothing.

"Camille!"

The faint shout came from Desiree's left. *Charles,* she thought. Charles was coming, finally. He must have heard Camille's scream.

The sound of his brother's voice seemed to break the spell of fury holding Philip. He released his hold on Camille with a little cry that sounded like a whimper. He stared down at her body floating in the water. "Dear God," he said.

Almost simultaneously, Desiree heard footsteps running along the path on the bridge side of the lake. Someone else was coming. Philip heard, too. He turned away from the water and slogged the few short steps to the shore. His head was cocked like an animal scenting danger as he turned first one way and then the other. Then he crossed the path and began to pick his way through the trees with as much speed and as little sound as possible. Desiree stifled a gasp. He was headed straight toward her!

She stayed as motionless as she could and prayed fervently that Philip wouldn't see her. Thankfully, he passed her, going deeper into the woods. At one point, he couldn't have been more than six feet from where she was hiding.

She was wondering what to do next when Rafael Perdido came running down the trail from the direction of the bridge. Glancing around, he spied Camille's body floating in the water. He cursed and ran into the lake.

Panicked, he stretched out a hand for her, but she was just out of reach. He grabbed for her again and managed to get hold of her hair. It floated over the surface of the water, spreading like an expanding pool of blood. Rafe tried to pull her closer, but he slipped on the muddy bottom and fell into the water with a splash. Sputtering, he got his feet under him and swapped his hold on Camille's hair for her blouse.

"My God!" The stunned exclamation came from Desiree's left. "You've killed her!"

"AND WHO SAID THAT?" the prosecutor asked, interrupting Desiree's story.

"Mr. Charles. He'd come running from the other direction. It was about that time Miss Mary came running from the same way Rafe Perdido had come."

"What was Mr. Perdido's reaction to Charles Delacroix's accusation?"

"He said he didn't do it. He said he heard her scream and came runnin'. Said he heard someone in the woods as he ran up. Then he told Miss Mary to look at Mr. Charles's pants. They were wet, too. Miss Mary was in a state of shock, I can tell you."

"What happened next?"

"Rafael Perdido told Miss Mary surely she knew he couldn't do anything like this. She didn't answer him, just turned back toward the house to go call for help. Mr. Charles, he was takin' on over Miss Camille. Mr. Rafe followed Miss Mary and tried to talk to her, but she wouldn't say anything to him."

"What did you do?"

"I waited until they took Miss Camille's body away

before I left. I sorta wanted to see what would happen next.''

"Miss Boudreaux, it's a matter of record that during the first trial there was no mention by Charles Delacroix or anyone else of Camille Gravier being pregnant. Can you tell the court why you didn't go to the police and tell them you'd overheard an argument between Charles Delacroix and Camille Gravier about that very matter?''

A look of sorrow crossed Desiree's face. "I've always been sorry I didn't. Most especially because Mr. Rafe, he got killed down in Angola. I know I didn't do right. I see that now, but as I recollect, there were three reasons.''

"Can you tell the court those reasons?''

"Yes, sir. First, if I'd told what I saw, the law mighta tried to blame Mr. Charles for what happened. They'd have said it was nighttime, that I couldn't see well and that he had a reason to kill Miss Camille.'' She smiled. "I been knowin' Mr. Charles all his life. He wouldn't hurt a fly.''

Desiree let her gaze drift to Philip. So much hatred in his eyes! She forced her attention back to the prosecutor.

"Second, if I'd come forward and said Mr. Philip did it, the law was gonna want to know what was I doin' in the woods, and Mr. Philip could just turn around and point the finger at his brother or even me. I knew no one would believe a quadroon wench in a fancy dancin' dress over a Delacroix.

"And third, everyone was sayin' they heard something in the woods that night, and everyone had seen a tramp in town. I figured Mr. Hamilton would make the jury believe it was the tramp, and it would all come out okay. Mr. Hamilton never lost a murder case, you know. Not till then. I felt really bad when Rafe Perdido went to prison. I sure did.''

"Thank you. Another question, Miss Boudreaux. Why did both you and Miss Gravier mistake Philip Delacroix for his brother? You've stated that the moon was pretty bright, and you could see what was happening fairly clearly.''

"Well, they're twins." One of Desiree's shoulders lifted in a little shrug. "No one had any idea Mr. Philip was anywhere around, and he came from the same way Mr. Charles went off to think. And he was wearin' a light-colored shirt, just like Mr. Charles was. You can't really tell colors at nighttime."

"Thank you. One final question. It's a matter of record that Mr. Perdido fled the scene and was arrested later at his boarding house, packing up his things. If he was an innocent man, why do you think he did that?"

"Rafe Perdido was like me—a nobody. Who's gonna believe his word over that of a Delacroix?"

COURT WAS ADJOURNED for the day. Shelby's stomach roiled sickly as she left the courtroom. She'd never been fond of her great-uncle, but to hear the details surrounding Camille Gravier's death brought home with a vengeance his coldness and hard-heartedness. It also brought home just how powerful the Delacroix family had once been. For the first time in her life, Shelby felt a twinge of unease. She'd always been proud of her family, proud of her name, but to know that an innocent man had died because Desiree had been afraid to tell the truth was a sobering thought.

Head down, Shelby pushed through the crowd in the hallway, intent on reaching some fresh air. She was at the head of the granite stairs when she ran headlong into some-one. The first thing she saw was a pair of expensive cow-boy boots. Travis.

With her misery at his earlier rejection compounded by the devastation of her thoughts about her family, she looked up and glared at him defiantly, saying the first thing that sprang to her mind. "Mission accomplished, huh, cowboy? You wanted to see a Delacroix pay for your great-aunt's murder. Well, it looks like you're going to get your wish.''

She just had time to register Travis's shock before she pushed past him and rushed down the courthouse steps.

CHAPTER FIVE

PHILIP DELACROIX'S children had varying reactions to the story Desiree told. Head high, emotions at an all-time low, Drew Delacroix left the courthouse wanting nothing more than to find a bottle. Only Katherine's presence at his side, her hand clasped tightly around his, kept him from doing so. For years, he'd fought to see only the good in his father, but there was a ring of authenticity in Desiree Boudreaux's story. Conviction in her voice. The clear, untroubled look in her eyes of one who had the truth on her side. When Drew and Katherine reached his car, he asked her how he could have been so blind for so long.

"Because he's your father and you love him," she said, touching his cheek with her fingertips. "None of us wants to believe our parents can be guilty of any wrongdoing."

"I don't love him. I hate him."

"No, you don't," Katherine said. "You're disappointed, hurt, shocked and outraged, but you still love him. If you didn't, it wouldn't hurt so much." She kissed him tenderly and looked him straight in the eyes. "You're going to get through this, Drew. *We're* going to get through this."

Drew pulled her into his arms and held her tightly. "How did I ever make it without you?"

"Wrong question, counselor," Katherine said. "The real question is how did I ever make it without you?"

DARK GLASSES FIRMLY in place, Annabelle Delacroix Trahan fought her way through the press of the crowd to the parking lot, wondering if she could contain her tears until she reached her car. All she could think of was getting away from the hundreds of pairs of curious—and sometimes malevolent—eyes. She pictured a long stretch of highway with no end.

As soon as the car door separated her from the world, teardrops began to trickle down her cheeks—not harsh sobs of distress and remorse, but quiet tears of sorrow. She started the engine and maneuvered her way through the throng of cars jammed into the parking lot and lining the street, wanting nothing more than for it all to be over.

There was no doubt in her mind that what she'd heard was the truth. A victim of her father's manipulation and a casualty of his single-mindedness and inflexible disposition—not to mention his cold rages—she could imagine the scenario all too easily.

The memory of all the years of loss and heartache he'd caused her and Jake and Cade spurred a sudden burst of anger and resentment. Outside the city limits, on the old Covington road, she punched the gas pedal, unmindful of the legal speed or the undulating curves. She had no idea how long she'd been driving or how far she'd gone when the unexpected wail of a siren brought her attention back to the present.

Engulfed in a feeling of déjà vu, she glanced in the rearview mirror and saw the flashing lights of an approaching police car behind her. Damn! The tears fell harder. She swiped at them with her fingertips as she pulled onto the shoulder. The cop car pulled in behind her and an officer got out. She lowered the window and cut the engine, fumbling in her pocket for a fresh tissue.

The man who approached the car was tall and lean and handsome. Mirrored glasses hid the expression in his eyes from her, but his mouth was set in a firm, unsmiling line.

Anger radiated off him in palpable waves. Her heart beat out a ragged, painful rhythm.

"Get out," he said without preamble, jerking open the car door.

He was angry. Furious, in fact. Darn it! She didn't need this. Annabelle complied, her teeth buried in her trembling bottom lip. She shut the car door and leaned against it, resting her palms against the sun-warmed metal, her bottom against the backs of her hands. She looked at him, waiting....

"You were speeding. Again."

"Was I?" She heard the surprise in her quavering voice. "I'm sorry."

"Sorry!" he exclaimed. "You might have been killed. Or killed someone else."

The severity of his tone brought a fresh rush of tears. Anguish and sorrow sharpened her own voice. "Maybe it runs in the family. Would being married to a killer bother you, Jake?"

He swore, and the strain on his face vanished in a single beat of her heart. He whipped off his sunglasses and hooked the earpiece in the vee of his shirt. She saw the same agony in his eyes she felt in her heart. He reached out and put a hand on the top of the car on either side of her head.

"Stop talking like a damn fool," he told her with soft ferocity. "Losing you would bother me. It would kill me."

Annabelle surged away from the car and into his arms. They closed around her, holding her securely in the shelter of his love. Jake lowered his mouth to hers in a kiss that was both punishment and enticement. When they were both breathless, he released her and cradled her face in his palms, brushing away the tears with the pads of his thumbs.

"I clocked you going ninety," he told her in a tender tone. "It scared me out of ten years' growth."

"I'm sorry. I was upset."

"I know." He pressed a kiss to the tip of her nose and rested his forehead against hers. "I don't know what to say to make you feel better."

"He did it, didn't he?"

"That's not for me to say."

"He did it," Annabelle said with conviction. "I keep thinking of what he did to us...how he's treated Uncle Charles—the whole family, really. And the strange part is I can't dredge up a lot of sympathy for him. That's terrible of me, isn't it?"

Jake straightened and let his hands fall to her shoulders. His smile was tinged with remorse. "I'd say it's more sad than terrible," he said. "But that's his fault, too. Your dad made his bed, Annabelle. He'll have to lie in it."

"KILLIAN WON'T BUDGE Desiree an inch," Joanna said as Shelby drove her cousin to Jax's house. Jax had gladly volunteered to watch baby Lori for a few hours while Joanna dropped by the courthouse. Jax's stepdaughter, Amy, was helping her tend both infants.

Shelby took her eyes from the road long enough to glance at her cousin. "For your dad's sake, I hate to agree, but I think you're right."

Joanna propped her elbow on the car door and rested her chin on her knuckles, staring out the window at the familiar scenery, but seeing nothing. "I hate this!" she said. "The way people stare, that considering look I see in their eyes. It makes me feel as if *I've* done something wrong."

"I know it's tough," Shelby sympathized, "but you've got to hang in there."

"I'm trying," Joanna said with a sigh, "but it's wearing

on my nerves. As young as she is, I really think the baby senses something's wrong. And it's making me terribly short with Logan and Nikki.''

''What does Nikki say about the whole brouhaha?''

''I think she's of two minds,'' Joanna said. ''On one hand, having it all brought up again brings back her own trial and all those fears. On the other, like any teenager, she's embarrassed. The one good thing to come from it is that she and Cade and Ty have drawn closer.''

''She's been through a lot the past year or so,'' Shelby said, ''but the times I've been around her, she seems much more mature than when you first moved here.''

''She's grown up a lot,'' Joanna said. ''I'm just sorry she had to be charged with murder to do it.''

''And Logan's okay with your moods?''

''The man's a saint. I don't know how he stands me. I can hardly stand myself.''

''You two have had an unusual year, too.''

''Don't I know it!''

Silence filled the car for several moments. Finally, Joanna asked, ''Didn't I see Travis come into the court-room this morning?''

''Yes.''

''I thought so,'' she said, a smile in her voice. ''There aren't too many guys around with shoulders like that. Did you get a chance to talk to him?''

''No.''

''Why not?''

''The man isn't interested in exchanging polite conversation with me, cousin,'' Shelby said. ''He just came back to gloat because we Delacroix are finally getting our just deserts.''

''Don't be ridiculous, Shelby. I'm sure one of the reasons he came back is because he has a vested interest in the trial, but I think you're forgetting the man was crazy about you."

"*Was* being the operative word here," Shelby said dryly. She shot Joanna a wan look. "Uncle Remy and Dad and I were having lunch at the Catfish Shack today. Travis pulled in, but when he saw me sitting there, he couldn't get back to his truck fast enough."

"Maybe he was intimidated by the thought of facing three Delacroix at once."

"And maybe he just doesn't give a darn anymore."

"There's only one way to find out," Joanna said. "Ask him."

"Ask him?" Shelby echoed. "I can't do that."

"Why not?"

"Because he turned his back on me. And because I told him off after Desiree's testimony today."

"So?" Joanna said with a lift of her dark eyebrows. "As you pointed out, this is a stressful time for everyone. If you two love each other, you can get beyond a few snipes and snubs."

Unbidden came the memory of a vow Shelby had made to herself the day before, after her great-aunt Mary had reminded her of the rarity of true love and warned Shelby not to let the family come between her and Travis. She had promised herself that when the trial was over, she'd go to Texas, look Travis up and throw herself at his mercy.

Now there was no need to go to Texas. Travis was right here in Bayou Beltane, staying at her cousin's bed-and-breakfast. All Shelby had to do was gather the courage to face him, tell him she was sorry and ask if they had a future together.

In theory, it sounded easy, but just thinking about it caused a sick feeling to congeal in her stomach. Did she have the courage to go to him and say she was sorry, that she'd been wrong, that she should have put their love first?

Or was she the coward her grandfather claimed to have been sixty years ago? Would she let the love she and Travis once shared die because she didn't have the courage to fight for it?

THERE WAS NO DOUBT in Travis Hardin's mind that his great-aunt Camille had been killed exactly the way Desiree Boudreaux claimed. Whatever label you put on it—crime of passion, heat of the moment, temporary insanity—it all resulted in the same thing. Philip Delacroix was guilty.

When Travis first heard about Desiree Boudreaux going to the police, he and his father had been happy that justice would finally prevail. When the D.A. contacted Travis about handing over his grandmother's letters from Camille to work up his case, Travis had done so gladly. But as more details were leaked by the press and Travis saw how deeply the lies and secrecy were imbedded in Shelby's family, the more potential he saw for heartache.

Yep, Philip Delacroix was as guilty as sin, and Travis's grandmother's dying wish was about to come true. The Delacroix would pay. But Travis was learning that vengeance wasn't always sweet. It was one thing to want revenge against a family he believed was ruthless, heartless and dishonest, but when that vindication hurt good people, it was something else. It was a darn shame Charles Delacroix's side of the family—and Philip's children, for that matter—had to suffer the consequences for something they'd had no part of.

It was also strange how insignificant retribution had seemed once Travis met Shelby. Funny, too, how unimportant the need to see her hurting the same way she'd hurt him became when he'd confronted the terrible anguish on her face earlier. When he'd unexpectedly run into her and her family at the Catfish Shack, he'd been so surprised, he'd tucked his tail and run, like a hunting dog that had come nose to nose with a polecat.

Seeing her again made him realize that he'd been fooling himself. He wasn't over her, and he wasn't likely to be—not in this lifetime. He had no idea where that left him. The only thing he did know was that for good or bad, his masculine pride—or what there was left of it after Shelby had done the two-step all over his heart—wouldn't allow him to make the first move. Not this time. Not even if it meant being alone forever.

He understood Shelby's need to support her family. Unfortunately, understanding didn't make it any easier to take. Selfish or not, he wanted to be first in Shelby's life, just as he wanted her first in his. He couldn't imagine a relationship—theirs or anyone else's—working any other way. Not for long.

When he'd gone back to Comfort, he'd told her he'd be waiting for her whenever she was ready to put him before her family. If there'd been any love left, she'd have contacted him. But she hadn't called, and Travis guessed he'd just have to get used to being alone and lonely.

MARY AND WILLIAM WERE waiting for Charles and Justin in Riverwood's mahogany-trimmed library. "Well?" Mary asked, her hands clenched tightly in her lap.

"She was very convincing," Justin said. He looked at Charles. "What do you think, Dad? Do you think Desiree is telling the truth, or is she just out to get Philip for what he did to Flora?"

Charles sank onto the burgundy leather sofa. He wiped a hand down his face and met his sister's eyes. "Everything she said was exactly as I remember it, but all that proves is that she was there. She said it herself—she might be the guilty party."

"What's her motive?" Justin asked.

"Who knows? Will you pour me a drink, son?"

"Surely." Justin went to the small bar and rummaged around for the brandy.

"What did she say?" Mary asked, leaning forward anxiously. "Tell us."

Charles recounted Desiree's tale, with the occasional comment from Justin. When they finished, Mary shook her head.

"I knew Camille all my life, but I never suspected—" she cast an apologetic look at Charles "—that she...slept around."

"You only saw what you wanted to see, Mare," Charles said. "We all grew up together. As far as you were concerned, Camille was family. You never saw the calculating side of her or how she used you—used all of us—to further her standing in the community. You have a tender, naive heart. There's nothing wrong with that, is there, William?"

Hearing his name, William, gave a startled jerk. "I'm sorry. I wasn't listening." He'd been too caught up in mental images of what had happened that night.

"I was pointing out to Mary how Camille used us all," Charles said.

"Indeed she did," William agreed. "God bless her soul."

"I've talked to Byron Calhoun, Mary, and you can be sure that it will come out this time that I might have been the one responsible for Camille's pregnancy," Charles said. "Not only that, but you know we'd been arguing about your having seen Camille with Rafe Perdido. I'm not going to keep quiet about that this time, either. I'm tired of living with the guilt."

William got up abruptly and moved to the window. His thoughts drifted on the ebb and flow of the conversation swirling around him.

"If you tell about your argument, the defense will try

to convince the jury that it could have been you—not Philip—who did the deed," Justin suggested. "You were at the scene, and it could be argued that you had motive."

"You're right, but I'm willing to take my chances. Desiree made a superb witness for the prosecution. James Killian will have a hard time shaking her or her story."

Desiree's story. A sudden pain clutched William's heart. If there was any remnant of tenderness left inside him for what he and Camille had shared, news of her betrayal with both his brothers had torn it from his heart.

It was hard to accept what Charles had told them at breakfast the day before—that Camille had been pregnant when she was killed. Harder still to accept that both Charles and Philip had known all these years and never said a word to anyone. Clearly Camille had allowed all three of the Delacroix men use of her body. William wondered how she could have been so callous and how she could have lied to them all so easily, apparently without remorse.

He wondered whose child it had been.

From what he had heard, he and Philip were the likeliest prospects, though no one else knew of the brief, illicit affair between himself and Camille. Like the other people involved in the old scandal, William had kept both his heartache and his secret well hidden. As hidden as Desiree had been that night.

William didn't like thinking about his birth mother. Doing so always brought a feeling of guilt. He knew he should make the first move, if for no other reason than it was his Christian duty to comfort those who needed comforting. Desiree Boudreaux was one of those people. As strong as she still appeared to be, she must be feeling alone and weary from carrying around such a heavy burden for so many years—not to mention that her family was disintegrating before her very eyes.

Yes, William thought, turning away from his view of the garden, he should go to her.

Should. But couldn't.

THE SATISFACTION FILLING Mary was almost palpable. Rafe had been innocent! This time it would be proved beyond a reasonable doubt. Despite the fact that Desiree's testimony had condemned her brother, a quiet joy filled Mary's heart. Part of her had always known that Rafe couldn't have committed murder, yet she'd turned her back on him and aligned herself with Charles. Telling herself that anyone in her situation would have done the same was little comfort, when, like Desiree, Mary's refusal to speak up was, perhaps, partly to blame for Rafe's incarceration and subsequent death.

Pleading weariness, she excused herself from the rest of the family and went home to lie down. Once there, she closed her eyes and imagined she and Rafe were twenty-two again. Twenty-two and falling in love, their lives stretching out endlessly before them....

March 1938

FINISHED WITH HER shopping, Mary headed toward the doors of the dry goods store, a satisfied smile on her lips. She needed some new clothes and was pleased as punch with her purchases, done up in brown paper wrapping: a lightweight, flower-sprigged cotton for a dress, blue chambray for a skirt and royal blue, navy and red plaid for a matching blouse. Since she was a far better cook than she was a seamstress, she would see if Mrs. Walters, who could make a treadle Singer sewing machine actually sing, would make the new things for her.

It was midafternoon, and Mary's mind should have been filled with thoughts of what she would fix her brothers and

father for the evening meal. Instead, images of various
dress styles paraded through her head. As she pushed
through the shop's door, a copper cooking pot displayed
in the window caught her eye, and she walked smack-dab
into a man who was hurrying by.

The force of the impact caused her to stumble, but a
strong hand closed over her upper arm to steady her. When
she looked to see who she'd careened into, the apology
that spilled from her lips came out in a breathless rush.

Rafe Perdido. What was he doing in Bayou Beltane in
the middle of the afternoon? He should be in the woods
cutting timber. Even as she asked herself the question, she
noticed the blood on his work shirt. "What happened?"
she blurted.

He pushed aside the lock of dark hair that had fallen
onto his forehead and revealed a blood-stained bandage.
"Logging accident. Had to come see the doc."

Mary's heart plummeted. "Are you all right?" She'd
grown up hearing horror stories of the things that could
happen while cutting down trees, and knew just how dangerous logging could be.

"I'm fine," he said, that slow smile taking possession
of his lips. "But thanks for your concern." Deviltry
danced in his eyes. "You are concerned about me, aren't
you, M-Mary?"

Her eyes widened and bright rose flagged her cheeks.
The color made her eyes brighter. Surprise at his audacity
gave her an animation usually lacking in her serious demeanor. "Of course I'm concerned. I know how dangerous
your work can be."

He smiled at her explanation. "How have you been?"
he asked. "You're looking particularly pretty."

The compliment caught her off guard and scattered her
few coherent thoughts to the wind. She knew she looked
as well as possible. Since she'd met Rafe a week earlier,

she'd been trying her hand at cosmetics, under Camille's tutelage. Today her freckles were muted by powder and her mouth and lips were rouged with a pale rose. She'd pulled her hair back at the nape of her neck and tied it with a white ribbon.

The dress she wore had a scoop neck and cap sleeves and hugged her slender waist and hips before flaring out to fall in soft folds around her calves. She knew the dress looked good on her. Her face might not be the prettiest in Bayou Beltane, but there was nothing wrong with her slender, full-breasted body.

Still, she was so unaccustomed to compliments—especially from a man as handsome as Rafe Perdido—and so afraid of being hurt by a casual flirtation, that she was compelled to end his trifling. "You're flattering me, Mr. Perdido. I'm well aware that I'm too tall and my nose is too big."

Rafe Perdido cocked his head to one side and stared at her for so long Mary felt naked.

"It isn't a big nose," he said at last. "It's just a strong one. Like mine." He rubbed at the aquiline angle of his own nose.

He didn't mind her nose? Forthright and honest as Mary was, it never occurred to her to say anything other than what was on her mind. "Strong, big, whatever. Somehow, a prominent nose suits a man, not a woman. Thanks for trying to make me feel better about it."

"Did I succeed?" he asked, the teasing glint in his eyes giving way to seriousness for a moment.

"Not much."

"Then I'll just have to keep trying, won't I?"

The implications of that statement swept through her, leaving her breathless and shaken. It intimated they would see each other again. That he would smile at her, tease her.

"I still have dreams about your coconut pie," he said, changing the course of their conversation.

"Do you?"

His gaze moved over her like a caress. His eyes were such a dark brown they looked black. "The pie...and other things."

She sucked in a sharp little breath and lifted a hand to her heart, almost as if she hoped to still its wild thumping before it burst from her breast. Darn the man! Why did he have to be so persuasive? Why did he have to sound as though he meant every word he said? "I believe you're flirting with me again, Mr. Perdido," she managed to say.

"You bet I am."

"Why me? There are girls a lot prettier."

"Pretty is as pretty does," he quoted. Then added, "And beauty is in the eye of the beholder."

"Talk is cheap," she countered easily.

"And you aren't," he said. "I can tell that. You're a classy lady, Mary, and you have a good heart. Maybe I like you because you take people at face value and don't make rash assumptions about their character because of what they appear to be on the outside."

Stunned by his praise, she said the first words that came to mind. "You can't judge a book by its cover."

He laughed softly, and, realizing that she'd inadvertently mouthed yet another platitude, she joined him.

"I hope we don't get into a war of clichés," he told her. "I really don't know that many." His smile faded. "I meant what I said, Mary. You're not judgmental. That's a rare gift."

"I got it from my father. As I told you, he's a fair man."

"I'd like to meet him someday."

Mary's smile would have done any coquette proud. "Perhaps you will."

"I look forward to it."

A neighbor of the Delacroix approached the store, and Mary was suddenly aware that she was standing on the street talking to Rafe Perdido. Everyone in town knew her, and they would all be wondering about her conversation with the handsome young drifter. She realized she was more concerned about someone calling her by her full name than she was about being seen conversing with a stranger.

"Hello, Mary," Laverne Dalrymple said, casting a curious look at Rafe. "How are you?"

"Good afternoon, Mrs. Dalrymple," Mary said in her most solicitous voice. "I'm fine. And you? How's your gout?"

"Much better lately."

"That's wonderful."

Laverne Dalrymple looked askance at Rafe as she stepped past them and entered the store.

"A neighbor," Mary explained unnecessarily.

"Oh." Rafe smiled. "I was wondering if I could impose on your kindness again."

"Of course," Mary responded—not too eagerly, she hoped. "If I can be of any help, I'd be glad to."

He gestured toward his head. "The doctor says the dressing needs to be changed this evening. I'm no good with that sort of thing. Do you think you could bandage me up again?"

"Certainly," Mary told him, thrilled that he'd asked her, more thrilled by the idea of seeing him again. "You'll have to come to Riverwood, though. Everyone will be out this evening, and I don't have any transportation."

"No problem," Rafe said. "What time should I come?"

"Eight?" she asked. "Everyone should be gone by then."

Rafe smiled. "Don't want the boss to know you're entertaining young men while he's away, eh?"

Mary couldn't quite meet his eyes. "Something like that."

"I understand. See you at eight, then."

Mary nodded. "At eight."

RAFE ARRIVED PROMPTLY at the designated time. Mary, who was just taking the last batch of sugar cookies from the oven, was surprised when she heard the knock at the back door.

He'd cleaned up. His hair was damp and carried the faintest scent of shampoo. Rafe Perdido might work at manual labor, but it was obvious he was fastidious about his personal hygiene.

"I didn't hear your car," she said, stepping aside for him to come into the kitchen.

"It's a truck, and an old one at that." He winked at her. "I parked it down the lane a bit and walked the rest of the way, so no one would hear me drive up—just in case someone was still here. I didn't want you getting into trouble for having me over."

He crossed the threshold and stepped into the room, looking around with interest at the gleaming floors, beaded lumber walls and the usual kitchen accoutrements. "Nice."

"Thank you. I baked some cookies. They should still be warm."

"For me?"

Not wanting him to think he was so important to her that she'd baked especially for him, Mary said, "It's always polite to offer a guest some refreshments."

He smiled at her, not one bit fooled by her nonchalance. "I don't suppose you have any of your delicious lemonade to go along with the cookies, do you?"

"As a matter of fact, I do," she replied with a smile of her own. If the way to a man's heart was through his stomach, then Mary intended to use her not inconsiderable culinary skills to the best of her ability.

They sat at the kitchen table and ate cookies and drank lemonade and talked about their likes and dislikes. Mary confessed that she wished she had the courage to go to Europe, get a flat and live the bohemian life while she studied art. She didn't mention that her father had taken her and her brothers to Europe the summer before.

"You paint?"

"Watercolors and charcoal sketches."

"Are you any good?" he asked with a smile.

"Of course I'm good!" she retorted. "Maybe I'll paint you sometime and you can judge for yourself."

"I'd like that."

Rafe's dream was to be a musician. He loved music, would like to make a living playing piano. Especially the kind of tunes played in the colored bars and nightclubs.

"But that's just a pipe dream," he told her. "You can't get ahead in this old world playing piano."

"Is getting ahead important to you?"

"Isn't it important to everyone?"

"I suppose."

"I'm tired of being looked down on. I'm tired of being thought of as a drifter. That's why I've decided to stay in Bayou Beltane. It's time to settle down in one place. If I do a good job for Hamilton Delacroix, maybe I'll be able to move on to something better."

Determination glittered in Rafe's dark eyes and infused his voice. He would do it, she thought. He would succeed. "Where did you learn to play the piano?"

"At the church orphanage."

"You were an orphan?"

He nodded. "The Depression about finished my family off," he told her. "My dad lost his job when I was a kid, my mom got sick, and when she died, Dad killed himself.

That left my older brother to raise me and my sister. He did the best he could. When the courts split us up, my sister and I were sent to an orphanage. When I was fourteen, I left.''

"You've been on your own since you were fourteen?'' Mary asked, aghast. His story was common enough, but she'd never personally known anyone who'd suffered so from the Depression.

There was a haunted look in his eyes, a look that said he'd often been lonely and frightened. ''Yes.''

"But that's terrible!''

"I don't want your pity, M-Mary,'' he said, with a fleeting smile.

Filled with a rush of excruciating sorrow, she reached out and covered his swarthy hand with hers, unaware that the gesture might be construed as bold. "What you have is my admiration. And my sorrow that you and your family were separated! My brothers are the bane of my existence sometimes, but I can't imagine being separated from them.''

"You aren't about to cry, are you?'' he said. His tone was teasing, but shadows still lurked in the depths of his dark eyes.

"And if I am?'' she said tartly.

To her surprise, he threw back his head and laughed. Mary started to move her hand, but he caught her fingers in the warm strength of his and held on tightly—almost, she thought, as if he'd never let her go.

"What a delight you are!'' he said when his laughter had died away. "I've never met a woman like you, Mary. One moment all prim and proper, the next shy and quiet, and then all fiery and indignant.''

Not knowing how to respond to that, Mary didn't reply. Rafe's thumb brushed across her knuckles, and her heart began to race.

"No one has cared about me since my parents died," he said quietly.

"No?"

"No." He gave a slow shake of his head. "It's a nice feeling."

Silence filled the kitchen. From the entry hall, the ticking of the grandfather clock seemed overly loud in the stillness of the room. Finally, Rafe said, "I'd like very much to kiss you, Mary. Would that offend you?"

Color rose in her cheeks, and her heart took off like a startled deer. "I'd like very much for you to do so," she replied with breathless anticipation.

He leaned across the corner of the table. Mary met him halfway. His lips were soft and firm and, after that first tentative moment, warm and alive against hers. She responded to the entreaty of his mouth by returning the pressure. And when he tested the seam of her lips with a tentative probe of his tongue, she parted hers with a small gasp of delight.

Nothing in her sheltered existence had prepared her for the dichotomy of feelings that unfurled inside her. Pleasure so acute it was almost pain. Full, tingling breasts. Heavy thudding from a heart that felt so light it could fly. An aching emptiness in the most feminine part of her, but a fullness of spirit that told her that this, then, was love. At long last.

At that moment, she truly believed she would do anything he asked of her. Would believe anything he told her.

In retrospect, she realized that when push came to shove, she hadn't loved him nearly enough.

CHAPTER SIX

PHILIP HARDLY SLEPT the night following the first day of testimony. There was another voodoo doll in his bedroom when he got home. Trembling with fear, he'd thrown it in the trash can and washed his hands with antibacterial soap, as if doing so could wash away its intended purpose. Flora was locked safely away, so who was responsible? Even though Philip didn't want to admit it, he knew the answer to the question. Who but Desiree had a desire to see him suffer?

For years, as he'd relived the events that had transpired that fatal night, he'd recalled his feeling of there being another presence in the woods. But as time passed and no one had come forward to put the finger on him, he'd chalked it up to guilt. Damn Desiree Boudreaux to an everlasting hell. Why now? Why wait so long to come forward?

Because you finally stepped over the line, Philip. Because you never should have done what you did to Desiree's daughter.

Philip didn't want to think about Flora Boudreaux. Just picturing the proud way she held herself and the smug expression on her face when Duffy McGhee had dragged her from the car the night of the kidnapping was enough to send Philip's blood pressure skyrocketing. The haughty witch had actually laughed at him. She hadn't laughed for long.

A self-satisfied smile found its way to his lips. If the

accounts of her madness were true, as they seemed to be, Flora hadn't been so proud after spending the night in the Delacroix tomb. He wondered how she'd liked spending hours with the spirits she conjured up to destroy others.

"How did it feel, Flora?" he asked the darkness.

Despite his hatred of her, Philip couldn't help wondering when and why it had all started going wrong between them. Both ambitious, passionate and determined, they had once been as close as two people could be. She'd certainly served him better in bed than Camille or even Gwen, the wife who'd betrayed him.

Even after sixty years, the thought of Camille and Charles together raised Philip's hackles. The child she'd carried must have been his own, Philip thought, and when he'd refused to marry her, she'd gone on to an easier mark. Manipulating Charles would have been child's play for a woman like Camille. It would have been easy for her to sleep with him a couple of times, then palm off the baby as his.

Charles would have married her, too. He had been smitten with Camille from their youth, and would have crawled over hot coals for her if she'd just said the word. He'd have gone against their father's wishes if necessary, or talked Hamilton around. A Delacroix always did the right thing.

Of course, it all came down to what was the right thing for a particular Delacroix, which was why Philip had never sought more than a physical relationship with Flora Boudreaux. If only she'd had a different lineage, Flora would have been the perfect mate for him. Or maybe not. Both headstrong, willful, they might have killed each other, instead.

As it was, they'd had a son, Jackson. Flora had never admitted whether or not her younger boy, Steven, was Philip's as well. Only recently had he learned via Jackson that he wasn't. Knowing Flora as he did, Philip realized her refusal to tell him the truth had been just another thing to hold over his head.

Jackson was his, no doubt about that, Philip thought. Like Camille, Flora had broken off with him after telling him of the pregnancy and suffering his refusal to marry her. Unlike Camille, Flora had made no big deal of his rejection. It was almost as if she'd known from the beginning what his attitude would be.

He and Flora had carried on a sporadic, half-hearted affair for several years after Jackson's birth. Philip had no illusions about their relationship. They'd used each other. Through the years, Flora came round whenever she wanted something—usually money for Jackson—and Philip sneaked off to the bayou whenever he craved some hot sex.

Eventually Gwen had found out about his affairs—all of them—and about Jackson. In retaliation, she'd taken up with a local banker. Her betrayal had caused Philip more embarrassment than heartache, but he'd made her pay for her transgression by seeing to it that she was forced to leave two of her children behind when she went off to California with her new banker husband.

Philip had always known it was important to keep your thumb on people, to find ways to bring them to heel. It was also important to promote good will—especially when someone had the power to ruin you—which was why, twelve years earlier, he'd allowed Flora to blackmail him into making Jackson a part of his life. A very fringe, very secret part of his life.

1986

"HE KNOWS I'M HIS FATHER?" Philip asked.

"He knows," Flora said.

"Who else have you told?"

"No one but your wife."

"Dear God! You told Gwen?" Philip asked, aghast.

Flora smiled that serenely sinister smile that sent chills down his spine. Her voice was flat, uncompromising. "Of course I did. And I'll tell others if you don't make Jackson part of your life."

"You want me to acknowledge him publicly?" Philip cried in disbelief.

"Why not?" Flora's eyes flashed in anger. "If he can own up to the fact of having a bastard for a father, you should be able to tell the world you have a bastard son."

"You know I can't do that. This is an election year. It would be political suicide."

"That's your problem, Philip, not mine. If you don't want all your dirty little secrets coming out, maybe you should have kept your pants zipped." She smiled at the double entendre.

Philip felt his face grow hot. "You'd do that?"

She gave a negligent shrug. "Jackson's as much your son as Drew is. He deserves what's his by right of blood."

A trickle of perspiration slid down Philip's spine. The hard look in her eyes said she meant business. Desperation had his mind working overtime.

"Can he keep a secret? This one and others? Can he do what needs to be done, no matter how distasteful it might be?"

"Of course," Flora said, frowning. "He's *our* son."

"What if I paid him to do things for me every now and then," Philip blurted, taking a chance with compromise.

"What kind of things?"

"I'm sure you know that when you're in my position, there are sometimes things that need doing, things I can't be connected to. As a cop, Jackson is in a good position to find out special information for me. He also knows how to get certain things done without getting caught. If he wants to help me out occasionally, I'll need to know I can depend on him. I need to know he'll do what I say, no questions asked.''

Flora's delicately arched eyebrows rose in consideration. "What would Jackson get in return?"

"I can be very generous," Philip said, being deliberately obtuse.

"I'll ask him if he's interested." She turned and left him standing beneath the shadow of a huge live oak.

TWO DAYS LATER, Jackson had accepted his deal. Surprisingly, he'd proved a valuable addition to Philip's organization over the years—until recently. Philip supposed he should have known Jackson wouldn't turn against his mother, but it never occurred to him that he'd turn against Philip himself.

The evening he and Flora first talked about Jackson, Philip had found a voodoo doll on his pillow, complete with a miniature bow tie. A pin pierced the juncture of the doll's thighs. Philip had panicked. It was a month before he could sustain an erection.

Ever since then, he and Flora had waged an ongoing, silent battle. Wits against witchcraft. Now it seemed that even though there was no love lost between them, the kind-hearted Desiree was siding with her evil daughter in an effort to bring Philip Delacroix down.

Even though Flora was at the mental hospital, and no matter how much he upped the security around the office and Belle Terre, the blasted dolls kept turning up. His blood pressure was sky high, his heart rate lethal most of the time. If he wasn't found guilty and sent to prison for the rest of his life, Philip knew Desiree would kill him. The old woman was in cahoots with the devil himself. She had the power.

As HAD BECOME HIS HABIT, William was sitting outside at dusk, thinking about the trial, the past and his own role in what had happened that long-ago night at Moon Lake. Charles had come clean to the family about his affair with Camille, taking responsibility for the conception of a child that might have been his. William knew he could do no less, but knowing the right thing to do didn't make finding the courage to take action any easier.

"William?" Mary's voice drew his attention to the door leading onto the back veranda.

"Yes?"

"You have a visitor."

As she spoke, Jackson Boudreaux stepped through the doorway. Jackson. Flora's—his sister's—son. His nephew. Surprise rendered William speechless as the younger man made his way to the lounge chair across from where William sat. There was torment on Jackson's face. His eyes were red-rimmed, as if he'd been crying—or drinking. Maybe both, William thought, catching a whiff of spirits as Jackson took his seat.

"Why have you come?" William asked.

Jackson clasped his hands and let them dangle between his knees. "I don't know. I was just…driving around, and found myself here. Maybe I need to talk to someone."

"What about Desiree? She's your grandmother."

"And your mother," Jackson said.

"So it seems."

"You could have done worse. Actually, *Grand-mère*'s been more of a mother to me than my mother has." William saw a brief flash of white in the dark shadow of Jackson's face. "Mom was always so eaten up with her hatred of my father and getting back at him that she didn't have much time left over for love. That was *Grand-mère*'s department."

William didn't know what to say, so he stayed quiet.

"She's old," Jackson said, "and even though she may not look it, she's frail. Everything that's happened the past year or so has hit her really hard."

Sudden concern stabbed William's heart. "She's all right, isn't she?" he asked.

"Do you care?"

"Of course I care."

"Then why haven't you gone to see her? She keeps waiting for you to come, and every day you don't she slips a little farther away."

"Why are you telling me this?" William asked, shame coursing through him.

"Because I love her. Everyone thinks I'm a callous, mean SOB with no conscience or heart, and maybe I am. I know I've done things for Philip Delacroix that will send me to perdition, and all because I was trying to get him to care about me."

Jackson laughed, a bitter, grating sound. "Drew and I were doing the same thing, only in a different way. We were stupid to think anything we did would be good enough. We should have known our old man would never love us. He doesn't know the meaning of the word."

"What do you mean, your old man?" William asked, a suspicion already growing.

"You didn't know?" Jackson laughed once more, again without mirth. "There are a heck of a lot of secrets in Bayou Beltane, aren't there? Philip Delacroix is my father. So I guess that makes you my uncle on both sides."

Even as the words sank in, William knew it was the truth. There was the look of a Delacroix about Jackson. The look of a younger Philip and Charles. Why hadn't he noticed before? He lifted a trembling hand to his forehead. Dear God, when would it end? Where would it end?

"Sorry to upset you," Jackson said, but he didn't sound particularly sorry. He pulled a flask from his pocket, took a long swig, recapped it and put it back. "I guess I thought I could win his respect if nothing else, but that hasn't happened in more than twelve years, so I figure it's a lost cause, too."

"As long as there's life, there's hope," William reminded him, the words coming automatically from a warehouse of trite but true phrases he'd relied on his whole life.

"C'mon, Uncle William, don't go spouting those religious platitudes. It's a little too late in the game for that."

Stung by the hopelessness in the younger man's voice, William replied in all sincerity, "No, Jackson, it isn't."

"Whatever." Jackson got to his feet, plunged his hands into his pockets and turned to stare out into the darkness. "I didn't come here to talk about me. I came for *Grandmère*."

"You've made your point," William said. "So maybe we should talk about you. I'm here to listen, if you want to talk."

"As an uncle or as a priest?" Jackson asked, over his shoulder.

"Whichever would be easier to talk to."

Jackson turned, a reckless smile on his handsome face. "I'll talk to Father William, then. Make my confession—you know? Confidentiality and all that."

"I'd respect your confidence even if you talked to me as your uncle, Jackson," William said.

Jackson nodded. "Yeah, I figure you would. I guess you heard I made a deal with the D.A. I spill my guts about my father, and I get immunity."

"What bothers you? Telling the things you did or exposing Philip?"

"Both, I guess."

"Telling the truth is never a bad thing."

"You know, I never realized just how low I'd sunk until my dad asked me to kidnap my own mother."

"You had nothing to do with Flora's kidnapping, then?"

"Absolutely not! I admit I broke into Katherine Beaufort's apartment to look for that diary for my old man, and I might know a little something about the fire at Delacroix Farms, but I draw the line at terrorizing my own mother. Duffy McGhee brought her in. My father threatened her, tried to make her admit she was planting the voodoo dolls he was finding, and when he didn't get anywhere, he had Duffy shut her up in the Delacroix crypt."

"Holy Mother of God!" William said. "We'd heard as much, but had no way of knowing if it was true or not."

"It's true. I know, because when I found out what Duffy had done, I let her out." Jackson cleared his throat, crossed his arms over his chest, threw back his head and looked up at the porch ceiling for a moment, trying to collect himself. Finally, he said, "She was all still and quiet, just staring off into space—you know?"

"Catatonic?"

"Yeah, I guess." The younger man wiped a hand down his face. "I had to carry her out. I took her to *Grand-mère*. She couldn't help her, so she got Remy to take her to the hospital."

"I'm sorry," William said, meaning every word. Jackson's longing for acceptance from his father had ruined his life. There but for fortune went Drew. After all, the motivating factor in both their lives was the same: Philip's approval and love. If Drew hadn't had guidance from Mary to counterbalance Philip's influence, he might have turned out to be another Jackson Boudreaux. As it was, Katherine Beaufort might have been the only thing to save him from himself.

Jackson strolled leisurely toward the steps of the porch.

Before descending, he turned. "I despise Philip Delacroix," he said.

"Your feelings are justified," William told him. "But you should repent of the sins you've committed and pray for forgiveness—both that the people you've wronged will forgive you, and that you can forgive Philip for what he's done to you and your family."

"It's too late for me, Father. I'm no sweet little altar boy who momentarily lost his way. I hope he rots in hell."

William watched Jackson hurry down the steps. When he reached the walk, William called his name. Jackson turned.

"Time changes a lot of things," the old priest reminded him. "And the forgiveness is for you, not him."

Without any sign that he'd heard him, Jackson disappeared around the corner of the house.

William thought about the visit long after the younger man had gone. He thought of what he'd told Jackson about forgiving Philip.

What a hypocrite he was! William thought, pushing himself to his feet and seeking his bed. Spouting banalities about forgiveness when he himself was unable to forgive his own mother for giving him away. If his attitude didn't change, Philip wouldn't be the only one rotting in hell.

ON THE SECOND DAY of the trial, as Justin predicted, the prosecution began its campaign to shore up Desiree's testimony. Shelby sat with family members near the front of the courtroom, this time on the opposite side from her uncle. She wanted to be able to see his reactions to what was said. She couldn't help turning from time to time, hoping—dreading—to see Travis come sauntering through the oak doors, knowing she should apologize but unable to find it in her heart to do so. Her emotions were too raw.

She didn't see Travis, but she saw Katherine and Drew

come in. An attractive, older woman with salt-and-pepper hair cut in a chic bob took a seat next to Katherine.

Then Charles was called to the stand.

"Did Camille Gravier tell you she was expecting a baby, Mr. Delacroix?"

"Yes, she did," Charles said, his head and his color high, his voice as steady as his reputation.

"Do you recall your reaction?"

"Shock, I think. And concern about how to break the news to my father."

"So you thought the baby was yours?"

"Yes. We'd only had—" Charles's voice trailed away in embarrassment "—relations twice, but it could have been mine. At the time, I believed it was."

The courtroom hummed with surprise. The venerable Charles Delacroix had been messing around with the hired help's daughter, the woman Desiree Boudreaux claimed was his twin brother's girlfriend?

"Miss Boudreaux has testified that your brother, Philip Delacroix, who overheard Miss Gravier's confession that night, believed the child was his. Miss Gravier wouldn't confirm this either way. In your opinion, Mr. Delacroix, is there a possibility that your brother could have fathered Camille Gravier's child?"

"Yes," Charles said gravely. "No one except me and William were supposed to know Philip was seeing Camille. He couldn't keep it a secret from us."

Charles further confirmed Philip's clandestine affair with Camille, saying his brother was just "sowing his wild oats" with Camille while planning to marry someone with higher social standing. When asked if he believed Camille was true to him, Charles admitted to *wanting* to believe it because he loved her.

"Mr. Delacroix, why didn't you tell the court about your

intimate relationship with Camille Gravier when Mr. Perdido was on trial for his life?''

All the color drained from Charles's face. Shelby was afraid he might have a heart attack right there on the stand.

''Because I was afraid that if anyone found out Camille was pregnant, and if they knew we'd been arguing over her having been seen in town with Rafe Perdido, I'd become a suspect. I'm ashamed to say so, sir, but I didn't say anything about it because I was a coward.''

MARY DELACROIX WAS ashamed of herself. Deeply. Ashamed she hadn't stuck by her guns and forced her father to let her keep her baby. Ashamed that she'd taken the coward's way out and hadn't stood up for Rafe. If she'd admitted he was at Belle Terre to see her, perhaps the law would have searched harder for the tramp who'd been seen around town.

But what if they'd caught the hobo and pinned the murder on him? That would have been wrong, too. Or they might have tried to prove Charles did it.

If Charles had been implicated, would Desiree have come forward to save him?

The questions roiled inside Mary's head, as they had for months, years, decades. She was no closer to an answer than she'd ever been. Her only consolation was that finally her conscience was clear. She and Charles had faced their dragons and slain them. Now all that was left to do was wait and see what the jury did with the information the district attorney's office was presenting to them about Philip.

As heartbreaking as it was to think Philip had taken Camille's life in the heat of his anger, it wasn't so hard to believe. He'd always had a temper, always been difficult. She'd taken his part over Charles's and William's more times than she could remember. She'd believed—or had

Play **TIC-TAC-TOE** and get **FREE GIFTS!**

HOW TO PLAY:

1. Play the tic-tac-toe scratch-off game at the right for your FREE BOOKS and FREE GIFT!

2. Send back this card and you'll receive TWO brand-new Harlequin Intrigue® novels. These books have a cover price of $3.99 each, but they are yours to keep absolutely free.

3. There's no catch. You're under no obligation to buy anything. We charge nothing — ZERO — for your first shipment. And you don't have to make any minimum number of purchases — not even one!

4. The fact is, thousands of readers enjoy receiving books by mail from the Harlequin Reader Service® months before they're available in stores. They like the convenience of home delivery, and they love our discount prices!

5. We hope that after receiving your free books you'll want to remain a subscriber. But the choice is yours — to continue or cancel, any time at all! So why not take us up on our invitation, with no risk of any kind. You'll be glad you did!

YOURS FREE
A FABULOUS MYSTERY GIFT!

**We can't tell you what it is…
but we're sure you'll like it!**

A FREE GIFT—

just for playing

TIC-TAC-TOE!

DETACH AND MAIL CARD TODAY!

First, scratch the gold boxes on the tic-tac-toe board. Then remove the "X" sticker from the front and affix it so that you get three X's in a row. This means you can get TWO FREE Harlequin Intrigue® novels and a **FREE MYSTERY GIFT!**

PLAY **TIC-TAC-TOE**

YES! Please send me all the gifts for which I qualify. I understand that I am under no obligation to purchase any books, as explained on the back of this card.

(U-H-DJ-08/98)

181 HDL CH6C

Name
(PLEASE PRINT CLEARLY)

Address _____ Apt.#

City _____ State ____ Zip

The Harlequin Reader Service® — Here's how it works:

Accepting free books places you under no obligation to buy anything. You may keep the books and gift and return the shipping statement marked "cancel." If you do not cancel, about a month later we'll send you 4 additional novels and bill you just $3.34 each, plus 25¢ delivery per book and applicable sales tax, if any.* That's the complete price — and compared to cover prices of $3.99 each — quite a bargain! You may cancel at any time, but if you choose to continue, every month we'll send you 4 more books, which you may either purchase at the discount price...or return to us and cancel your subscription.

*Terms and prices subject to change without notice. Sales tax applicable in N.Y.

If offer card is missing write to: Harlequin Reader Service, 3010 Walden Ave., P.O. Box 1867, Buffalo NY 14240-1867

BUSINESS REPLY MAIL
FIRST-CLASS MAIL   PERMIT NO. 717   BUFFALO, NY

POSTAGE WILL BE PAID BY ADDRESSEE

HARLEQUIN READER SERVICE
3010 WALDEN AVE
PO BOX 1867
BUFFALO NY 14240-9952

NO POSTAGE
NECESSARY
IF MAILED
IN THE
UNITED STATES

wanted to believe—that Philip wasn't really selfish, self-centered and mean. She'd wanted to believe that he'd needed his mother's love, that somehow she herself had failed him by not providing the emotional balance he'd needed while growing up.

She'd known for years that was hogwash. Had known Philip *was* self-indulgent, egotistical and, while not truly evil, certainly greedy and covetous. Whatever happened when he testified, Mary knew Desiree was telling the truth. Philip had killed Camille, and in his selfish desire to protect himself, he'd let Rafe take the blame.

Like Camille, Rafe had died because of Philip. Now Mary wondered whether or not she could forgive her brother for it. She had no immediate answer for that question. Her emotions were too raw, her own shame too great.

William could offer her no comfort; he, too, was suffering through his own private hell, trying to come to terms with the notion of being Desiree's son and Flora's brother.

The only solace Mary could find was in the past and the warm memories of her brief, precious time with Rafe. No one but Camille had known Mary was seeing Rafe, and she'd worried constantly about what would happen if anyone in her family found out.

She'd known Charles and William would worry. Philip would be furious. She'd feared her father would beat her to within an inch of her life, or worse, send her off to a convent. She had dreaded his finding out almost as much as she'd dreaded telling Rafe she was Hamilton Delacroix's daughter.

She'd finally gotten the courage to tell him the night she'd sneaked out of the house after everyone was asleep and gone with Rafe to Boogie's, a honky-tonk on the outskirts of Covington. She'd never been in a bar before, and even though going against her strict upbringing had been frightening, it had been exciting, too.

Mid April 1938

THE LIGHTS OF BOOGIE'S were dim, and the room was filled with smoke, people in flashy clothes, and easy laughter. Between sets of hard-hitting blues, the clink of glassware punctuated the sounds of a dozen conversations.

Mary got her first taste of alcohol, which went straight to her head. When Rafe pulled her onto the dance floor, she found herself helpless to resist, even though she was a poor dancer at best.

It didn't matter. What they did could hardly be called dancing. Guiding her to a dark corner of the room, Rafe clasped his arms around her waist, wrapped hers around his neck, like links of chain locking them together. They were so close her breasts were crushed against his chest, and she felt the strength of his thighs and his masculinity moving against her.

When she looked up at him, Rafe smiled. She licked her lips. He groaned, spun her around in a wild pirouette and bent his head to kiss her. The room seemed to explode in a flash of brilliance. Her head whirled dizzily, making her feel giddy.

She felt the gentle probe of his tongue and opened her mouth for him. Dear heaven! They were French kissing! It was a scandal! It was wonderful. Every stroke of his tongue ignited another small blaze that licked along her nerve endings and stoked the smoldering fire at the very heart of her womanhood. She pressed closer.

Rafe drew back to look at her, his eyes glittering with a strange and slumberous excitement. Whatever he saw in hers, made him guide her to a dark hallway. There, in the comparative privacy of the darkness, away from the prying eyes of the other customers, he backed her against the wall and slid his hands down to cup her bottom.

She gasped at the urgent feel of his male hardness as

his hips ground against hers with slow, mind-destroying thrusts. His mouth captured hers again, the stroking of his tongue keeping rhythm with his hips, wringing a response from her she was helpless to deny.

The implication of what they were doing—of where this was leading—was obvious and more intoxicating than the rum she'd consumed. Mary felt dazzled by the emotions coursing through her, dazed by the expertise with which he coaxed a response from her.

She was burning up inside, her bones dissolving beneath the heat of his kisses. When moisture dampened her brow and her cotton underwear, she had no idea what was happening and felt a wave of embarrassment sweep over her. Then Rafe's teeth closed gently over her lower lip and his hand slid up to her breast. Her humiliation vanished before a swell of desire so strong her knees buckled.

Her thought processes shut down like the saws at the mill at five o'clock.

She whimpered but didn't know why. Blindly, her hands moved to his face. Desperately, she whispered his name.

"Come on." His own voice was breathless, hardly more than a whisper. He grabbed her hand and led her down the hallway to the back door.

The fresh nighttime air hit her like a bracing slap in the face, cooling her fevered skin, restoring her sanity.

What was she doing? she wondered as he pulled her across the parking lot and helped her into his truck. Rafe Perdido was handsome, exciting, desirable—and a virtual stranger. She couldn't give herself to him so easily....

"Rafe," she began, intending to tell him she wasn't that kind of girl, but he kissed her again and her feeble attempt at protest died on her lips.

"Shh," he whispered, smiling in the darkness. He pulled her close to his side, cranked the engine and started back toward Bayou Beltane, their fingers laced together.

Neither spoke during the trip, but the emotions seething between them were palpable. Need. Hunger. Fear. Curiosity. Love.

There was no doubt in Mary's mind that she loved him. She told herself he loved her, too, but he hadn't said it. She'd been warned by Camille that *love* was a word men bandied about to get what they wanted from a woman. Still, she felt love in everything he did—from the way he looked at her to the way he touched her. It was evident in his gentleness and his tender teasing. Or did she only imagine it?

When Rafe pulled into the lane leading to Belle Terre, he turned off the motor and cut the headlights. Then he drew Mary close and kissed her again. The kiss was long and leisurely, almost gentle, nothing like the kisses they'd shared on the dance floor of Boogie's.

She felt him smile against her lips. "You're driving me crazy, you know that, don't you?" he said.

She drew back to meet his smiling gaze. "I am?" she asked in wonder. "How?"

"I'm trying very hard to be good, because I know you're a nice girl. But being good is hard, because I want you so much."

Thrilled that she—plain Mary Delacroix—could wring such an admission from a man like Rafe Perdido, Mary felt it only fair to be equally honest. "I want you, too."

"Sweet mother of God," Rafe said, clutching tightly at her hands. "Do you know what you're saying?"

"I...I think so."

"I know you've never—"

"No!" Mary interrupted. "Never."

"I don't want to hurt you. I—"

She pressed her finger against his lips. "You won't. I know that. You'd never hurt me."

"I have a blanket. We can put it in the back of the truck."

"No," Mary said with a shake of her head. "Not there. This is a special time. I want it to be at a special place."

"Where?"

"Riverwood. There's no one there."

"Hamilton Delacroix's other house?" Rafe exclaimed. "No. I don't want to be accused of breaking into my boss man's house."

Mary felt a momentary pang of guilt. It was time to tell Rafe the truth. Past time. And she would. Soon. "Don't worry. We're not going to break in. Remember the magnolia tree where I was reading the day we first met?"

"Yes."

"That's my special place. That's where I want to be."

Rafe nodded. "Yes," he said. "It's perfect."

Without another word, he started the truck. They made the drive to Riverwood in less than ten minutes and walked to the tree hand in hand. Rafe held aside the branches so Mary could precede him into the cozy sanctuary.

Wordlessly, and together, they swept away fallen seed pods and spread out the blanket.

Together they lay down face-to-face and began a slow journey into uncharted territory. Hands skimmed over curves. Lips worked slowly over small rises to claim peaks and crests. Caverns were explored, their depths plumbed.

With only the moon as a witness, Rafe staked his claim on Mary, and Mary, ultimately conquered and feeling utterly feminine and truly beautiful for the first time in her life, wept with the splendor of it.

They must have dozed, for the hooting of an owl roused her. It took her a moment to orient herself, and when she did, she felt a flutter of alarm that had more to do with the passage of time than with what she'd done. She pressed her mouth to Rafe's cheek and called his name. He stirred, smiled, pulled her close and kissed her again—quite thoroughly.

"We should go," she said, running her palm over the crisp hair of his chest.

"You're right. It's late." They both scrambled for clothes. Getting dressed became a matter of concentration. Both kept getting waylaid by a kiss or a touch.

Mary was twisting her hair back when she said, "I have something to tell you."

"That sounds ominous," Rafe answered, pulling on his socks.

"I haven't been exactly truthful with you."

"Oh?"

"I haven't lied," she said quickly, fearing an anger she'd never yet seen in him. "I just haven't told you the whole truth."

"About what?"

"Who I am."

Rafe drew her close and smiled in the darkness. "Don't tell me. You don't really work for Hamilton Delacroix at all. You're an international spy, working for the German government," he said lightly.

"You're partly right," she told him, pulling back. "I'm not a spy, but I don't work for Hamilton Delacroix, either. At least not for pay." She took a deep breath. "My name is Mary Delacroix. I'm Hamilton Delacroix's daughter."

"You're joking."

Mary heard the incredulity in his voice. "No. You never asked my name. Weren't you curious?"

"Sometimes. But it never seemed that important. When we were together, that was enough. You were just Mary. You were smart and had a sharp tongue and you believed in me. That was all I needed to know."

Mary's heart swelled with love at his acceptance of her.

"Why didn't you tell me sooner?" he asked.

"I started to tell you that first day, but then I realized you thought I worked for my father. You were so nice, and seemed to like me, so I decided not to. It was wrong, I know, but I wanted you to like me for what I was, not who I was or what I could do for you. On the extremely rare occasion when a man has made a play for me, it's because he's hoping to latch on to the Delacroix money."

"What makes you think they do that?"

"Well," Mary said, spreading her arms wide, "look at me. They certainly wouldn't be interested in me for any other reason, would they?"

Rafe took her in his arms. "When I look at you I see a woman with a big heart. A loving heart. One who is kind and caring and beautiful in all the ways that count. I was drawn to that, Mary. I am drawn to that."

The tenderness in his voice was her undoing. She felt the dampness of tears slipping down her cheeks and held him more tightly. "Oh, Rafe!"

"I love you, Mary."

The whispered words stirred the hair at her temple and fell on her ears like a benediction. "Oh, Rafe!" she said again.

He took her shoulders and drew back until he could look into her face. "I mean it. You've given me a belief in myself I haven't felt in years. Because of you I know I can make something of myself besides a logger."

She framed his face with her hands. "There's nothing wrong with being a logger. It's good, honest work."

He circled her wrists with his fingers and pressed a kiss to one palm, then the other. "I know that. Once it might have been enough. But I want more from life now. Because of you. For you."

"I don't need *things*. I've had *things* all my life. What I need is a man who'll love me forever."

"You have him. I want to marry you, Mary."

She sucked in a surprised breath.

He placed his fingers over her mouth. "Don't say yes or no. Not now. I know your family wouldn't accept me. Not yet, anyway. But maybe in time...in a few months if I get a better job and prove to your father I'm not just a drifter. If I show him and everyone in Bayou Beltane that I want to make something of myself and I can take care of you, maybe he'll be more accepting."

Mary's heart felt full to overflowing. She nodded.

He kissed her then, the gentle pressing of mouth against mouth. The kiss was like the sealing of an agreement, a promise for the future. When it was over, he helped her to her feet. "We should go."

"Yes."

He gathered the blanket and together, arm in arm, they made their way to his truck. "Maybe it's a good thing I didn't know who you were," he said when they were back on the road leading to Belle Terre. "I'd never have flirted so outrageously with you."

"You wouldn't? Why?"

"I'd have been scared to death of you. Rich girls frighten me."

"That isn't what I've heard. I heard you made a play for Judge Alvarez's daughter."

"Well, Miss Delacroix, you heard wrong. Bianca Alvarez made a play for *me*, but she only did it to show off to her friends. She was just slumming."

"Slumming?" Mary said aghast. "She said that about you?"

"That's what the lady said. To my face. Thank God I was smart enough to see her for what she was. Her father found out somehow and put pressure on her to stop. No skin off my nose. That woman is trouble with a capital *T*."

"She's very pretty," Mary said.

Rafe cast her a sideways glance. "So is a black widow spider."

Mary laughed and Rafe joined her. Then he shook his head. "I can't believe it. Hamilton Delacroix's daughter."

CHAPTER SEVEN

THE THIRD DAY of the trial began with Mary's videotaped deposition, shown on several small television screens set at strategic places around the courtroom. Unlike the first trial, this time Mary was composed as she told the prosecutor something she'd never admitted to Rafe's jurors, something he'd never explained, even though to do so might have meant a different ending to the trial, might have saved his life.

"Miss Delacroix, according to the transcripts of Camille Gravier's murder trial, Mr. Perdido offered no explanation for his presence in the woods the night in question. All he said was that he was meeting someone. He refused to elaborate. Do you know who he was meeting?"

"He was meeting me," Mary said. "We'd been seeing each other secretly for some time."

"Secretly? Just as your brother Philip was seeing Camille Gravier?"

"Yes."

"Why secretly?"

"I didn't think my father would approve of my association with Rafe. To the people in Bayou Beltane, he was considered a drifter, a nobody. Rumor had it he was a ladies' man."

"Do you remember where you were when you heard Camille Gravier's scream?"

"I was at the house, pacing up and down the yard."

"The house. Belle Terre plantation house where you

lived, correct?'' Mary answered affirmatively, and the prosecutor asked, ''Where was Mr. Perdido?''

''He'd gone off to be by himself for a while. We'd argued earlier about my having seen him kissing Camille in town. I'd told him I didn't want to meet him anymore, but he persuaded me to let him come over so he could explain what had actually happened. I was...expecting his child, and I loved him, so I agreed to meet him and hear what he had to say.''

Another murmur of shock rippled through the courtroom, like a wave at a football stadium.

''And what did he tell you?''

''He said Camille had pursued him for weeks. Relentlessly. He said *she'd* kissed *him*, not the other way around, so that I would see them together and break off with him. He told me, as he said he'd told her, that he wasn't interested in her, that he loved me.''

''Isn't it true that Miss Gravier was your closest friend?''

''I thought so at the time. Now I'm not so sure.''

''Why do you think she tried to break up your relationship with Mr. Perdido?''

''Because she wanted him for herself. The more he rebuffed her, the more determined she would be to have him.''

Mary looked down at her hands for a few seconds, then looked into the camera again. ''It's taken me many years to come to this conclusion, but now I realize that Camille Gravier was selfish and self-centered. Everything she did was calculated so she'd reap the benefits. She dated Philip hoping she could talk him into marrying her. When that didn't work, she went after Charles, who was mad about her and far more easily influenced. She played them against each other.''

''And Mr. Perdido?''

"She went after him simply because he struck her fancy. Maybe because, for the first time in our lives, I was getting the attention of an exciting man. Camille didn't like competition. That's why she pretended to be my friend. Homely Mary Delacroix was no competition."

"Do you think Camille Gravier was successful in her pursuit of Rafe Perdido? Do you think they had a sexual relationship?"

"No, I do not." Mary spoke firmly, with conviction.

"Why not? You said she was determined, and she was beautiful."

"Because Rafe Perdido truly loved me. And because of that love he would never betray me with another woman."

"By your own admission, he was a ladies' man. What makes you so certain he was loyal to you?"

"When I saw him in the water with Camille's body, I couldn't believe what my eyes were seeing. Charles believed Rafe had killed her, and it did seem that's what had happened. But he looked at me and said I should know he couldn't do anything like that. He was right. I *did* know him, and I *didn't* believe he could do anything like that. But the only other thing to believe was that Charles had done it. And that was impossible, too."

Mary pressed her trembling lips together. "I went to call the police. Rafe pleaded with me all the way to the house to look into his eyes and tell him I believed him. I couldn't. I can only guess that he loved me more than I did him. He left then, and when the sheriff found him, he was packing to leave town."

"And how does that prove he loved you?"

"If he hadn't truly loved me, he would have told my father—who defended him—why he was on our property that night. But he didn't say anything, because he didn't want me to suffer for it."

"You made the statement that he loved you more than you did him. Why?"

"Because I wouldn't say I believed him. I wouldn't put him before my family, and because I let my father force me to give up our child."

During both Charles's and Mary's testimony, Philip sat at the table, his gaze fixed unerringly on his siblings' faces, his expression intent. He might have been carved of stone, a perfectly sculpted statue with no discernible emotion on his visage.

There was another stonelike countenance in the audience, that of a woman past middle age. A woman with salt-and-pepper hair, who sat clutching her purse with a white-knuckled grip. A woman whose eyes shone with the glitter of tears she refused to let fall.

WHILE THE SPECTATORS in the courtroom viewed her taped deposition, Mary Delacroix lay at home on her bed with one arm flung over her eyes, thinking of the past. It was how she seemed to spend most of her time these days. She wondered what the citizenry of Bayou Beltane would say when they learned both Philip and Charles had slept with Camille and that she herself, the town's chaste old maid, had given birth to a child out of wedlock, then given that child away.

It was strange, she thought, that once she would have panicked at the thought of being talked about. Now she couldn't summon up the energy to care one way or the other. It was one of the perks of growing old. She remembered Desiree saying that when you got old you'd earned the privilege of saying and doing what you wanted. Maybe as you grew older you realized that what people thought about you didn't matter nearly as much as your opinion of yourself.

Early May 1938

MARY STOOD NEAR the fallen tree at the lake, a woven crown of honeysuckle in her hands, waiting for Rafe. They had been seeing each other secretly for almost a month, and the more time Mary spent with him, the more deeply in love she was. Though her initial interest in him had sprung from his rare good looks, his easygoing way and the aura of the forbidden that surrounded him, it hadn't taken her long to realize he was more than just a handsome, charismatic drifter, and that there was far more to their relationship than the physical one they shared.

He'd surprised her with the fact that he'd finished school, though he was quick to add that he wasn't particularly proud of his grades. It was his good fortune to be blessed with intelligence and the ability to grasp concepts quickly and easily. With her help, he could do anything he wanted to do, be what he wanted to be, she was sure.

Mary watched Rafe as he strode briskly down the path toward her, hands in his pockets, shapely lips pursed as he whistled a popular tune. He'd just come from a job interview as a buyer for her father's timber company and looked particularly handsome in a pair of gray trousers with black braces over a white, collarless shirt.

Rafe put his arms around her waist and brushed her mouth with his. "Mmm. You smell good. And you taste like dewberries."

"I've been nibbling on them while I waited for you," she said, gesturing toward a tangle of brambles that sported a profusion of berries easily an inch long. "Are my lips blue?"

"No," he said, brushing her mouth with his again. "They're rosy red." He grinned. "I'm going to be blue, though, if you don't bake me a berry cobbler. I don't suppose I could talk you into making one?"

"Perhaps," she said, smiling up at him and brushing back a persistently errant lock of dark hair. "If you asked very sweetly. Now, stop fooling around and tell me what happened."

Rafe looked pleased with himself. "Well, Festervan didn't hire me straight out, but he did seem impressed at how well I could figure timber on the stump. I think he's narrowed it down to me and another fellow, so I guess all we can do is keep our fingers crossed."

"And pray."

"By all means. If you think it will do any good."

"Of course it will. I'll have William pray, too." She gave Rafe a saucy smile. "He ought to have a little pull with God."

Rafe laughed and gave her a brief, hard hug and an equally hard, brief kiss.

"What was that for?" she asked breathlessly.

"For being you. For being so smart and so supportive and for making me laugh."

Mary felt her cheeks grow red. She wasn't used to praise, and hearing it from Rafe still made her both proud and uncomfortable.

"I mean it, Mare," he said, laying his hand against her cheek and brushing the crest of her cheekbone with his thumb. "I never knew life could be so good until I met you."

Mary's throat tightened with emotion. "Oh, Rafe," she murmured, turning her head and pressing a kiss to his palm.

"I love you, Mary," he said. "And as soon as I get this job and save some money, I want to marry you."

It was what Mary wanted more than anything in the world. "We could elope."

"No," Rafe said firmly. "I want to do this right. I want your father to know I can take care of you. Maybe not in the style you've grown accustomed to, but I want him to know I can keep a roof over your head and clothes on your back. I want you to be proud of me, and I want him to approve of our marriage. Can you understand that?"

"Yes," she said softly, tears springing into her eyes. "I can understand that."

At the time, she'd understood exactly, and Rafe's determination to make something of himself made her respect him that much more. What he didn't understand was that her father would never approve of a marriage between them...something that became clear when he found out about her pregnancy not long after. After fainting at the trial, she'd felt it necessary to tell her father why. After all, pregnancy wasn't a secret that could be kept indefinitely.

Mid June 1938

"YOU'RE WHAT?" Hamilton asked in a quiet tone when Mary said she was expecting a baby.

"I'm expecting a baby," she repeated, "Rafe Perdido's baby."

"You're pregnant by Rafe Perdido?"

"Yes." Mary's confession was little more than a whisper.

Hamilton spent the next five minutes ranting and raving and cursing and demanding to know how she could shame the family this way. Mary, who had seldom seen her father angry, feared he'd have a heart attack.

When he calmed down, he said, "Well, that explains why you begged me to take this case, doesn't it? How long has this been going on?"

"A few months."

"A few months. Dear God! How did you meet him?"

"We met when you sent him to cut up that fallen tree."

"I'll give him this," Hamilton said. "He certainly knows how to choose his mark. But then, his kind usually goes after rich women if they can."

Mary gasped in shock and pain. Shock that her usually mild-mannered father was being so unreasonable about the whole thing and pain because he thought so little of her attributes that he didn't believe a man could love her for herself and not her name.

"That's unfair, Papa! And it isn't true. He didn't know I was a Delacroix for weeks."

"So he told you."

"He *didn't* know," she said in a firm voice. "He loves me. Me. And not because I'm a Delacroix. If I tell him about the baby, he'll marry me to give it a name."

"He doesn't know?" Hamilton asked sharply.

"No."

"Who else knows you were sneaking around like a slut from Boogie's to sleep with Rafe Perdido?"

Shame flooded Mary. How could her father make something so beautiful into something that sounded so sordid? "No one knew but Camille."

"Your brothers?"

"No."

Hamilton pinned her with a hard stare that sent a frisson of discomfort down her spine. "And they won't."

"I beg your pardon?"

"You'll not say a word about this to anyone, Mary, do you understand?" Hamilton said.

"But, Papa—"

"Do you understand?"

"No, I don't understand!" she said in bewilderment. "If I don't tell Rafe—don't marry him—what will I do?"

"What you'll do is forget about marrying Perdido. In fact, you'll forget you ever met him."

"I can't do that!" she cried, raising her voice to her

father for the first time in her life. "Haven't you heard a thing I've said? I love him. He loves me. He isn't the kind of person you think he is, Papa, and he didn't kill Camille."

"Who did, then?" Hamilton retorted. "Charles?"

Mary sucked in a sharp breath. There it was again—that impossible choice. Who to believe? Charles or Rafe?

"What about the noise Rafe heard in the woods?" she asked, her voice rising along with her desperation. "Charles thought he heard something, too. Why aren't you and the police looking for that tramp who was in town? Why are you letting Rafe take the blame?"

"Damn it!" Hamilton roared. "How dare you imply I'm doing anything but my level best for Rafael Perdido?"

Seeing how high his color was, Mary reached out and touched his arm in a soothing gesture. "I'm sorry, Papa. I didn't mean to imply you weren't."

Hamilton pulled a hanky from his pocket and mopped his perspiring forehead. "I am doing all I can, Mary. Not necessarily for Perdido, but because I take pride in my ability and my reputation. But something's gotten into Neville, and with these ridiculous, incomprehensible decisions he's making, there's no way the jury can come to any conclusion but that your Mr. Perdido is guilty."

Mary gasped at the cold, unemotional statement. She stared at her father with eyes gone wide with disbelief, her anger replaced by an inability to understand. "B-but you've never lost a murder case. That's why I wanted you to represent him."

Hamilton's anger was spent, too. "Well, my dear," he told her heavily, "there is, as they say, a first time for everything. Perdido is bound for the gallows as surely as God made little green apples, and there is no way I'll let a daughter of mine marry a convicted murderer."

"Then what will I do?" Mary demanded, her fury rising again.

"I'll speak to Neville. He knows a lot of people. You'll go away and have your baby and we'll put it up for adoption."

"I will not give this baby up!" Mary cried. "It's the only thing I'll have left to remember Rafe by."

"You'll do as I say, young lady, or you'll pack your things and find another place to live."

IN THE END, NO AMOUNT of pleading or tears had budged Hamilton Delacroix. Mary knew there was no way she could make it on her own, so she had acquiesced. They told the people of Bayou Beltane she'd gone to Europe for an extended trip, when in reality she'd gone no farther than a convent in Baton Rouge. Long-time friend that he was, Neville Alvarez had arranged the adoption.

Now, finally, Mary knew who had adopted her child. Judge Alvarez's mistress had had a sister who couldn't conceive. She and her husband had adopted Rafe and Mary's child, the daughter who had been born just days before Mary received word that Rafe had been killed in a fight at the prison.

Even though Mary had loved her father, there were times, even after all these years, when she wasn't sure she'd ever forgive him.

AFTER A TWO-HOUR lunch recess, and obviously feeling that he'd established a convincing account of what had happened on the night Camille was murdered, the D.A. began to add to the strength of his case. By calling Jake Trahan to the stand, he reinforced the importance of the information in Patrice Forêt's diary. Jake testified that Jackson Boudreaux had broken into Katherine's apartment solely to gain access to the diary, a crime Jackson had already been arrested for and confessed to doing at Philip's instigation.

The prosecutor also laid the groundwork for the role someone had played—according to the information in the diary—in slanting the decisions Judge Alvarez had made, ultimately causing Rafe Perdido to be sentenced to death, despite his well-mounted defense. That someone, the D.A. claimed, was Philip Delacroix. Calhoun used Katherine Beaufort's testimony to shore up his stance.

Called to the stand, she explained how the diary of Judge Alvarez's mistress had come into her possession. The news that she was the niece of the daughter Mary Delacroix had borne Rafe Perdido sent another hum through the courtroom.

Katherine told the court how she and Drew Delacroix had spent weeks deciphering the code—written in French—and how despondent Drew had grown with each new piece of evidence against his father.

"You're saying that the defendant's son helped translate the diary entries that would ultimately help place blame for a farcical trial on his own father?"

"Yes."

"Why would he do that, Ms. Beaufort?"

Katherine's gaze found Drew's in the crowd. She lifted her chin, and the look in her eyes was just short of adoration. "Because unlike his father, Drew Delacroix is an honorable and just man."

"Objection!" the defense thundered.

"Sustained," the judge droned. "Ms. Beaufort, please keep any feelings you have about the defendant's personal traits to yourself in the future."

"Yes, your honor," Katherine said, sounding properly chastised.

"Miss Beaufort, do you believe the information in the diary is true?"

"Yes."

"Why? Why would Patrice Forêt write down information that was basically pillow talk?"

"As insurance."

"Insurance? Can you explain, please?"

"A rich man's mistress doesn't have much security. She's important to him only so long as she's...performing to suit the man's needs or whims. Or until someone prettier, younger or sexier comes along and catches his eye. Aunt Patrice wrote down the things Neville Alvarez told her that she thought were important. Things she believed she could use to bring him to heel, if that need ever arose, which it did."

"Thank you. And were there such important entries in the diary you found?"

"There were."

"What kind of information did they contain?"

"Information that implies that Philip Delacroix was blackmailing Neville Alvarez."

A murmur swept through the courtroom.

"How?"

"Well, there was mention made that Philip had been to New Orleans with some of his fraternity buddies and seen Judge Alvarez with Aunt Patrice. The information was vague, but evidently, Philip said something along the lines that the judge should know who his friends were and that he should be extra careful about his rulings on the Perdido case, or Mrs. Alvarez might get word of how he was really spending the nights he was supposed to be working late. I know it isn't concrete, but why would Philip Delacroix blackmail Judge Alvarez if he didn't have something to hide, himself?"

"And what do you think that something is, Ms. Beaufort?"

"Truthfully? I think he killed Camille Gravier."

A low roar spread through the courtroom. The media buzzards almost trampled one another in their haste to spread the news.

AFTER KATHERINE, Jackson was called to the stand. He admitted that even though he was a law officer, sworn to serve and protect, he had performed unlawful deeds at Philip's behest to satisfy his gambling debts and his need to have what he called "a better life." He admitted he'd made a deal with the D.A.'s office. As a witness, he was forthright and brutally honest, refusing to downplay his role in the crimes he'd committed but making it very clear that he'd done what he'd done because he hoped to score points with Philip Delacroix.

"And why did you want so badly to get into Mr. Philip Delacroix's good graces, Mr. Boudreaux?" the D.A. asked.

"Because he's my father, and I wanted him to be proud of me."

The journalists went into a frenzy. Several seats in the courtroom were abdicated in a noisy furor as various newshounds hurried to relay that startling tidbit to their offices. After several attempts to restore order, a disgusted Judge Ramsey adjourned for the day.

Philip left the courtroom, his usually regal carriage somewhat bowed, his eyes shadowed for the first time since the proceedings had begun.

"IS IT TRUE, DAD?"

Though Drew hadn't set foot in his father's house in months, anger and pain and an insatiable need to know just how low his father had sunk had driven him and his sisters to Belle Terre to confront Philip with this newest blow to their pride and hearts.

As hurtful as it had been to hear Jackson's confession,

it hadn't escaped Drew's notice that his half brother had been motivated to do harm by the same thing that had prompted Drew's own behavior: a longing for Philip's love.

Now, as they all gathered in the cherry-wood library, Drew watched his father pour out two fingers of whiskey and toss it back as if it were nothing more than sweet tea. Philip shuddered, thunked the glass onto the bar and poured another. "Is what true?"

"Was Jackson...my brother—" Drew grimaced "—doing your dirty deeds while he was supposed to be upholding the law?"

"Unfortunately, yes."

"Why?" Drew asked, the word dripping bitterness. "To see which one of us would jump the highest at your bidding and be the worthiest of your love?"

"To keep Flora's mouth shut," Philip said. He sipped at the second shot of whiskey, a thoughtful expression on his face. Then he faced Drew with a look of censure. "Until that little incident with Flora, he always did as he was told, no questions asked about the wrong or right of it, no worry about the consequences. I couldn't get him to bring his mama to me when I asked him, though. I had to get Duffy to do that. I guess Jackson has some scruples after all."

Philip tipped back the last of the Old Turkey amid startled cries from his daughters that masked the ringing of the doorbell.

"So Jackson was telling the truth? You did order Flora kidnapped and put into the vault?" Drew asked, aghast. Despite everything he'd suffered at his father's hands, he'd wanted so badly to believe at least that was a mistake.

"Of course I did," Philip snapped, reaching to tweak his bow tie.

Joanna and Annabelle both gasped in shock. "Dear God, why?" Joanna asked.

"I had to try and stop her. The witch was hell-bent on killing me with her damnable voodoo dolls and setting fire to my house. Still is."

"What do you mean?" Joanna asked, struggling to recover from this new bombshell. "Flora isn't leaving any dolls, Daddy. She's in the mental hospital."

"Well, someone is." Philip's voice was as flat as the expression in his eyes.

"Excuse me, Mr. Delacroix, sir."

Clovis stood in the doorway. His café au lait face with its road map of wrinkles and strange mismatched eyes wore no discernible expression. It was impossible to tell if he'd heard any of the conversation. But Joanna knew there was little going on in the house that Clovis missed.

"What is it, Clovis?" Philip snapped.

"You have a caller."

"Who?"

"No need to be so formal, Clovis." A tall woman with rich auburn hair and green eyes swept past Clovis on a fragrant wave of White Diamonds perfume.

"Mother!" Joanna said, her surprise rendering her speechless. Annabelle gave a shocked gasp and Drew cursed.

"Hello, Jo," Gwen said, going to her older daughter and embracing her warmly. "I know you're wondering what on earth I'm doing here."

"What the hell *are* you doing here, Gwen?" Philip asked, reaching for the bottle again.

Gwen, who was a little more than twenty years younger than Philip, whirled. The smile on her still-beautiful, carefully made-up face was bright with faux good cheer; the look in her eyes said she was spoiling for a fight long past due. "Hello to you, too, Philip. It's been a long time."

"Not nearly long enough."

"Still into intimidation, I see." She took a couple of steps toward him. "Are you feeling well, Philip? Your color is a little off."

His color and his blood pressure rose a notch, as she'd known they would.

"What the devil are you doing here?" he repeated.

Gwen raised her eyebrows in feigned surprise. "Why, I've come to see my children through this terrible ordeal, Philip."

"They've managed just fine without you for twenty-odd years, Gwen."

"Oh, we've all managed. But I doubt they've done any better without me than I have without them."

Gwen turned to Annabelle and Drew, tears in her emerald green eyes. Her smile wavered and a breath whooshed out in a shuddering sigh that revealed both her anguish and her nervousness. "You've grown from beautiful children into beautiful adults." She clasped her hands to her ample breasts and pressed her lips together for a second to stop their trembling. "I've missed you so!"

"Let's not get maudlin, Gwendolyn," Philip said. "It's a little late for regrets."

"It's never too late to make things right if you can, Philip, which is one of the reasons I've come. Considering your situation, maybe you ought to think about that, too."

Annabelle was the first to speak, the first to recover, her fluid, creative mind fixating on the obvious. "Was Flora the reason you left Daddy?" she asked, gazing upon the mother she hadn't seen since she was a teenager. The mother who'd sent birthday and Christmas gifts without fail. The mother Annabelle had never done more for than send the obligatory Christmas card.

"One of them."

"The other was that banker fellow, if my memory

serves me correctly,'' Philip snapped. He pointed a finger at his younger daughter. "And don't you forget that she didn't just leave me, missy. She left you and Drew, too.''

"Yes," Gwen said. "There was Emerson. But there's a little more to it than that, isn't there?''

"Daddy...Mama," Joanna said in her most placating voice. "Now isn't the time to go into all this.''

"Of course it is," Gwen said. "It's why I came back. I saw that a lot of ugly truths were coming out and I decided to add mine. God knows I've suffered enough for my sins. It's time your father suffered for his, and that's the real truth.''

"Truth!" Philip scoffed. "The truth was you were sleeping with Emerson.''

"You're right, Philip, that's a fact. Another fact is that you were not only seeing Flora, but a whole bevy of women on the side. I was miserable—not that my being unhappy excuses what I did.''

She pinned him with an unfaltering glare. "And since you're the one who brought it up, maybe you should tell Annabelle and Drew why I left them.''

"How would I know what was going on inside that head of yours?" Philip growled evasively.

"Tell them!" Joanna was startled to realize the words had come from her. More startled by the bitterness in her voice. "Tell them how you went behind her back and told them you'd be miserable if they didn't stay with you. Tell them—''

"I didn't!" Philip said loudly.

"I heard you!" Joanna said, her own voice rising, tears in her eyes. "Tell them the truth. That you *made* her leave them here.''

"Made her?" Philip thundered. "How could I *make* her do anything? She was a grown woman.''

"I believe the term is *blackmail*, Philip," Gwen said,

her voice surprisingly steady. "Something you've used to your advantage on more than one occasion, it seems. You found out about my affair with Emerson. I said I'd end it if you'd stop seeing all those other women. You said not to bother, that you had no intention of curtailing your extramarital activities. You told me to get out and to leave you and the children in peace. I refused to leave them. We argued for weeks. Finally you said I could take Joanna because she was so stubborn and difficult. You wouldn't let me take Drew or Annabelle."

"Lies!"

"I don't lie, Philip, but if you don't remember, maybe it's because you're getting senile." Philip swore, and Gwen turned to Drew. "He told me I couldn't take you, the Delacroix heir, or Annabelle, because she adored him. He said that if I did, he'd smear my name and Emerson's across the papers from Shreveport to New Orleans. He told me he'd ruin Emerson's career, and prove I was an unfit mother. He'd get custody and I'd never see any of you again. He said if I agreed to do it his way, I could see you during the summers."

"And all the time he was going behind Mom's back, bribing the two of you and doing his damnedest to talk you into staying with him," Joanna said.

"Why didn't you fight for us?" Annabelle asked, her tortured gaze fixed on her mother's.

"I would have if I'd thought there was any hope. But the Delacroix name is very powerful. Your father had the money, influence and power to do everything he threatened. My parents ran the local grocery store. There was no way I could fight him and win."

Gwen's shoulders lifted in a helpless shrug. "So, rather than have you all taken away from me, I did what I thought was best. I married Emerson, took Joanna and went to California. I lived for the summers when I could have the two of you with me.''

Her brief laugh held no humor. "Obviously, that didn't work out too well. I soon saw that your father spent September to May filling your heads full of nonsense about me. There was no way I could win your love or your respect in three short months, so after a while we all stopped trying.''

She turned back to Philip. "That's exactly what happened, isn't it, Philip? At least have the guts to tell them the truth about this.''

"And if it is?''

A ragged sob escaped Gwen's lips. "You deprived my children of a mother who loved them. Who still loves them,'' she said, her eyes awash with tears. "You're a bastard, Philip Delacroix, the kind that has nothing to do with birth. I pray God will forgive you for what you've done. I'm not sure I ever can.''

She turned her tear-glazed eyes on her children. "I'm sorry for all of it. Not for loving Emerson. He's a good and decent man, and we've been very happy. But I'm sorry that I couldn't take you with me and sorry you were told I didn't care about you. I'm especially sorry for all the things I've missed in your lives.''

Her gaze moved from Drew to Annabelle and she smiled through her tears. "Whew!'' she said. "I feel better. The truth really does set you free.''

Then she grew serious once more. "I don't know if you can forgive me, but I pray you can. What you do with the things I've told you today is up to you, but I felt the time had come for you to find out what really happened. I'm not sure if there's a chance for us to have any kind of relationship or not, but I want you to know I'm willing to work at it if you are.''

Without another word, Gwen started for the door.

Amazingly, Clovis was there to open it for her. She left them all feeling as if a tornado had just swept through the room, her children uncertain if her visit had destroyed what little was left of their belief in their father or if it had blown away the miasma of pain and betrayal, the legacy she'd bequeathed when she left them.

As soon as Gwen left, Philip excused himself to go upstairs and rest. If his children hadn't been so upset with him they might have been concerned about his high color and his shortness of breath.

Clovis showed them to the door and they walked abreast down the wide walkway to Drew's Mercedes. "Why didn't you tell us Mother was coming, Jo?" Drew asked.

"I didn't know. Normally I talk to her every few days, and she's called every day for the past week or so to see how we were all faring, but she never said a word about coming. She told me earlier she might come back for the trial, but when it started and she didn't show up, I assumed the thought of facing Daddy again was too much for her."

"She might have been intimidated by him once, but it didn't seem like she was scared of him today," Drew said, an appreciative grin brightening his face.

"That's the way she is," Joanna told them. "Once she decides to do something, she comes on like gangbusters. She'd made up her mind to come here and get this all off her chest, and by golly she did it."

"It's the truth, isn't it?" Annabelle said. "I barely remember Dad swearing how he'd cry his eyes out if I left him. Why didn't you tell us before that Mom left us because he was blackmailing her emotionally?"

Joanna shook her head. "Would you believe I didn't remember? Not until she started talking about it? Maybe it's that repressed-memory syndrome."

"I'd forgotten, too," Drew said. "It's funny the tricks

your mind can play. All these years I convinced myself I chose to stay with Dad because I wanted to be with him. The truth is I stayed for the same reason I've done everything else for him. Because I was trying to please him, to make him love me.''

No one spoke while they all struggled to deal with the truth they'd just realized. Finally, Annabelle said, ''Mom still looks so young and pretty. It's funny, but I see a lot of Cade in her.''

''I always have, too,'' Joanna said, and added, ''Look, it's not my place to tell you what to do or feel, but whatever you decide, remember that she loves you both and, despite what Daddy may have said about her, she's a wonderful person. I've never had a phone call from her that she didn't ask about you both as well as Cade.''

''She asks about Cade?''

''Of course she does. She's missed being a grandmother, Annie, as much as she's missed being a mom. And you and Cade can add that to your list of things to thank Daddy for.''

CHAPTER EIGHT

WHEN THE JUDGE BANGED his gavel, ending the third day of testimony, Travis was one of the first spectators to leave the courtroom. He didn't want to chance running into Shelby and receiving another tongue-lashing. She'd sat closer to the front today, and from his own seat, he could watch the emotions racing across her face as the prosecutor revealed new information about her family.

Watching her had been an exercise in both pain and pleasure. He knew she probably had some idea about what the various witnesses would disclose, but having the whole world privy to the deepest, darkest Delacroix secrets had to leave her feeling exposed and vulnerable. Neither was a state he could imagine the confident, cocksure Shelby enduring very well.

He hated to think of her hurting, which pretty much summed up what a colossal sap he was over her. He told himself that whatever they'd felt for each other was over, that he shouldn't give a darn what she felt, but none of his arguments had any impact on his heart. The woman had treated him like a second-class citizen, and he still wanted to hold her until all her pain went away.

CLAIRE BEAUFORT HAD TRULY believed that coming to Bayou Beltane and hearing about the family that had rejected her, seeing the mother who had given her away, would end her uncertainty and her pain.

It hadn't.

Katherine, her niece, had been begging her to come and meet Mary Delacroix ever since she'd learned that the first lady of Bayou Beltane was Claire's mother. But the thought of facing the woman who'd given birth to her and then given her up for adoption had held no interest for Claire, who had fought feelings of self-doubt all her life.

Unlike so many people who couldn't wait to find their birth parents, she wanted no part of the woman who had given her away. Even when Katherine's growing association with the Delacroix and her meeting of various family members brought new information, Claire refused to consider a meeting. She'd lived her whole life without any of them, and she'd done just fine. Lorraine and Brice Beaufort had been wonderful parents, and except for the sorrow of her adoption, Claire had had a happy childhood, a fulfilling life. Why would she want to meet the woman who'd given birth to her and then given her away?

"It isn't for you," Katherine had told her during a phone conversation a few days before Philip Delacroix's trial started. "It's for Mary."

"Why should I care about her?" Claire had asked. "She didn't care about me."

"I don't believe that's true," Katherine said. "She's really a wonderful old lady. Everyone in the family adores her. Besides, I'm going to be marrying Drew, and Mary is his great-aunt. Surely you'll both be at the wedding."

Claire shrugged. "I'll cross that bridge when I come to it."

"At least come and hear what happened from her point of view. Find out what happened to your father. Maybe it will give you new insight into who you are."

"I know who I am," Claire had said, determined not to give in to the curiosity Katherine's arguments aroused.

But the conversation stayed with her, haunting both her dreams and her every waking hour. Just before the trial, she'd called Katherine and told her she would come and hear what was said, but she didn't want to meet any of the Delacroix.

Hearing Desiree Boudreaux's testimony about what had happened the night Camille Gravier was killed had done nothing to endear Mary Delacroix to Claire. But when she'd watched the videotape of Mary's statement, seen the anguish in her eyes and heard the sorrow and regret in her voice when she'd told how her father had forced her to give away the child she and Rafe Perdido had created, Claire had felt a crack in the shell she'd constructed so carefully and deliberately around her heart.

As much as she wanted to believe otherwise, Mary Delacroix wasn't uncaring and selfish. She was just a woman who had paid the price for falling in love with a man unsuitable to her station in life. She was a woman who'd given up her baby because she'd had no other choice.

"So what are you going to do about that, Claire?" she asked herself aloud.

She didn't know. She needed time to think this through. Unbidden came the memory of a conversation between her mother and her Aunt Patrice she had overheard one spring evening as they'd rocked back and forth in the front porch swing. Claire had been playing with her dolls at the other end of the veranda. She couldn't have been more than seven or eight, and she hadn't understood what the conversation meant, but she'd been acutely aware of her aunt's pain.

1946

"WHEN ARE YOU AND JOHNNY going to have a baby, Patrice?" Lorraine asked her sister as she pushed the swing with one bare foot.

"Never."

Lorraine looked at Patrice in surprise. "Never? Why?"

"Because I had an abortion five years ago, Lorraine, and there won't be any more babies. Ever."

"Oh, Patrice! Are you sure?"

Patrice's mouth twisted into a sardonic smile. "I'm sure. I didn't have to go to some backwoods midwife. Neville knows lots of people. He gave some doctor a bundle of money." The smile made another brief, humorless appearance. "All very sanitary and painless. Get on the table, Miss Forêt. Shot of something to kill the pain. Scrape, scrape, scrape. No more baby. But something went wrong, and now that same doctor says I won't ever be able to have another baby."

The veneer of composure she clung to with the thin thread of sarcasm cracked. Claire watched helplessly as her aunt burst into heart-wrenching sobs and her mother held her and murmured words of comfort. When Patrice's tears were spent, she wiped her eyes and blew her nose on a floral print hanky.

"That's why you broke it off with him," Lorraine said, putting two and two together.

Patrice nodded.

"I despise Neville Alvarez for doing that to you," Lorraine said.

"That makes two of us." Patrice laughed hollowly. "Of course, that's how I got my new house and car."

"What do you mean?"

"I mean that all the years Neville and I were together, I kept a diary of things he told me after we—" Patrice cut her eyes to Claire "—you know."

"You're blackmailing him?"

"Not anymore. But it gave me and Johnny a start, and the old SOB could afford it."

"Did you give him the diary?"

Patrice shook her head. "It's tucked away in a safe place in case I ever need it again."

"Patrice..."

"Don't go trying to make me feel guilty, Lorraine. What I did may be wrong, but it's no more wrong than him making me kill my baby." The tears flowed down her cheeks again. "I wanted that baby, Lorraine. I wanted it real bad...."

THE MEMORY FADED, leaving Claire feeling strangely sad. Maturity had taught her that things weren't always black and white. Sometimes people made the best decisions they could at the time, and then had to live with the consequences.

Which was why she was going to think long and hard about meeting Mary Delacroix.

TRAVIS WAS AVOIDING HER, Shelby decided as she drove to Riverwood. No doubt about it. As soon as the judge banged his gavel and ended the day's proceedings, Travis had skedaddled out of the courtroom like a scalded dog.

Can you blame him?

Actually, she couldn't. It was true that he'd hightailed it away from the Catfish Shack rather than speak to her, but she'd certainly gotten back at him when she'd lashed out about his need for revenge.

The ball was back in his court.

Or was it? she wondered, chewing on her lower lip. She and Travis weren't kids trying to see who could get in the most licks at the other. They were adults—though she'd be the first to admit that neither of them was acting like it.

Whipping her car into the garage at the back of the house, Shelby grabbed her briefcase and went inside. The spring day was hot and humid, and the coolness of the air-conditioning was welcome even after the short walk to the back door.

She was being ridiculous, she thought, dropping her briefcase on the kitchen table. And so was Travis. It had to end, and she knew it was up to her to make things right. Her heart sprinted at the memory of how things once were between them. It cramped in sudden pain at the sure knowledge that it was her fault it had all fallen apart.

Shelby had already acknowledged that her great-aunt was right. The kind of love she and Travis had shared was rare indeed. She'd also conceded that it was up to her to try to fix things. If they couldn't be fixed, then it was up to her to at least make some sort of peace between them.

She went upstairs to her room, kicked off her shoes just inside the door and headed for the bathroom. Drastic action called for drastic preparation. If she was going to bare her soul and lay her emotions out for Travis to either accept or trample, she had to be prepared, both mentally and physically.

Knowing it was all or nothing, Shelby drew a hot bath. She was about to add some bath crystals when her gaze fell on a concoction Marie had made up for her months before, when Travis was still in town. According to her sister, a practicing aromatherapist, this particular combination of scents was guaranteed to stir a man to unequalled passion.

The mental image that came to mind sent shivers of longing down Shelby's back. Why not? she thought, reaching for the decanter and dumping a generous portion of the exotic-smelling oil into the water. In for a penny, in for a pound. If she was going to make a colossal fool of herself she might as well do it right.

That thought was uppermost in her mind when she got out of the tub twenty minutes later. After blowing her hair dry, she used a big-barrel curling iron to give it some bounce, then pinned it loosely on top of her head, dragging tendrils down to frame her face. She took her time with her makeup, careful to use the cosmetics to enhance her looks. She wanted to look beautiful, not made up.

Satisfied with the results, she went into the bedroom to survey the contents of her closet, settling on a sleeveless dress of clingy black knit. What there was of it, with its scoop neck and mid-thigh length, fit her like the proverbial glove. The fabric molded her curves with the intimacy of a lover's caress. She drew on black-tinted hose and slipped her feet into high-heeled black pumps with an ankle strap that made her feel extremely sexy. After a spritz of cologne that echoed the fragrance of the bath oil, she was set.

She regarded herself in the cheval mirror and was surprised to see a look of apprehension in the eyes staring back at her. Would seeing her make Travis remember the nights they'd spent in each other's arms, or would he take one look at her and slam the door in her face?

"You won't know until you go and see," she told her reflection. Blowing the woman in the mirror a kiss, Shelby grabbed a small black purse, headed out the door and down the stairs.

IF THE NUMBER OF CARS in the parking lot at the back of the house was any indication, Annabelle's bed-and-breakfast looked filled to capacity. Shelby recognized Travis's truck and found herself torn between thankfulness and apprehension. She pulled up to the curb at the front of the house, cut the engine and got out, not locking the doors.

The better to make a quick getaway, my dear.

Shelby loved Annabelle and Jake's house. The fernery—essentially a deep bay window where ferns were kept during the winter—was a particular favorite of Shelby's for its architectural interest. She also admired the two turrets, which gave the house a castlelike appearance.

Shelby rang the doorbell and was thankful her cousin answered the summons. Annabelle looked Shelby up and down and smiled, a knowing little woman-to-woman smile. Then she raised her hands to her cheeks in mock surprise. "Don't tell me. Let me guess. You're here collecting for the heart fund."

Shelby's smile was less smug, more a grimace. "In a matter of speaking. I'm here to collect a heart. If it hasn't already been given elsewhere."

"I doubt that," Annabelle said. "You look wonderful."

"Thanks." Shelby hugged her cousin. "How are you holding up?"

"Fair," Annabelle said, closing the door behind them. "It helps having the house full. When you're changing sheets, scrubbing toilets and serving high tea, it doesn't leave much time to think about your father going to prison."

"That may not happen."

Annabelle met her eyes squarely. "He did it, Shelby. I know he did."

"Even if he did, it wasn't premeditated. It sounds as if Camille provoked him."

"What's that? A crime of passion?"

"Yes. Probably with a manslaughter charge."

"What kind of sentence does that carry?"

"Up to forty-four years," Shelby said. "But Uncle Philip isn't a threat to society, he is old and in poor health, and he does have friends in high places. It's very possible—even probable—that he'll get a commuted sentence."

"Do you think so?"

"Yeah," Shelby said. "I do."

Annabelle smiled and gave her another hug. "Thanks, cuz. You always make me feel better."

"I'm glad. Now, which room is my man in?"

"Top of the stairs, first door on the left."

"Thanks," Shelby said. She held up her crossed fingers and started up the steps. "Wish me luck."

"Always."

Shelby paused outside Travis's room. The television was playing softly. She took a deep breath and rapped smartly on the door before her courage failed and she backed out. She heard his footfalls on the floor and thought about running, but before she could do more than consider the option, he opened the door and she was trapped by the surprise in his eyes. The surprise was followed by pleasure, but that expression vanished so quickly she wondered if she'd imagined it.

"What are you doing here?"

The harshness in his voice and the sight of his naked chest—all smooth flesh, solid muscle and crisp, curly hair—almost robbed her of the boldness that had carried her this far. This was going to be harder than she expected. Shelby forced a smile. She hoped Marie's concoction was doing its thing.

"I came to talk to you," she said with a bravado she dredged up from her high school drama days.

TRAVIS HOPED HIS SURPRISE didn't show. The last thing he'd expected to see when he opened the door was Shelby Delacroix all dressed up in something black and sexy and short...extremely short. He'd forgotten just how shapely her legs were, forgotten how shapely she was all over. She looked good enough to eat and she smelled divine. Somehow all his hurt feelings paled when he looked into her regretful eyes. The woman was a threat. Not only to his heart, but to his rational thinking.

"May I come in?" Without waiting for his reply, she brushed past him into the room. The scent of something exotically floral wafted up with the warmth of her body as she sauntered past him. Travis drew in a deep breath, filling his senses with it.

This will never do, Hardin. You can't let her tie you in knots again.

With that reminder ringing in his brain, he dredged up a dark look and enough sarcasm to reply, "Sure. Why not?"

Shelby cast him a mocking look over her shoulder, her eyebrows arched. "I see you still have that inimitable Texas charm."

The saccharine sweetness of her voice was enough to give him a toothache. "Yeah, well, some things never change."

And a lot of things did.

He closed the door and Shelby turned to face him. "Have you?" she asked. With her usual bluntness, she was getting right down to the nitty-gritty. And why not? he asked himself. What was the point of mouthing a lot of meaningless banalities about how they'd been and what they'd been doing? Still, she was moving a little too fast for comfort, especially since she was so close that every breath he took filled his nostrils with that delicious scent that was playing havoc with his reasoning.

He frowned. "Have I what?"

"Changed." She stepped nearer. "Do you still love me, or have you found someone else?"

For a moment he just stared at her, dumbfounded by her directness. Then he retreated a step, clearly staggered. "What kind of question is that?" he growled.

"An honest one," she said with a lift of her chin. "One that deserves an honest answer."

Travis regarded her warily for a moment, then began to laugh. "Damn, Shelby," he said with a disbelieving shake of his head. "Do you ever stop to think before you speak? Look before you leap?"

"Not often," she said, with more of that disarming candor. "It's a bad habit of mine."

Travis offered her a wolflike smile. "Like I said, some things never change."

"I have."

The words hung between them. Awkward admission. Tentative promise. Fragile hope. What did she mean? he wondered, his mind racing. Where was she headed with all this? One thing was for sure—he had to be careful or she'd lead him down the garden path again. Though Travis usually was one to keep his head, Shelby managed to undermine his common sense and his better judgment with very little effort.

When he made no response, her troubled gaze found his. "I've thought a lot about things—about us—the past few months," she told him, "and I've come to the conclusion that you were right."

She was apologizing, Travis realized with shock. Shelby Delacroix, who stormed in where angels feared to tread, was actually apologizing. He knew it was good for her, a character-building experience if you will, but he couldn't stand to see her humble herself in front of him.

"I did put my family first," she said. "I—I can't seem to help it, but if you'll give me another—"

He held up his hand. "Stop!"

She blinked at the harshness of his voice. "Wh-what?"

"Just stop," he commanded softly. "I can't stand to see you so—so... Oh, hell, I don't know! Mealymouthed." Under the influence of her perfume, his reasoning had disappeared. Drunk as he was at the sight of her, his frown vanished, and a smile—no doubt a sappy one that showed just how happy he was to be breathing the same air as she was—claimed his lips.

Her breath left her in a low sigh.

"Groveling doesn't become you, darlin'," he drawled. "But that dress sure does. What there is of it. And what kind of perfume is that? It's sexy as hell."

The sudden change in his manner must have thrown her for a second, but then her smile was there, as bright as the dawn of a summer day. With a little cry, she launched herself at him.

The impact of her body was one of the sweetest sensations of his life. His lips covered hers with a hunger that was nearly brutal. He couldn't help it, he was so starved for the taste and feel of her. She welcomed the onslaught, plowing her fingers through the thickness of his hair and giving him kiss for kiss.

Then somehow they were on the bed, his weight bearing her down onto the mattress, his hands skimming beneath the short skirt of her dress to caress her hip.

"I've missed you so much," she gasped between kisses. "So much."

"I've missed you, too, darlin'," he said, his voice a husky rasp against her ear, a rasp that matched the downward slide of her zipper.

Common sense told him he was making a big mistake, that they should talk first, but his common sense had deserted him the minute she'd stepped into the room. He was about to slip the shoulder of her dress down, and she was about to let him, when a panicked voice came from the door, accompanied by the pounding of a fist.

"Shelby!"

Travis froze. His eyebrows snapped together in a frown as he met her wary gaze.

"It's Annabelle," Shelby said. "Something's wrong."

"Shelby! Are you in there?"

"Yeah. Just a sec."

Without a word, Travis rolled away and let her up.

Shelby struggled with her zipper as she made her way to the door. A hysterical Annabelle stood there, tears streaming down her cheeks, her hands knotted at her breasts.

Trepidation spread through Travis like wildfire on a dry Texas prairie.

"What is it, Annabelle?" Shelby asked.

"It's Flora. She escaped from the mental institution, and she's taken Daddy hostage at Belle Terre."

"Hostage?" Shelby exclaimed. "Flora?"

Annabelle nodded. "Jake's already gone over there. He's had some experience in hostage negotiations, and he's going to try and make her see reason."

"How did you find out?"

"Flora had Daddy call here. Jake called Uncle Charles."

"What does she want?"

Fresh tears trickled down Annabelle's cheeks. "I think she wants Daddy dead."

"Dead!"

"She has a knife."

"Dear God!" Shelby breathed.

Annabelle struggled for control. "I'm so worried about him. You know how high his blood pressure has been this past year or so. I'm afraid all this will cause him to have a stroke or something."

Shelby reached out to offer her cousin a comforting embrace, but Annabelle took a step back and squared her shoulders. "Don't offer me any sympathy, Shelby. If I let go, I might not be able to get through this."

"What can I do?"

Annabelle shook her head helplessly. "I don't know. Go check on Uncle Charles, I guess. Jake said he was taking the news pretty badly."

"Are you going?"

"I can't," Annabelle said. "I just can't."

"I understand." Shelby cast a look at Travis that begged him to understand. "I've got to go."

"Shelby," he said, holding out his hand. His eyes held her captive.

"My family needs me."

"*I* need you."

Annabelle slipped down the stairs, leaving them alone. The raw agony in Travis's voice was like a giant hand squeezing Shelby's heart. It occurred to her with sudden clarity that she was doing it again. Once more the Delacroix family needed her, and once again she was putting them ahead of Travis.

The look in his eyes said he realized it, too. That if she walked out the door, it was over. This time for good. She couldn't do that to him. Couldn't do it to herself.

She put her hand in his. "Come with me," she said. "I don't know what we'll find, and I need you there."

Travis didn't move, but his gaze probed hers with an unsettling intensity.

"My family is important to me, Travis. But you're important to me, too. Aunt Mary told me not to lose you over them, but I love them—" Shelby wasn't even aware that tears rolled down her cheeks "—and everything's such a mess right now I can't just abandon them to move to Comfort, open up a country law practice and have your babies. Not now. Not until the trial is over. Dad's worried and Granddad is a basket case. Aunt Mary is wasting away, and Uncle William is so withdrawn...."

Her voice trailed away and she raise her hands helplessly, more unsure of herself than she'd ever been in her life. "I can't change the way I am, Travis, but I don't want to lose you."

"You've thought about moving to Texas?"

She nodded and swiped at her cheeks with her fingertips.

"Opening a law practice there?"

She saw the hint of humor in his eyes and nodded again. "I figure even Comfort must have some crime. Chicken thieves. Cattle rustling."

"Illegal moonshine," he said, as serious as she. "Land scams." He pulled her closer. "You said you wanted to have my babies."

She wouldn't look at him. "I do," she whispered, splaying her palm over his bare chest. "Lots of babies."

"Do you plan on having these babies out of wedlock?" She looked up at him, her eyes wide with surprise.

"You didn't say anything about marriage."

"Didn't I? I meant to. You will marry me, won't you, Travis?"

"Darlin'," he said, bending to kiss her, "I thought you'd never ask. Of course I'll marry you. It would be my pleasure." His smile was slow, chagrined. "And my own personal hell."

BY THE TIME TRAVIS and Shelby got to Belle Terre, a news team from New Orleans was unloading its cameras. Gator Guzman was there and most of the Delacroix family had arrived. Drew and Joanna—Drew looking pale and serious; Joanna looking wild-eyed and distraught—were talking to Jake near his patrol car when Travis and Shelby pulled up. If any of them wondered why Travis was with her, they were too polite to ask. Instead, they smiled at him, shook his hand and greeted him as if he'd never left Bayou Beltane, as if he and Shelby hadn't been apart all these months.

"I saw you in court today," Drew said to Travis, "but you got out before I could say anything. When did you get into town?"

"I've been here for the whole shebang." Travis looked uncomfortable. "I hope there are no hard feelings over my giving my grandmother's letters to the district attorney."

"None," Drew said. "This whole thing has been festering for so long, it was bound to blow sooner or later. I'm for getting the whole truth out, no matter how painful it is."

"You have to admit, though, brother dear, that there have been a heap of surprises along the way," Joanna said.

"Oh, yeah," Drew admitted with a wry grin. "A heap of them, including Dad's numerous infidelities. Not to mention that it looks pretty much like he—" Drew broke off, afraid of offending Travis.

"Accidentally killed my great-aunt Camille. It's okay. Contrary to what my grandmother believed, I don't think Aunt Cam was a very nice person."

"You think it was an accident, then?" Joanna asked.

"From what I've heard, I don't think he went to Moon Lake to kill her. I think when he saw what she was doing to him and Charles, how she was playing them against each other, he lost his cool, got a little rough. When she screamed, all he could think of was shutting her up." Travis shook his head. "I don't think it was premeditated."

"That's big of you," Drew said.

"It's the conclusion I've come to from the testimony I've heard. I have a feeling it'll be the jury's, too."

"Maybe," Drew agreed.

"I hate to run, but I see Dad over there," Shelby said to her cousins. "Will you excuse us?"

Drew and Joanna waved them on, and Shelby led Travis to where Justin stood alone, his haunted gaze focused on the house. She went straight into his arms.

"Are you okay?" she asked.

He pushed her hair back with hands that trembled. She didn't recall ever seeing her father any way but composed. "I've been better."

He held out his hand to Travis, as if he'd just noticed

his presence. Justin was too well bred to let any questions or concerns he might have about Travis and Shelby being together show on his patrician features. "Hello, Travis. How have you been?"

"Just fine, Mr. Delacroix. I'll be better when the trial's over, though."

Justin's smile was brief and lopsided. "Assuming it ever is."

"Yeah," Shelby said. "Just when I think we've had all the bad news we can possibly take, something else happens. What's the situation with Flora?"

"It seems she was out in the garden during hospital visiting hours and just walked away."

"How could that happen?" Travis asked. "Don't they have some kind of security?"

"Evidently, the person who was in charge got busy with another patient, turned his back for a few minutes...." Justin shrugged. "Flora had been comatose. No one paid her much mind. Mentally, she came back from wherever she'd been, and lit out. It happens all the time."

"Is she totally nutso?" Shelby asked. "Has she said what she wants? Has she threatened Uncle Philip?"

"Evidently she's behaved in a very lucid manner since she arrived at Belle Terre, which, as we all know, doesn't necessarily equate to sanity."

"Annabelle said Flora has a knife and wants to kill Uncle Philip."

"That's the general consensus," Justin said. "Jake has been trying to make contact, but she's taken the phone off the hook, and she won't answer when he talks on the bullhorn."

"Has anyone contacted Desiree?" Shelby asked. "She should know what's going on."

"Jake sent Remy out to tell her."

"All this can't be good for her," Shelby said. Like the rest of the family, she'd always had a soft spot for Desiree.

"None of this is good for any of us," Justin clarified.

"Where's Granddad?"

"At Riverwood. I wouldn't let him come. Your mother stayed with him."

"It's his brother who's in danger," Shelby reminded her father gently.

"And he's my father, Shelby. I don't like the way all this is affecting him. He's aging before my eyes. His being here won't change the outcome of whatever happens. And it won't stop it."

"Your dad's got a point, darlin'," Travis said, dropping his arm across Shelby's shoulders and drawing her to his side.

Shelby sighed. "I suppose." Her attention was snagged by a car coming much too fast down the lane. It skidded to a stop and Jackson Boudreaux got out. He didn't bother to shut the car door, but headed for Jake Trahan in a dead run.

"Wonder who put the burr under his saddle?" Travis asked.

"I don't know," Shelby said. "Let's go see."

The closer Travis and Shelby got to them, the clearer it became that Jackson and Jake were arguing about something, and Drew was throwing in his two cents' worth.

"It's my responsibility to get Philip out of there alive," Jake said.

"That may be so, but I have a better chance of doing that than you do," Jackson argued.

"Back off, Boudreaux!" Drew commanded. "You don't have any business going in there."

Jackson looked at Drew, the half brother he'd spent so much time envying, hating. The brother he had so much in common with.

"No?" he said, smiling slightly. "The way I see it, Flora Boudreaux is my mother. And in case you've forgotten, Philip Delacroix is my father. So, big brother, that makes it my business, whether you like it or not."

Norman had nothing to lose. The way I see it, even Clovis got a fair portion. And in case you reckon you're better than the jury, Clemens, my mother that's got you on trial ain't nobody whether you like it or not.

CHAPTER NINE

THE CRAZY WITCH MEANT to kill him. Philip knew that as well as he knew his name. He pulled a monogrammed handkerchief from his pocket and dabbed at the sweat beading his upper lip and forehead. The small cotton square had about reached its capacity of absorption.

He'd retreated to the chair behind the desk in his library to put some distance between him and Flora. How had she gotten out of the hospital, anyway? he wondered. How she had gotten into his house was easy. Since he spent most days in town, he couldn't be sure the doors were kept locked during the day as he had demanded. Even with Clovis there, it would have been simple for her to just walk in when no one was looking. The same way Desiree had done the past few months, he surmised with sudden comprehension.

Thank God Flora had settled down. When she'd first burst into the library, he hadn't known her. Her hair had gone mostly gray in the few weeks since her incarceration—first in the crypt, then the mental hospital. With the long, slightly curly mass a wild tangle about her once beautiful, angular face, she'd slipped into the room brandishing a knife, her eyes savage with purpose.

Philip recognized the knife with the scrimshaw handle as one he'd given Flora long before Jackson was born. He'd used the blade himself, to cut away her clothes while she tore at his, their appetite for each other raging out of control the way it had for many satisfying years. How could anything so right go so wrong? And why? A sigh of something as close to regret as Philip ever felt soughed from his lips. The feeling passed, replaced with fury that she dare come into his home and do this to him.

He watched her, this woman with whom he had once shared the closest physical communion—the woman who had mothered one of his sons—as she paced back and forth in front of the windows, drawn there by the sound of a siren and the strobe of police lights. It seemed the cavalry, or its twentieth-century equivalent, had arrived along with Gator Guzman and what looked like Drew's Mercedes.

Never one who liked being around a lot of people, Flora watched the gathering crowd with growing agitation. It was evident in the tightening of her lips, the alternately flashing anger and concern in her dark eyes. In the jerky way she turned, so unlike her usual graceful movements.

"Quite a throng out there, isn't there, Flora?" he said, the ingrained urge to needle her conquering his fear momentarily.

Flora didn't answer. Instead, she silenced him with one heart-stopping, malignant look. All thought of goading her vanished. He gasped and his hand fluttered to his chest, where his heart resumed its rapid, erratic beating. She was crazy, he realized. Insane.

And whose fault is that?

Certainly not his. He couldn't help that she'd sold her soul to Satan and that the price for that was her sanity. Any drunk in the Quarter with two brain cells left to rub together would tell you it was impossible to mess around with black magic without it affecting every aspect of your life. Like drugs or power, it was an addiction, one that ate you up from the inside out.

Yes, she meant to see him dead, but she had no intention of using such quick and relatively painless methods as a bullet to the head or a stiletto through the heart. With his own testimony just hours away—a mere formality, since there was no way he could escape sentencing any longer—he would welcome a quick and easy death over time in prison.

But Flora's temperament didn't lean toward clemency. Never had. Her way was to exact a lengthy and painful ruin, something he realized now she'd been doing ever since Jackson's conception. Like a child who picks at a scab, Flora had been plucking away at Philip in dozens of different ways the past thirty-four years, causing him more trouble than pain, more misery than grief, but nudging him closer and closer to the place she wanted him with every verbal encounter, every clash of wills, every bit of voodoo used to mock him.

She meant him to die a slow death.

First she would intimidate him with the force of her power. Then, with the combined strength of her cohort, the devil, she would drive him over the brink of sanity. And when he was a slobbering, blathering idiot—the way she had been when Jackson freed her from the burial vault— she would pin him with one of those malevolent looks, point a finger at him, and he would die of a stroke or a heart attack, but only after he'd suffered long enough to satisfy her twisted need for revenge. He knew all about that. He himself had a close relationship with that need.

Or perhaps she would twitch her nose like that television witch the children had liked so much when they were little, and he would burst into flame—what was it called? spontaneous combustion?—and disintegrate into a pile of ashes before her very eyes. Whatever it was she had in mind for him, Philip was sure of one thing. It wouldn't be pleasant.

Fueled by a nervousness he was helpless to control, he rose from his chair and went to look out the other library window. It *was* Drew's car. Joanna was with him. Shelby, with her unrelenting curiosity, was talking to her father,

her long, tall Texan in tow. Justin stood looking at the house, his concern clear even at this distance.

Charles was nowhere to be seen. Neither was Annabelle. Philip hadn't expected them to be. It was obvious that Gwen's impromptu visit had had a considerable impact on Annabelle, who hadn't made an appearance in the court-room today. Jake was out there, though, doing his best to uphold the law, even though it was clear to Philip that he wasn't his son-in-law's favorite person. After all that had transpired, Philip was surprised so many members of his family had shown up.

While he watched, another car came barreling down the lane. The driver got out and headed toward Jake.

"Jackson!" Flora's voice held dismay and excitement.

Indeed. It was Jackson—the turncoat—and he looked quite agitated. He must have come out of concern for his mother. Philip didn't flatter himself it was for him, not since Jackson had sold him out for the proverbial thirty pieces of silver, accepting a suspended sentence in return for telling all about his and Philip's dealings. Since the stupid ingrate was so hell-bent on seeing that he went to jail, Philip hoped they had to share adjoining cells. And that Flora was right there with them. Or better yet, that she was in a mausoleum. This time for good.

Before Philip could deny Jackson entrance, he pushed a startled Clovis aside, stepped into the room and crossed over to his mother. He wore jeans, a T-shirt and athletic shoes. A lock of dark hair fell across his forehead—the way Philip's had in his youth—giving him a rakish look. He really was quite a handsome young man, Philip thought. He'd inherited the best from both parents.

"You all right, *Maman?*" he asked, taking her into a loose embrace and casting Philip a reproachful look over her shoulder.

"Yes." Flora stepped back and brushed at the errant lock of hair. "Why have you come?"

"To take you out of here before someone gets hurt."

Flora smiled serenely. "Oh, someone is going to get hurt, all right."

The conviction in her voice chilled Philip's blood. "They'll get you, you know," he said, once again unable to curb his tongue.

Flora turned to him, her dark eyes blazing with an unholy fire, the knife pointed at him. "But only after I get you. All you Delacroix are gonna pay."

Philip's brief flare of bravado shriveled. "What do you mean?" he asked.

Flora offered him a diabolic smile. "I mean that after I get through with you, I'm gonna take care of the rest of your high-and-mighty family. I'm gonna start with that fancy lawyer daughter of yours and her girl. Or maybe I'll wait until she and her high-falutin' man go out to pass a good time and I'll sneak into their Garden District mansion and steal that new baby of theirs. How'd you like that, Mr. Philip Delacroix?"

Jackson was silent. The look on his face said without words that he was seeing a side of his mother that alarmed him.

Philip's heart pounded. Flora fully intended to hurt Joanna and Nikki and baby Lori. His relationship with his children might not be the best, but he loved them, in his own way. Flora was demented. A lunatic, he thought with rising anxiety.

"Joanna Delacroix's done nothing to you, *Maman*," Jackson said.

"Her daughters are alive. My boy is dead. An eye for an eye, as they say."

"Save your breath, boy," Philip said. "You can't reason with a crazy woman."

She advanced on him, knife at the ready. "What did you call me?"

"Crazy," Philip said, his voice harsh, his trepidation fading in the face of her threat against his family. He knew he had to try to stop her, even if he died at her hand. He had to try to spare his family her vengeance.

In the most noble act of his conniving, contemptible life, Philip took a step toward her. And another. "You're a crazy swamp witch. A raving lunatic!"

Seeing the murderous glint in his father's eyes, Jackson darted between his parents, his arms outstretched to keep them apart. With a strength none of them suspected in a man of his age, a power born of adrenaline and desperation, Philip ducked his head and ran at the younger man, shoving him aside.

Jackson went sprawling backward, his arms flailing. He fell against a wing chair, cracking his temple on the wood of the arm. With a moan, he slumped to the floor.

With a feral screech of maternal outrage, Flora launched herself across the space separating her from Philip. Her mane of gray hair streaming out behind her like ribbons of smoke blown by a turbulent wind, her lips drawn back in a grimace of pure hate, she raised the knife over her head, ready to plunge it into his heart.

Their eyes met and Philip's brief surge of boldness died. There wasn't time to say a prayer, the first he would have uttered in decades. There wasn't time to move out of her way. Knowing that the grim reaper wasn't a man at all, but a woman in a flowing floral tunic, he squeezed his eyes shut and sketched the sign of the cross over his chest in a feverish attempt to jump-start the religion of his youth.

"Flora!"

The name, spoken in a familiar voice, thundered through the room, echoing inside Philip's head. He heard Flora gasp, and opened his eyes. She stood a scant yard away, the blade still aloft, murder in her eyes.

"Flora," the voice said again. "Put the knife down."

She turned her head toward the doorway. Clovis, his shoulders squared in their customary military manner, crossed the room slowly—almost majestically, Philip thought. There was a look in the old retainer's one good eye that Philip had never seen before. A firmness, a hardness totally unlike the submission usually residing there; a look at odds with his usual calm and genial demeanor.

The hand gripping the scrimshaw handle wavered, lowered a bit.

From his place on the floor, Jackson moaned. The sound seemed to remind Flora of what had set her off. She glanced at Jackson, then back to Clovis. Her arm rose again. "He hurt Jackson. He's been hurting Jackson for years. It's time to end it."

"Put the knife down," Clovis repeated, advancing toward her with slow purpose. A harsh breath hissed from between Flora's clenched teeth, but she didn't move, held immobile by the expression in the old man's eyes.

He came to a stop mere inches from her, putting himself between her and Philip. Without a word, he reached up and closed his arthritic fingers around the wrist of her upraised arm in a grip that turned the knuckles of his café au lait hand white. They stood there for long seconds, staring into each other's eyes.

Jackson roused and pushed himself up on one elbow. Neither Philip, Clovis nor Flora moved. Catching sight of Philip's horrified expression, Jackson turned groggy eyes to Flora and Clovis and froze in turn.

Philip held his breath. He could hear the ticking of the grandfather clock against the far wall, the chirp and twitter of birds outside the window. Could feel the ragged pulse of his blood beating in his veins, pounding in his head, which felt as if it was in a vise. From far away, came the lonesome wail of another siren.

Finally, Flora's gaze wavered beneath the weight of the old man's stare. The tension seeped from her body, like air from a child's balloon. Clovis reached up with his free hand and took the knife. Flora lowered her arm and her resistance.

Clovis slipped his arm around her waist. "Come on, child. We're gonna take you somewhere and get you all fixed up." He looked at Jackson. "You all right, boy?"

Jackson reached up to finger his temple. His fingers came away sticky with blood. "Fine, sir."

"Take your mama outside. Chief Trahan may be needin' to talk with her."

Wordlessly, Jackson did as the old man asked. To Philip's astonishment, Flora made no move to resist, even though she must have known she was headed back to the mental home, or possibly even to jail. Clovis followed behind them toward the front door.

He was in the hall before Philip realized that the standoff was over and he was all right. He reached up and straightened his bow tie, then took a couple of unsteady steps toward the chair Jackson had fallen against, gripping the back to brace himself. He cleared his throat, trying to find his voice.

"Clovis!"

"Yes, sir?" the old man said, turning.

"You saved my life. How can I thank you?"

"Don't owe me nuthin', Mr. Delacroix, sir," Clovis said. "It was my duty."

WHEN JACKSON LED his mother out of the house, there was no sign of the mad woman who'd threatened another human at knifepoint. Flora seemed docile, weary looking and old as Jake handcuffed her and recited the Miranda.

The television crew filmed the whole process from a distance—Jake's deputies saw to that. Gator Guzman strained to see, and when the cruiser took off for the jail, he jumped into his car and followed, a newshound hot on the trail of a story and hopefully a statement.

As soon as they drove off, Joanna headed toward the house. Drew followed at a more leisurely pace. When he reached Jackson, he paused.

Seeing them standing side by side, Shelby was stunned by how much they looked alike, amazed she hadn't seen the similarity in their build, in the way their hair grew, the shape of their jaw—all typical Delacroix traits.

Obviously unable to think of anything to say, Drew turned and followed his sister to the house. Jackson plunged his hands into his pockets and regarded Drew's retreating figure for a few seconds, then turned and saw Shelby staring at him.

Like Drew, she wasn't certain what to say, but inbred Southern manners required something. Telling Travis she'd only be a minute, she crossed the few yards separating her from Jackson.

"I'm sorry." As inadequate as it was, it was the best she could do.

"Yeah," Jackson said solemnly, "so am I."

She gestured toward his head. "You ought to go get a couple of stitches in that cut."

"It'll be okay."

Shelby nodded. "Jake's a fine man. He'll take good care of her."

"Why would you care?" Jackson asked, a hint of his old, cocky self making a fleeting appearance.

"Because she's a human being, she's your mother, and as you pointed out a little while ago, for better or worse, we share Delacroix blood."

"It's been pretty much worse for me," he said, meeting her gaze steadily.

Shelby's smile was tinged with sarcasm. "I'm sure you've already figured out that it hasn't been a bed of roses for any of Uncle Philip's kids."

"Yeah." He looked down the lane, where the chrome of Gator's car could still be seen glittering in the early evening sunlight. "What's going to happen to her?"

"I imagine her attorney will have her plead temporary insanity."

"We can't afford a fancy lawyer. She'll get a public defender."

Shelby rummaged around in her purse and found a scrap of paper. She jotted down a name and phone number. "Call her. She's damn good."

Jackson took the paper, read the name and looked up with astonishment. "You? You gotta be kidding."

Shelby shrugged. "I take a lot of pro bono cases. My side of the family, including me, thinks a lot of Desiree." She drew a deep breath. "We've all had a heck of a year or so. We can hold grudges or point fingers, or we can deal with it and get on with our lives. Sometimes you have to cauterize a wound or pour salt in it before it can heal. Maybe that's what's happened to all of us. Maybe we can all be healed, if we don't keep picking at the scab."

Jackson's face held disbelief.

"You and your mother have both done wrong, Jackson, but my uncle isn't without blame. I think Drew and Joanna would tell you the same thing. They have their own Philip Delacroix crosses to bear. I don't know if we can ever be friends or if you, Joanna, Drew and Annabelle can ever have more than a cursory relationship, but the important thing is for you to all realize none of you is to blame. You're victims. The same way Rafe Perdido was a victim sixty years ago."

Shelby held out her hand to the man who was her cousin.

Silently, he took it.

"WHAT WAS THAT ALL ABOUT?" Travis and Shelby had just bade her father goodbye and Travis was following her to her car, enjoying the sway of her hips in the short black dress.

She tossed him an over-the-shoulder smile that seemed to say she knew exactly what was on his mind. "Just offering the olive branch to Jackson."

Travis opened the car door and she turned to face him. "You could do that, after what he's done to your family?"

Shelby shrugged. "It's like I told him. He's a victim. Neither of his parents is a saint, nor is he. Flora has probably poisoned his mind against us, but I can't forget or ignore the fact that we have the same blood flowing in our veins and that Philip and my grandfather are flip sides of a coin. No matter what Flora and Philip are like, Jackson is Desiree's grandson, and she's a good and decent person. As far as that goes, Uncle Philip must have a few good qualities himself or his kids wouldn't have turned out the way they did."

"You're saying that no one is all good or all bad."

"Exactly. Environment plays a big part in which traits develop."

"You're a good person, Shelby Delacroix," Travis said, backing her against the car and pulling her into his arms. "I knew there was a reason I loved you."

She slid her hands into his rear jeans pockets and fit herself more intimately against him. "And here I was thinking it was the hot sex that kept you coming back."

"That, too," he said with a little laugh that was partly a groan of frustration. "As a matter of fact, I was wondering if we could go back to my room and pick up where we left off.''

''Not on your life, buster.''

Travis looked like a kid who'd just been told he couldn't have a much coveted toy.

Shelby giggled softly at his dismay and pressed a kiss to his whisker-rough chin. ''It's been a while. Poor Annabelle would never be the same, not to mention her other guests. I've got someplace better in mind, but we have to wait until after dark, and we have to be very quiet.''

''Why?''

''It's on private property.''

''Hmm,'' Travis said thoughtfully. ''Trespassing. Adds a little spice.'' He nodded. ''Okay. We'll wait. But I need a big kiss to hold me off.''

''No problem, cowboy,'' she said, tilting her head and offering him her lips. One kiss turned to two, and two into half a dozen. They were both breathing heavily when Shelby pulled back to get some air. They both knew they were kidding themselves. A kiss wasn't nearly enough to hold off either of them.

''Do you?'' Shelby asked when she could breathe again.

''Do I what?'' Travis asked with a frown.

''Love me?''

''Of course I love you, Shelby,'' he told her, brushing back her hair with a clumsy gesture. ''I never stopped. And I never will.''

WILLIAM TURNED OFF the cordless phone and set the receiver on the glass-and-wrought-iron table on the back veranda. ''That was Justin,'' he told Mary. ''It's over. Philip is fine, and Jake took Flora off to jail.''

''Jail?''

William nodded and sat down in the Adirondack rocking chair across from her. ''I'm sure they'll transfer her back to the hospital as soon as they satisfy all the legalities. This time with proper surveillance and hopefully proper help.''

"What did she want?" Mary asked.

"To kill Philip." William related the tale as Justin had told him. "She had a knife and fully intended to use it on him, but Clovis intervened."

"Clovis?" Mary asked in surprise. "That's strange. I can't imagine Clovis getting involved." She laughed. "Actually, he's been around so long he's like part of the furniture. Sometimes I forget he's even there."

They sat in the comfortable, companionable silence that comes with knowing each other well, rocker creaking, glider squeaking. Finally William spoke. "Will you be all right if I leave for an hour or so?"

"Of course I'll be all right," Mary said tartly. "I don't need a baby-sitter just yet. Where are you going?"

William met her questioning gaze, his own eyes filled with a sad determination. "I'm going to drive over to Belle Terre, take the pirogue and go into the swamp. To see my mother."

Mary nodded. "I think that's an excellent idea, brother of mine."

The simple statement told William three things. That Mary understood. That she approved. And that even though Desiree might be his mother, they would always be siblings in spirit. Which, William thought as he pushed himself to his feet, was what counted most.

IT HAD BEEN YEARS—at least twenty or more—since William had paddled across Moon Lake's placid surface to the winding bayou where Desiree made her home. Surprisingly, he hadn't forgotten how. Perhaps it was like riding a bicycle—once learned, never forgotten. The single oar scooped the greenish water out of the way, on one side and then the other, shooting the pirogue forward like a sleek bullet.

A weary sun had eased below the line of trees to the west, giving over to the encroaching evening. The scarlet glow above the treetops looked as if a giant fire burned out of control somewhere beyond the horizon.

As William neared the opposite shore, he startled a great blue heron, whose wings beat clumsily in an attempt to get airborne and escape the unfamiliar creature headed its way. Though the sunlight was fading, a quintet of turtles still sat on a mossy log, like a police department lineup. Water striders hopped over the surface of the lake and dragonflies buzzed around him like a fleet of miniature helicopters with no flight plan.

William propelled the small boat along the shore to the mouth of the bayou, guiding it through the all-but-hidden opening and slipping into another world. Though it was still plenty hot beneath the shady canopy, the temperature dropped several degrees. The coolness was a trade-off for the mosquitoes that hovered around him like a black, miasmic cloud. Thankfully, mosquitoes had never been too fond of his blood type, but just to be on the safe side, he'd doused himself with repellent before leaving the house.

He'd also brought a powerful flashlight in case it grew dark before he started back. Even so, he knew he was courting danger. The swamp could become a confusing maze for anyone unfamiliar with its twists and turns.

A kingfisher called, reminding him of the harsh yet dreamy beauty of his surroundings. Several varieties of trees made a leafy arch overhead, allowing brief glimpses of the darkening sky. Cypresses waded in the water like swamp witches with bony knees raised, their locks of Spanish moss trailing in the murky waters like skeins of ragged, unkempt hair.

The deeper into the swamp he went, the more it felt to

William as if he were going back in time, which, in a way, he was. He was going back in time to when he was born and his mother had chosen to give him away.

By the time he saw Desiree's place in the distance, shadows were starting to congregate for the evening symphony. The nighttime orchestra was tuning up, the first tentative baritone chirp of crickets against the occasional bass bellow of a bullfrog. It was music he'd always loved, an appreciation passed on through the genes. A legacy, perhaps, of his mother's.

She was waiting on the porch, rocking slowly in an ancient cypress rocker, a clay pipe clenched between her teeth, her dark, arcane eyes focused on him with unblinking intensity. For a brief, foolish moment, William felt as if she'd forced him to come by sheer dint of will. Feeling like a misbehaving child being called to the principal's office, he tied the boat to a post and started up the pier to the house.

When he reached the porch, Desiree stopped rocking. "I'd about given up on you."

The statement implied she'd felt he would come, that she'd known he would, but how could she when William hadn't even known himself? He stepped onto the porch. "May I sit down?"

She nodded, and he took a seat in a metal lawn chair someone had painted bright yellow. The sweet scent of tobacco filled his nostrils. When she made no move to speak, he said, "Remy told you about Flora and Philip?"

Desiree nodded. "Said she left the hospital and took Philip hostage at knifepoint."

"Yes." While Desiree rocked and smoked, William related what Justin had told him during their phone conversation. "According to Jackson, Clovis stopped her."

There was the briefest halt in the rocker's movements. Then the creaking started again. Desiree sucked on the pipe, and smoke wreathed her head like the evening fog collecting on the surface of the water.

"Flora always was a headstrong child, and when she loved, it was with all her heart. Got that from me, I suppose."

"What does love have to do with what she tried to do to Philip?" William asked.

The rocker stopped again. Desiree fixed her potent, all-knowing gaze on him. "It has to do with everything. Affects every decision you make. You of all people ought to know that."

William felt uncomfortable suddenly. She might have been talking about his life in the church and how he'd heard things—sins—committed in the name of that elusive thing called love. Yet somehow he felt that his life as a priest had nothing to do with her observation. It was as if this woman who had given birth to him had somehow peeked into his soul, his past. It was as if she knew about Camille.

William told himself he was being fanciful, that it was just the old guilt rearing its head. How could she know? Then he remembered her testimony. She'd known about Philip and Camille and about Camille and Charles. There was the distinct possibility that Desiree had seen him with Camille, too.

"Funny thing about love," the old woman observed, staring out over the water. "It can turn to hate in the blink of an eye. Guess you know all about that, too," she said, slanting him a shrewd look. "As much as Flora loved Philip Delacroix when she became *enceinte* with Jackson, she learned to hate that man."

"Hate should never be used as an excuse for wrongdoing," William said, falling back on his theological training.

"Shouldn't," she agreed with a nod. "But is. Philip

should never have done what he did to my baby girl, and that's a fact.''

William had given considerable thought to how he would have reacted to the atrocity Philip had committed against Flora had it been done to him. Right or wrong, William had concluded that he, like Flora, might have sought revenge.

''No,'' he agreed, ''he shouldn't. Having her put in that burial vault was extremely cruel and heartless.''

Desiree drew on her pipe. ''Philip has always been that.''

''You say it so calmly,'' William said, turning to search her face.

''How else should I be?''

''By wronging Flora and Jackson, Philip has wronged you, yet you don't seem to hold any animosity toward him.''

Desiree's eyes were as calm as the waters of the bayou. She took the pipe from her mouth and gently tapped the ash into a Folgers can sitting by her rocker. ''Never cared for him much, even when he was a boy. They's a whole heap of difference between Mr. Philip and Mr. Charles, now, isn't there?''

''Yes,'' William agreed. ''They're very different.''

She brought her gaze back to William. ''But you were askin' about animosity. I don't feel any. Not anymore. It all left me when I got up on that courtroom stand and told the truth about what I saw in the woods that night. Your faith says the truth will set us free. It's true. That's why I'm glad you found out about me bein' your *maman*.''

said out. My mama had had a bunch of mouths to feed and no daddy'd take care of me and by then—"

William was silent. Somehow her faith, and her trust in no one but herself, his mother.

...with all her... Hamilton and Marguérite. They had him. She'd given...

CHAPTER TEN

WILLIAM'S BREATHING stopped momentarily. Desiree had made the transition from forgotten malice toward Philip to being William's own mother with such ease that he was taken aback. He'd known the conversation would turn to this sooner or later. It was why he'd come. He'd thought a thousand times of what he would say to her, practiced trite little speeches about forgiveness and putting it all behind them to prove to her that he'd learned his seminary lessons well, to show her that in spite of what she'd done to him, he was a civilized man, a devout man who practiced what he preached.

But, as usual, when he was caught off guard, his thought processes shut down. All the pompous things he'd planned on saying to her flew from his mind like bats flying from a cave, accompanied by the noisy cacophony of beating wings and shrill squeaking. William recognized that the noises drowning out her simple words were the wild beating of his heart and an internal shriek of resentment.

Reduced from intellect to raw emotion, he said the first thing that came to mind, asked the question that burned in his brain and ate at his heart. "Why did you give me to Hamilton and Marguérite Delacroix? Why didn't you want me?"

Desiree looked at him, her surprise clear. "It had nothin' to do with wantin' you," she told him. "I was sixteen years old when I got with child, barely seventeen when I had you. My mama had died a couple of months earlier, and my daddy'd gone off to God knows where.''

William was silent, searching her face, as if by doing so he could discern the truth.

''I worked for Mr. Hamilton and Miz Marguerite. They had Miss Mary and the twins, and her and me, we came *enceinte* at the same time. She was havin' a hard time, so Mr. Hamilton hired a nanny for the children and sent Miz Marguerite down to Galveston Island to take it easy. He asked me did I want to go down with her. I'd learned a lot about doctorin' from my mama, and he thought my powders and tisanes could help her. Don't know if he ever told you, but I saved Charles's and Philip's lives once when they were babies.''

''Yes,'' William said. ''I heard.''

A soft smile of reminiscence dallied with the corners of the old quadroon's puckered lips. ''Anyway, Mr. Hamilton, he wanted me to go and see to Miz Marguerite. I hadn't ever been anywhere but Bayou Beltane, so I said yes.'' She chuckled. ''That was a big mistake. I hated all that water. Too noisy for me. And way too big. I missed the trees and the frogs and the mud. That sand would get in my shoes and eat up my feet.''

''What happened to Mama's other baby?'' William asked, forgetting for a moment that the woman sitting next to him was his mother.

''Her baby was born dead.'' Desiree shook her head at the memory. ''I never saw a woman take on so. She wanted a big family, Miz Marguerite did. It broke her heart when her little girl died. And there I was, healthy as a horse, not knowin' how I was goin' to work and take care of a baby of my own.''

Desiree's eyes held a faraway look. ''We stayed on at Galveston Island. Mr. Hamilton was hopin' the sea air would perk Miz Marguerite up, but she was grievin' real bad. Then you came along about three weeks after she lost her baby girl. I think the idea to give you to them came to me when Miz Marguerite handed you to me for the first time. She looked at you like she might not ever let you go, and there were tears in her eyes."

William recalled how gentle Marguerite Delacroix had been, how much she had seemed to love him. No. She *had* loved him. She'd loved him as if he were truly her own flesh and blood. He'd never had any doubts about that.

"I knew the Delacroix were good people," Desiree said, "and I knew they were good parents. I figured they could do better by you than I could ever think about doin'. If you grew up as a Delacroix, you'd have a good family and a chance to be somebody someday. If you stayed with me, I'd be lucky to feed you. I knew a boy needed a daddy. And there was the fact that Miz Marguerite had this empty place in her heart that needed fillin' up."

William nodded. In spite of his pain, her rationalization sounded reasonable.

"I went to Miz Marguerite and told her what I had in mind. She was thrilled. She called Mr. Hamilton, and he was excited because she was. That man loved her, I'll tell you that. He'd have done anything for her. He agreed, but made me and Miz Marguerite both swear we'd never tell a soul that you were really mine. As far as the world knew, you were the baby she'd gone to Galveston Island to have."

"And neither of you ever said anything? Not until Philip wanted to sell off the land last year?"

"Not a word," Desiree said. "Mr. Hamilton offered me a lot of money, but I wouldn't take it. I told him I wasn't sellin' my child, I was givin' it to someone who'd love it. He insisted on doin' something for me, so I told him I wanted to be close enough to you that I could watch you grow up and be a part of your life in a small way. I asked him could I build me a house on his swamp land. I'd grown up with that life, and it suited me. That's when he deeded me that forty acres free and clear."

William sat, trying to absorb what she'd said. It made sense, especially considering the circumstances. But it was still a bitter pill to swallow. "Did you ever regret what you'd done?"

Again she looked surprised by the very thought. "How could I regret something that was so right? I had peace of mind, William, that's what I had. The Delacroix were crazy about you. You were growin' up like a little prince. I saw you every day or two."

Seeing the bleakness of his expression, she reached out a knotted hand and touched his arm. William stared down at the arthritic fingers and fought the urge to cry. It was the first time she'd touched him in years—since he was ten or so.

"I didn't have any regrets," Desiree said, "but there were times I sure missed havin' you and wished you were with me. Times I knew you were sick or troubled and wished I could advise you. But then I reminded myself that I'd made a deal, and you were doin' just fine without me."

"Why did you keep Flora?" William hated the resentment he felt.

"I was a good bit older when I had Flora. I had a lot more sense, and I was doin' all right by myself. I had a grown-up cousin who kept Flora when I was out collectin' my herbs and things. And when Flora was older, I took her along. Her bein' a girl made things easier, somehow. But just because I kept her never meant I loved her more."

Desiree smiled. "Truth be told, you were a lot easier to love than Flora ever was. And when you became a priest, I was truly proud that you'd followed your heart to your calling. I always knew your heart was good."

There was more silence. More thought.

"Were you proud of me when you saw me with Camille Gravier?" William asked with brutal bluntness, perhaps needing to clear his conscience more than he needed to hear her answer.

"I knew about you and Camille," Desiree said, her eyes meeting his with disconcerting directness. "I saw you, just like I saw her with Charles and with Philip. I knew it wasn't right, but I didn't feel like I was one to cast stones. I knew what kind of woman she was, how she was playin' Philip and Charles against each other, and how she'd set her cap for you just to see if she could make you turn your back on God. I figured you'd give in, but I also figured she'd do what she did. I knew you'd be hurt, but I thought you'd come out a stronger man, and make a better priest. It's easier to understand where folks are comin' from if you've walked down the same road."

"If you know all this, then you know the baby she was carrying when she died could have been mine."

Desiree nodded.

"Why didn't you come forward back then and tell the authorities?"

"You're my son, William. I was trying to protect you. Even though I saw Philip do what he did, I didn't want you implicated in any way. Philip was a liar. Is a liar. The Delacroix were powerful people. Still are. I knew it could all come down to whether the jury believed him or the others. As it was, they took Charles's word over Rafe Perdido's. Even though I knew Hamilton loved you, I was afraid to test that love. Afraid which side he'd take if it came down to believing you or his real sons."

William tipped his head back. "Oh, God!" he murmured. He thought it was a prayer, but he wasn't sure. After long moments of staring up at the roof of the porch, he looked at Desiree. "I should tell them."

"Who?"

"Jake Trahan. Or at the very least, I should tell my brothers and sister."

"Why?" Desiree asked.

"Charles had the courage to tell us about himself and Camille, and he had the courage to get up on the stand and say that the baby could have been his. I should do the same."

"Why?" Desiree asked again.

"Because it's the honorable thing to do."

The old woman shook her head. "William, Charles was there that night. He had to tell about his relationship to Camille. Philip killed Camille. Tellin' everyone you slept with her won't serve any purpose but to rid you of the guilt you've been carryin' around all these years."

She was right, William thought. The guilt over his affair with Camille and the way he'd betrayed his calling had eaten away at him for decades. Telling *wouldn't* change what had happened at Moon Lake.

"If you tell Charles and Mary and the rest of the family, all you're going to do is destroy a bit of their belief in who you are."

"But I'm living a lie."

"Your life is no lie, William Delacroix," she said. He heard anger in her voice for the first time. "You haven't pretended to be a good and godly man all these years. You *are* a good and godly man. One who made a mistake as a young man and who has never forgiven himself for that mistake even though God has."

Was she right? William wondered. He believed in divine forgiveness. Why was it so hard for him to believe God could forgive him?

"Let it go, William. Just let it go."

From across the bayou an owl hooted and was answered by another. A firefly blinked like a miniature beacon in the sky. And in that moment, with his mother's hand resting on his forearm and the sound and scent of the bayou surrounding him, William felt a perfect peace steal over him. For the first time in sixty years, he felt as if he might be able to do what she asked. He drew in a deep breath. The air had never tasted so sweet.

"It's almost dark," Desiree said. "You should be gettin' back."

"Yes." William pushed himself to his feet. "I'd like to come again, if I may."

"I'd like that," Desiree said.

William was down the porch steps when he turned. "One more question."

"You want to know who your father was," she said, with that uncanny ability to read his mind.

"Yes."

The expression in Desiree's eyes was flat, emotionless. "Neville Alvarez."

The name fell into William's mind with the impact of a physical blow. He grabbed at the handrail. "Judge Alvarez?" he whispered, feeling all the strength leech from his legs.

Desiree nodded. "Judge Alvarez. He was just a lawyer back then, a partner of Hamilton Delacroix's. But he was comin' into his power even then. You might not believe this, William, but I was a pretty girl. Real pretty. Maybe even what they'd call sexy nowadays. And I bloomed early. Neville took a shine to me."

She'd turned inward to her memories again. William saw that the distant look was back in her eyes.

"There was no denyin' him. And after the first couple of times, I just stopped fightin' it."

"Dear God!" William cried softly. "Are you telling me that Neville Alvarez raped you?"

Desiree nodded. "That's exactly what I'm sayin'.

Turned out okay, though. He soon found someone else, and I got you from it.''

William stared at her for several seconds, then turned and made his way shakily down the ramp to the dock. He climbed into the boat, his mind a jumble of facts, his heart a hodgepodge of feelings. Desiree giving him away. Marguerite losing a child. Neville Alvarez—his father—raping Desiree. Flora trying to kill Philip...

William tried to pray. Thought he swore. Finally he understood why people in the Bible tore at their clothes. He understood more of what Job must have experienced as God allowed Satan to have his way with him.

He would never recall the trip back to Moon Lake through the trees and the darkness. His only coherent thought was to wonder if the nightmare would ever end.

SHELBY AND TRAVIS WHILED away the evening hours by having dinner in Covington. Afterward, she stopped by a house with a sign out front that pronounced Quality Quilting Done Here and roused the owner so she could look at her collection. Travis knew better than to question Shelby. There was always a method to her madness, and besides, he had a pretty good idea about what the quilt would be used for.

Fifteen minutes later, she'd picked out a gorgeous wedding-ring quilt done in white and off white. When the woman quoted a price of several hundred dollars—inflated, Travis was sure, because they'd had the audacity to interfere with her viewing of the movie of the week—Shelby wrote out a check, declaring the quilt was the buy of the century. They left, a satisfied smile on both women's faces, the purchase stuck in a huge black trash bag.

Travis stowed the quilt in the trunk and turned what he hoped was a pitiful, pained look on Shelby. "Is it dark enough yet?"

Shelby shook her head in pseudo sorrow. "You have absolutely no control, Travis." She grinned and stepped into his embrace. "That's one of the things I love about you."

"Yeah? What else?"

She pulled his head down and whispered in his ear. Travis felt his face going hot. When she finished, he asked again, "Is it dark enough yet?"

"Yeah, it is. Or it will be by the time we get there."

"Where are we going?"

"Riverwood."

"Riverwood?"

She nodded. "I want to make love with you under the magnolia tree. Aunt Mary and Rafe Perdido spent a lot of time there, and I figure it's a lucky place."

"Lucky? Things didn't turn out so good for him," Travis said darkly. "Your aunt, either, for that matter."

"Yes, they did, in the ways that count. She really loved him, Travis, and after hearing her testimony, I believe he really loved her. If I've learned anything this past year, it's that forgiveness is mandatory to true happiness and that love—in whatever form—is what makes you rich."

Travis couldn't argue with that, no matter what else had happened in Mary's and Rafe's lives. He and Shelby got into the car and he drove to her house...slowly.

Instead of pulling into the garage, they parked down the lane and used the pencil flashlight hooked to Shelby's key chain to guide their way around the house. With Travis carrying the quilt, Shelby walking slowly, hampered by her high heels, they walked arm in arm, whispering, laughing softly, making the short trek an adventure.

A sudden thought stopped Travis in his tracks. Shelby stumbled against him. "You haven't bought any dogs since I was here last, have you?"

"Nope. Ow! These shoes are killing me."

Travis knelt at her feet, unbuckled the narrow straps encircling her ankles and slid the high heels off. He hooked them over his fingers. "I'll buy you some new panty hose. Unless you want to take them off."

Shelby shook her head in the darkness. "I want *you* to take them off."

"It will be my pleasure, ma'am." He handed her the shoes, pulled her back to his side and they started off again.

When they reached the backyard, Shelby took his hand and led him unerringly to the massive magnolia, slipping between the branches the way she had the afternoon she'd found her great-aunt there.

Travis followed. He set down the quilt and aimed the penlight this way and that.

"Help me spread out the quilt," she said in a hushed voice.

But Travis was caught up in his awe. "It's like a hidden room under here."

"I know. Cool, huh?" Her voice was hardly more than a loud whisper. "Now, will you put out the light before someone catches us, and help me with the quilt?"

Travis turned off the flashlight and shoved her keys into his pocket. He spoke in a low rumble tinged with humor. "Well, if they do catch us, I know this female lawyer who might be able to get us off."

Shelby laughed softly. "Yeah, and I know this federal judge. Nice guy. I might be able to do something about trespassing. But indecent exposure? I'm not too sure about that."

Together they spread out the quilt. "Will it ruin it, putting it on the ground?" Travis asked.

"I don't think so. It hasn't rained in a while. If it gets dirty, I'll have it cleaned before I put it on our bed."

"Our bed?" Travis asked, sitting down and pulling off his boots.

Shelby dropped to her knees and tossed her hair back. "Yeah, our bed. In case you didn't notice, this is a wedding-ring quilt, and if I remember correctly, you refinished your grandmother's old bedroom suite recently."

"That I did."

It seemed fitting to him somehow that he and Shelby would sleep on the bed where a Gravier had once slept, that their children would be conceived there. It was a sort of symbolic end to hostilities, a proper way to bring things full circle. It seemed fitting, too, that the quilt would become one of their family heirlooms. The thought pleased him.

He got to his knees, facing her. "Come here," he said, and she did. As Mary and Rafe had done that night so long ago, they knelt together beneath the tree and pledged their love and their determination to beat the odds. The tree and the night seemed to approve.

"I can't just pack up and come to Comfort when the trial is over," Shelby said as he unzipped her dress. "We'll have to hire someone to take my place. It may take a few months to get everything squared away."

"I know. I can wait." He pressed a kiss to the hollow where her neck and shoulder met. She shivered.

"You're awfully slow," she complained as he worked her arm out of her dress.

"I'm out of practice," he said in a distracted tone, starting on the other arm. "You could help."

Shelby laughed softly and pulled her arm free. "Do you think I'll fit in in Texas?" she asked.

"Well, you've got the first prerequisite down, but you need help on the second."

"Oh?"

He slid the dress down to her hips. "You look darn good

in a pair of jeans, but you talk way too much. Texans are notoriously closemouthed.''

''Oh.''

Smiling, he tipped her head back and looked into her eyes. ''I could use a little help, here, darlin'.''

Shelby reached up and gripped both sides of his shirt near the neck. She gave a grunt and a mighty jerk. The sound of tearing fabric rent the stillness of the night. Buttons flew.

Travis uttered a mild curse. ''What the heck are you doing?''

''Helping,'' she said sweetly.

''That's not helping,'' he grumbled even as he pulled his shirttail from his Wranglers. ''It's destruction of property. It's—''

''So sue me,'' she said, sliding her palms over his bare chest.

He laughed then. ''You know, Shelby, until now, I never realized you had a sense of humor. I like that in a woman. A woman who—''

''Travis,'' she interrupted.

''Can laugh at herself, who can make other people laugh, is—''

''Travis!''

''What?''

''For a Texan, you talk a lot. You know that Mary Chapin Carpenter song?''

''Which one?'' Travis asked.

'''Shut Up and Kiss Me.'''

''Yeah. It's one of my favorites. I know it well.''

''Well, why don't you try doing it?''

Travis's smile was a white flash in the darkness. ''It would be my pleasure, Ms. Delacroix, ma'am.''

And he did. But the pleasure wasn't just his. It was Shelby's, too.

MUCH LATER, WHEN THEY were both boneless with satiation, Travis propped himself up on one elbow and looked down at Shelby, who lay motionless on her back, staring up at the darkness.

"While I've got you in an agreeable mood, I want to ask you something."

"Ask away, cowboy. At the moment, I'm feeling very kindly disposed toward you."

"Will you marry me?"

She reached out a languid hand and caressed his cheek. "I thought we'd already settled that," she said with a weary, satisfied smile. "Of course I'll marry you."

"No, I mean I want to get married now. Tonight, if possible."

Shelby rose up on one elbow to face him. "Tonight! Why? You said you could wait."

"I know I did, but I've been thinking about everything that's happened the past few months. Just look at what went down this afternoon with Flora and Philip. Life is too unpredictable, Shelby. We talk about forever, but none of us knows how long that might be. I don't want another day passing without knowing you're mine for however long forever might be."

"Travis, you know as well as I do that there are laws that have to be satisfied."

"I thought you said you know a judge. Your dad can pull a few strings, call in a few markers, can't he?"

Shelby was silent for long seconds. "Kiss me," she said.

"Why?"

"Just kiss me."

Travis did so, thoroughly. Thirty minutes later, Shelby pulled away from him and shook her head. "Wow."

"Is that a yes or no?" Travis asked, brushing her hair away from her face.

"Help me get dressed, cowboy," she said. "I've got a wedding to plan."

WHEN DREW AND JOANNA LEFT, after assuring themselves that Flora hadn't harmed him, Philip went to his room to rest and found two things that shook him to his soul. A picture had fallen from the wall, its frame shattered, the glass broken. He also found another voodoo doll on his bed.

His heart skipped several beats as he stared at the malicious handiwork. Flora must have put the crude figure there before she accosted him in the library. Though the bow tie proved the image was of him, this doll was different from the others. It looked like a cadaver, with a small black cross hanging around its neck. A pearl-studded straight pin pierced its heart.

Philip told himself he should be used to finding the dratted effigies. So far nothing serious had come from their being left here and there. Still, he couldn't ignore the clear signs that Flora had stepped up her campaign to drive him insane. The cadaver and black cross, both symbols of *wanga*, were far more sinister than an ordinary gris-gris.

With hands that trembled only slightly, he picked up the doll and tossed it into the bathroom waste basket. As he looked into the mirror, he saw that it was cracked for no apparent reason.

Philip wiped a shaking hand down his face, then grabbed a hand towel and wiped feverishly at the perspiration there. He went back into the bedroom and sought the comfort of his bed. A cracked mirror. A fallen picture. According to old superstitions, both were signs of imminent death, even without the added influence of the voodoo doll.

He cursed Flora Boudreaux and her mother, hating them both with every fiber of his being. If Desiree hadn't come forward, he wouldn't be in this fix. Without her, he wouldn't have to take the stand. It might be better if he didn't, but at this point he felt it was imperative to give his side of the story. He hadn't followed Charles and Camille with the intention of drowning her. He'd only wanted to spy on them and see what sort of line Camille was feeding his twin. Wanted to feed his own jealous fury.

Philip hadn't been so torn since that fateful spring. Despite their differences, he loved his brother. Actually, it was the knowledge that he'd never be the kind of person Charles was that made crossing the line a favorable pastime of Philip's.

He'd learned early in life that Charles was smarter, kinder, better behaved—the perfect son. Philip's reaction was to become impudent, mean and manipulative. Notoriety was better than being ordinary any old day. Like any behavior done over and over, his had become habit. Even worse, he'd come to like the power he wielded because of his actions. Power was a terrible addiction.

He and Camille had always had a lot in common, and as they'd grown up, those similarities in the way they looked at life had brought them together. Camille was the first girl Philip had had sex with, and even though he'd been innocent, he'd suspected he wasn't her first.

The more time passed, the more he learned about Camille. Her outer beauty was just a facade for a cold and calculating mind. Camille Gravier meant to be someone someday, and she didn't care how she reached that goal. Philip had watched her use Mary throughout their youth, relying on his sister's good graces to get invitations to parties she would never have received had she not been Mary Delacroix's best friend. He had seen her interest in Rafe and known it wasn't reciprocated, even though he'd had no idea that Rafe's lack of interest stemmed from his preoccupation with Mary.

Still, Philip was crazy about Camille, obsessed with her, which was why he'd waited so long to marry and why he'd married Gwen, who was as close to a carbon copy of Camille as he was ever likely to find. In looks, anyway.

In temperament, the two were complete opposites. Gwen was basically a good and decent person. Camille was like the little girl in the nursery rhyme with the curl in the middle of her forehead. When she was good, she was very, very good, and his life was perfect in every way. When she was bad she was horrid, as she'd been the day he told her he couldn't marry her.

He knew now that he, the master manipulator, had been out-maneuvered by the auburn-haired, green-eyed beauty. She'd never really cared for him at all. All she wanted was the Delacroix name, and it hadn't mattered to her which brother gave it to her. Only William had escaped her grasping clutches and the heartache she'd doled out so indiscriminately. Lucky fellow.

Now it seemed even Mary had suffered because of Camille's single-minded determination to have her way. His big sister Mary and Rafe Perdido had had a child... The fact that she'd managed to keep that a secret for so long had angered Philip at first. He prided himself on keeping tabs on all the events concerning his family. But as more things happened and more old secrets were revealed, he'd quickly figured out that expending his energy on anger was a waste of time. There were more pressing problems to worry about than his sister's love child.

Like what he would say on the stand the next day. He couldn't go to jail. Somehow he had to make the jury believe he was innocent of cold-blooded murder. He had to make them see that what had happened was spur-of-the-moment, heat of passion. He hadn't meant to hurt Camille, he'd just wanted to stop her screaming....

He had to make them see that he'd hidden in the woods

afterward because he was just a frightened kid who realized he'd done something very wrong. So frightened he'd
kept quiet even when it became clear that Charles might
become a suspect, too. By not coming forward, Philip had
not only forced the blame on Rafe Perdido, he'd thrown
his own brother to the wolves. If public opinion and prej-
udice against Perdido hadn't been so strong, Charles might
have wound up serving time at Angola...might have been
killed there himself.

That, Philip knew, was at the root of his rift with
Charles. Charles had always suspected that Philip had been
in the woods that night, that he'd killed Camille. Philip
had drawn away from his twin for the same reason. Once
again, he'd known he was inferior to Charles.

It wasn't Charles's fault, though. It was his. Philip felt
the sting of tears in his eyes—tears of self-pity and no
small regret. There was another secret, too, another death
on his hands. But that one he would take to his grave.

Outside, a dog howled, another harbinger of death.

CHAPTER ELEVEN

JUST AFTER DAYBREAK on the morning of Philip's testimony, Joanna, who, along with the baby, had spent the night with Mary and William, sat with Gwen in the kitchen drinking coffee and wishing the day were over. For countless, different reasons, neither had slept well the night before. "You look like death warmed over, Mom," Joanna said, pouring more chicory-laced coffee into Gwen's fragile china cup.

"How indelicate of you to say so," she answered, but Joanna saw the glimmer of humor in her mother's eyes. "You look a little worn yourself."

"Lori had colic." Joanna's eyes widened in understanding. "She kept you awake, didn't she? Probably Aunt Mary and Uncle William, too."

"I heard her, but that isn't really what kept me from sleeping. I kept thinking about Philip and how I could ever have convinced myself he loved me—or that I could ever have loved him, for that matter."

"Simple," Joanna said. "He dazzled you with a mile-long line and kept you guessing by not committing himself."

Gwen cradled the cup between her palms and laughed. "You do know him."

"I know how he operates. That doesn't necessarily mean I know him. It isn't the same thing."

"You're right." Gwen sipped at her coffee. "I asked myself a hundred times why he married me, but it wasn't until I spoke with Mary and William last night that I found out."

"Why?"

"Because I look like Camille Gravier."

"Really?" Joanna asked.

"Mary and William both said the resemblance was uncanny. It was the first thing they noticed about me when I started seeing Philip."

"Do you think he really loved her?" Joanna asked.

"Honestly? I don't think your father knows the meaning of the word. Maybe he wanted her. Maybe he just thought he wanted her. But Philip is too wrapped up in his own quest for power to love anything or anyone overly much."

"It's sad, isn't it?"

"Yes."

Joanna's laughter was tinged with bitterness. "He'd be furious if he knew I pitied him, but I do. I've hated him for manipulating my life. But since I went to work for Uncle Charles, I've learned to accept Dad for what he is. I've even learned to tolerate him. I have regard for him because he fathered me, but I don't love him."

"He always was a control freak. Look how he coerced me into giving up my children! Look what he did to Jake and Annabelle, and how he's treated Drew." Tears sparkled on Gwen's eyelashes. "I'm so glad they've finally worked their way out from under Philip's thumb and so glad that I at least got you children from the marriage." A sad, bitter little smile touched her face. "Maybe I should say I at least got you. It remains to be seen if I'll ever have Drew or Annabelle."

"They're smart people, Mom," Joanna said, taking her mother's hand and squeezing it. "It may take a while, but they'll work through it all and see that you were as much a victim as they were."

"I have to take some responsibility, Jo," Gwen said.

"And you did. The other day. They see that. They both have to take responsibility for the way they let Dad dominate them, too. Let's face it, he's a tough guy to buck up against. Greater mortals than the four of us have folded under his pressure."

Gwen pulled a tissue from her robe pocket and wiped at her eyes. "I know it may not be possible, but I'd like to have some sort of relationship with them. And with Cade."

"You have to believe it will happen. I do."

Gwen smiled and nodded. "Annabelle's really happy, isn't she?" she asked in a trembling voice.

"Ecstatic," Joanna said. "And about time. Drew is, too. Katherine Beaufort is exactly the kind of woman he needs."

Gwen's eyes brimmed with tears again.

"What's the matter?"

"I don't know," she admitted. "In spite of what's happened and what may happen, and despite the ugly scene with your father, I'm glad I came. I think I needed to see him again to have closure on the past and all the hurt we caused each other. In a strange way, coming here has made me happy. Isn't that weird?"

"No," Joanna said. "It's normal, I think. You've closed the last page of one part of your life, and you're about to start a new one." She smiled. "And this time, I promise you, the story will have a happy ending."

The phone rang. Fearing the worst from such an early call, Joanna looked at her mother, a frown drawing her dark eyebrows together. She picked up the receiver before the ring woke her aunt and uncle. "Hello... Annabelle! What's wrong? You can't be serious! At seven-thirty? Well, I suppose so. What do you need? Okay. Bye."

"What on earth was that all about?" Gwen asked as Joanna hung up the receiver.

"Annabelle wants us to drive into Bayou Beltane—by seven-thirty. Shelby and Travis are getting married."

SHELBY STOOD IN ONE of Annabelle's guest bedrooms and gazed at herself in the mirror. She looked like a bride, she thought, thanks to all that she and Annabelle had done to put together the impromptu wedding in less than eight hours.

When she and Travis had gone inside to tell her parents of their decision, Justin had been shocked but glad to accommodate them. He'd made a few calls, got the waiting period waived and agreed to perform the ceremony himself.

Madeline had been thrilled at the news, even though it was short notice—especially since she'd missed her other daughters' wedding ceremonies. Wanting it to be as special as possible, Madeline had raced up into the attic and come down cradling a sheet-wrapped wedding gown in her arms.

"It's your grandmother's dress," she said, offering it to Shelby. "I think it should fit. If it does, it can be your 'something borrowed.'"

The gown, of creamy satin and antique lace, was a scoop-neck style with a close-fitting bodice that flared out at the hips. The veil was an illusion of cream-tinted flowers and tulle.

The dress, which smelled faintly of cedar, fit Shelby to a T. She thanked her mother with a hug and told her she'd be proud to wear the wedding gown. With that hurdle out of the way, they'd gone to call Annabelle, to ask if the wedding could be held in her backyard early the next morning, before Philip took the stand.

Though Annabelle was as surprised as the rest of the family, she agreed readily. No, she didn't need a thing, she assured them. Because of the bed-and-breakfast, she always had sweets in the freezer, made up ahead, and she could bake a cake herself if she had to stay up all night—which she did.

As Shelby looked out the back window at the white gazebo, the profusion of spring flowers and the white-draped table set with delicate antique china, she was astounded at how professional things looked on such short notice.

She and Travis would take their vows in the gazebo, which was covered with clematis vines bearing white, saucerlike blooms. Potted ivy topiaries flanked either side of the main entry. Annabelle had accomplished a miracle.

In fact, the whole thing was a miracle, considering all they'd been through. As frightening as it was, her heart told her she was doing the right thing. Like Travis, she saw how life could get in the way of happiness. Like him, she wanted to hold close every moment of their time together.

A knock sounded at the door. Madeline, who'd been helping Annabelle with last-minute preparations, stepped inside. "It's time," she said, crossing the room to take her daughter's cold hands in her warm ones.

"I'm ready."

"You look lovely, Shelby," Madeline said, her eyes awash in tears. "And I'm so happy for you."

Shelby felt her own eyes tearing up. "Thanks, Mom. I'm glad you're here."

"So am I." She gave Shelby a tentative smile. "May I give you a word of advice?"

"Surely."

"Be patient and supportive with each other. Don't let life smother the feelings you have for each other. Love takes tending, just like any living, growing thing."

Shelby nodded. "Thanks, Mom." She kissed Madeline's cheek and together they went outside to the gazebo, where everyone was waiting.

There was no music, and Shelby walked into the gazebo alone, the long gown making a soft swishing sound. Her family—everyone from Uncle William and Aunt Mary and her grandfather Charles, to Jax's and Joanna's baby daughters—were there. Her brother, Beau, and Holly, her sister Marie, with Lucas at her side—everyone was sitting in folding chairs or standing outside the perimeter, their faces beaming. Even Charly and Marshall had dropped everything to be there, driving much of the night from an investigation case near Houston.

Travis and her father stood together, Justin handsome in a black suit, Travis looking the farthest thing from cowboy in a black tuxedo with a tucked and pleated shirt. Shelby wondered briefly how he'd found one on such short notice.

Then he smiled at her, and everything fled from her mind but the fact that soon—very soon—she would be Mrs. Travis Hardin. *Shelby Hardin.* It had a nice ring to it, she thought as she returned his smile. Her only regret was that Travis's father couldn't come. T.C. claimed he didn't have enough time to get there, but Shelby figured he was still having a hard time with the idea that his son was marrying a Delacroix.

Travis took her hand in his, and Justin began the simple ceremony. Shelby felt slightly outside herself as she recited the beautiful passages of loving until death. Before she could fully grasp that they were really getting married, it was over, and Travis was kissing her. Kissing her thoroughly.

When they broke apart and Justin introduced them as Mr. and Mrs. Travis Hardin, there was clapping and excited laughter. Then Shelby and Travis were swarmed by family members who enveloped them in hugs and a love that brought tears to her eyes.

They linked arms and drank the traditional champagne; they fed each other bites of cake while Jax and Logan and

Charly took pictures. Finally, Annabelle rang a small bell and announced, "I have a buffet breakfast fixed, and if you want to eat before the trial, you'd better come and get it."

At the mention of the trial, a bit of the golden glow seemed to evaporate, but Travis grabbed Shelby's hand and dragged her toward the table. He made a sweeping bow and said gallantly, "Ladies first."

With a smile, Shelby reached for a rose-patterned china plate and prepared to have her first meal as a married woman.

AT THE BAYOU BELTANE courthouse, the day of Philip's testimony got off to a bad start. The air-conditioning in Judge Ramsey's courtroom was out. The only weapons left to battle the oppressive heat were the old-fashioned cardboard and tongue-depressor-style, hand-held fans advertising the caring way Whittington Funeral Home could handle your loved one's burial preparations, and two squeaky ceiling fans—no doubt as old as the building—that beat at the moisture-laden air like butter paddles whipping heavy cream.

The minor inconvenience didn't deter the curiosity seekers. The courtroom, with its eight-foot-high windows flung open to let in as much airflow as possible, was packed. Everyone wanted to hear what Philip Delacroix had to say. In an unspoken show of family cohesiveness, Philip's and Charles's children sat clumped together midway back of the same side of the room Philip sat on.

Clinging to the memory of Shelby's wedding, Joanna leaned against Logan's broad shoulder, taking comfort from his nearness and strength. Once again, Nikki was happily baby-sitting Lori. Katherine sat next to Drew, their fingers laced together tightly. Because of his job, Jake couldn't be with Annabelle, but Cade was there that day, looking solemn and grown up and very protective of his mother, who clung to his arm.

In the row behind them Justin and Madeline sat with Charles. Shelby and Travis, who'd exchanged their wedding finery for everyday clothing, sat next to Beau and Holly. Uncle William, whose dark eyes held a sad, haunted expression, was there, but again Mary had elected to stay home. Marie, Charly and Jax were present with their spouses.

Only they knew their front of unity wasn't as much to show their support of Philip as it was to tell the world they stood by each other, that the famous family feud had ended with them. Several members of the media would make a note of it.

Gwen came in and managed to squeeze in beside Claire Beaufort—strangers with a common dilemma. In the back, on the opposite side of the courtroom, segregated from the rest of the Delacroix family as effectively as if a sign forbade his fraternization with them, sat Jackson Boudreaux. The patch at his temple showed starkly white against the lock of hair that fell over it. The flesh around his dark eyes was bruised from lack of sleep.

Philip's eyes had a similar look. When his alarm had gone off at six-thirty, he hadn't yet shut his eyes from the night before. His mind was too busy sifting through the implications of the death symbols he'd found in his room and the relevance of the dog that had howled periodically throughout the night.

There were other sounds, too, sounds he might not have noticed at any other time. The squeaks and groans of the old house as it settled more deeply on its foundations. The scratch of a tree limb outside his window. In contrast, the grandfather clock that had chimed the quarter hour for as long as he could remember was silent. It occurred to Philip that a stopped clock was also a portent of death.

Was it coincidence that all these things had happened the same night, or were they planned? Both Flora and Desiree knew how superstitious he was. Was Desiree in cahoots with Flora, now locked up someplace where she couldn't hurt him? Was she out to drive him crazy, or did she have something else in mind?

Philip hadn't been to confession in years, not since the day following the incident with Camille, when he'd gone to the small Catholic church in Bayou Beltane and confessed to the old priest what he'd done. Father Desmond, who'd served the parish all his life, had retired soon after Philip's confession of killing Camille. There was no doubt in Philip's mind that the cleric had recognized his voice. He'd been hearing Delacroix confessions for years.

Philip often wondered if his confession had been the point at which the old man had decided he could no longer hide his disappointment and horror, could no longer put up a front of love and compassion for the selfish, disobedient people who spilled their guts to him and expected him to make everything right with God.

Last night, as he had that night so long ago, Philip had lain in his bed and felt a sudden need to make things right with his creator. For once in his life he was honest with himself and admitted the need was prompted by fear of retribution, not love or even sorrow for his sins. It was the best he could do.

But there was no one he could call except William, and he couldn't bring himself to bare his soul to the son of Desiree Boudreaux, even though that man had been brought up as his brother. And so he'd lain awake fighting his fears, torn between hoping the pain in his head and the pounding in his heart weren't signs of a stroke or a heart attack and praying they were. A swift death would be preferable to whatever Desiree had planned for him, wouldn't it?

A perfect calm had come over him at some time just before dawn. When his bedside alarm went off, he'd risen to prepare for the day. Now, as he sat waiting to be called to the witness stand, that calm was still with him. He would get up there and tell his side of the story. The jury would either believe it or they wouldn't. All his worry couldn't change that. One way or the other, it would all be over soon.

At the appropriate time, Philip rose and moved slowly toward the stand. His back held its usual ramrod straightness, but there was some indefinable something that suggested for the first time that he was an old man.

He answered his attorney's questions in a clear, confident voice that resonated throughout the courtroom and reminded everyone listening just why he'd become so successful both in his law practice and in politics.

He was telling his version of what had happened the night of Camille's death when he saw the double doors open and noticed some confusion near the doorway. There were quiet murmurs among the people standing there and a subtle shifting of bodies as the crowd parted to let someone through.

Desiree moved through the doors with slow majesty. Her dark eyes glowed with a zealous energy that seemed at odds with her physical frailty. Jackson, who was sitting next to the aisle in the back row, got up and offered his grandmother his place. She patted his hand as she sat down, then turned to fix her gaze on Philip once more.

He skimmed his tongue over his lips and realized all his saliva had dried up. Contrarily, his armpits grew damp and his palms began to sweat. He gasped for breath and reached up to tug at his bow tie, which had grown far too tight. He was vaguely aware of people staring at him, of concern on their frowning faces.

"Mr. Delacroix? Mr. Delacroix, are you all right?"

The attorney's voice seemed to come from a distance. Philip could hardly breathe, much less answer.

"Mr. Delacroix!" This time it was the judge calling him, but Philip could do nothing but stare into Desiree Boudreaux's dark, hypnotic eyes. His head felt near to bursting. His chest tightened in sudden pain.

Desiree's eyes narrowed. She pushed herself to her feet.

"No! Please!" he cried, reaching out a hand as if to keep her away. He grabbed the railing in front of his chair and slid to his knees. Desiree started forward. Philip heard the air rasping in and out of his lungs, like a man who'd just finished a marathon. He clutched his pounding head and looked at the attorney standing mere feet from him. The defense lawyer's eyes were wide with shock.

"Keep her away from me!" Philip cried. "She wants to kill me."

"Mr. Delacroix!" the judge said sternly, banging his gavel. "I will have order in this courtroom. Everyone take your seats or I'll have this room cleared. Bailiff!"

Uncertain whether to answer Philip's cry for help or ignore him in favor of pleasing the judge, the bailiff looked from one to the other. Amid murmured speculation, the spectators settled down. Jackson took his grandmother's arm and said something in her ear.

A second later, a loud shriek rent the air, echoing throughout the vaulted, high-ceilinged room. Beating the air around her head, a woman jumped up from her chair, and pandemonium broke loose. Philip saw Joanna rise, saw Charles pointing upward.

A barn swallow circled the room, as frightened by the bedlam below it and the fans whirling all around it as the woman who'd screamed when it flew through the open window in a whir of fluttering wings.

A bird! Another sign of death. Philip gripped the railing more tightly and forced himself to his feet. He looked at

Desiree, who was now back in her seat, her unwavering gaze probing his. The doors behind her opened and a tall, spare man stepped through. Philip checked to see who the new intruder was. Clovis!

A feeling of relief washed over Philip like a gentle ocean wave. He took one staggering step toward his faithful family retainer before he saw the look in Clovis's eyes.

Hatred. Pure, pristine hatred. It was then that Philip realized it wasn't Desiree who'd been deviling him for so many months. It was Clovis. But why?

Philip sucked in a shocked breath, marginally aware that people had turned to stare at the man in the doorway. He saw Clovis lift his arm and point a bony finger at him, saw the blaze of malice burning with feverish brightness in his strange, mismatched eyes.

He saw Desiree get up. Saw Jackson try to stop her. Heard the judge's hoarse voice yelling something. Heard the banging of the gavel.

The band around Philip's chest tightened. His head felt as if it were going to explode. The bailiff started forward, but stopped when Desiree stepped in front of Clovis. The old retainer didn't even look at her. He just shoved her out of his path, the same way Philip had pushed Jackson aside the day before. Only Jackson's quick reaction now kept his grandmother from falling.

Then Clovis raised his arm above his grizzled head and brought it down in a sharp forward motion, like a pitcher releasing a fast ball.

Philip wasn't sure what he expected. Balls of fire. Bolts of electricity. Fiery sparks shooting off the tips of Clovis's fingers, at least. But all Philip saw was the brief shimmer of something bright and shiny before that something struck his chest. He staggered backward and fell into his chair.

He didn't hear Gwen's scream of shock blending with the other feminine cries in the room. Didn't hear Drew's curse or Annabelle's sob or Charles calling his name in a harsh, despairing voice. Philip Delacroix would never hear anything again. The blade of Flora's knife was buried in his heart, all the way to the hilt.

WHEN THE COURTROOM was cleared, and an ambulance had taken Philip's body to the morgue, the judge dismissed the case. Philip Delacroix had already faced his punishment. Drew and Joanna had gone to the Whittington Funeral Home to see if their service was as good as the promise on their cardboard fans.

Four hours later, at Charles's request, both sides of the family gathered at Riverwood, where Odelle, the housekeeper, plied them with sandwiches, strong coffee and lots of sympathy. Even Toni, seven months pregnant though she was, drove out from the city with her husband, Brody. It was the first time they'd all been under the same roof since Mary's eightieth birthday, two years ago come July. It saddened Charles that it took something like the death of his brother to bring them all together, and he prayed that now—finally—things would be different, that they could be a real family again.

"I should have done something to stop him," Drew said, pacing the length of the library and back.

"Stop beating yourself up over it, Drew," Shelby told her cousin. "There's nothing you could have done. You were too far away. Besides, who would have thought Clovis would do something like that?"

"Shelby is right, Drew," William murmured.

"I can see Desiree or even Flora pulling something like that, but Clovis? Why?" Beau said.

"Desiree would never have hurt Uncle Philip!" Marie exclaimed, a hint of irritation in her voice. "It isn't in her to hurt people. She's a *traiteur,* a healer."

"Aunt Marie is right." The unexpected comment came

from Cade, who was again sitting close to his mother. As if, Shelby thought, he was trying to keep any harm from coming to her. "Desiree was going to help him. That's why she got up."

"You're crazy, kid," Beau said.

Cade shook his head. "No, I'm not. I saw it in her eyes. When Grandfather grabbed his head, she got a real worried look on her face. She was going to try and help him, but the judge told everyone to sit down. Then Clovis came in."

"I have to agree with Marie and Cade," Charles said, speaking for the first time since they'd arrived. "Desiree is many things, but she isn't a killer. But Clovis! Why did he, of all people, do it? He's been with Philip since we split up the firm and the houses. What makes a person turn on you after a lifetime?"

"My dad will get a reason out of him," Cade said.

"Poor Jake!" Joanna said. "He's had his hands full the past few days."

Odelle refilled coffee cups, Holly passed around more sandwiches, and Drew turned from the window to face them. "I've been thinking about Jackson," he said.

"What about him?" Charles asked.

"He's had a pretty rotten deal, knowing he was a Delacroix and not being able to claim his birthright. Doing whatever Dad asked blindly, on the slim chance he'd wake up and discover Jackson was worth something. Worth Dad's love."

"That's a pretty deep insight," Charles said.

Drew's mouth curved in a wry smile. "Yeah, well, you've heard the old saying, it takes one to know one. I've come to the conclusion that I know what drove Jackson because the same thing drove me. The only difference is that we used different techniques and I stayed within the law."

"Jackson said as much to me the night he came to visit," Mary said.

"Jackson came to see you?" Shelby said.

"Actually, he came to see William."

"Why, Uncle William?" Shelby asked.

"I'm not really sure," William said, rubbing his chin thoughtfully. "I think it was to tell me to go see Desiree. But he stayed quite a while, and we had a nice chat. When he left, he told me the same thing Drew just said. He didn't make any excuses for the things he's done. He knows there aren't any. But at least I understood his motivation."

William picked up his coffee cup. "It's sad, really. If Jackson had grown up in a better environment, he might have turned out differently. Unfortunately, Flora's ambitions for him and her hatred for Philip got Jackson started down the wrong path in life."

A knock sounded at the door, and, as if the conversation had conjured them up, Odelle announced that Desiree and Jackson had come to see the family.

"What do you think she wants?" Justin asked.

"I have no idea," Charles said. He turned to Odelle. "Show them in."

Desiree and Jackson came into the room. The old woman leaned heavily on her grandson's arm, as if the latest in a long list of bizarre happenings had robbed her of whatever meager reserves of energy she might still possess. Beneath the scrutiny of so many Delacroix eyes Jackson looked uncomfortable.

Solemnly, Charles greeted the woman who had been such a part of the whole family drama and offered her a seat. Jackson helped Desiree into a chair and stood at her side. His hands clasped behind his back, he stared straight ahead, focusing on a painting across the room.

"I suppose you're wondering why I've come," Desiree said.

"Yes."

"I came to tell you about Clovis...and why he did what he did."

"You know?" Charles asked, stunned by the news.

Desiree nodded. Her dark gaze moved from one family member to the other, as if to make certain they were all included in her answer. "Clovis is Flora's father."

"What?"

"Mother of God!"

"Damnation!"

The responses came from Justin, William and Jackson, respectively. Mary simply nodded. The rest of the assemblage seemed unable to find any words at all.

"I met him when I was twenty-eight or thereabouts. He was a handsome young man, and set on makin' something of himself. He swore he was goin' to live in a big house with lots of fancy things." Desiree's smile was wryly humorous. "I guess when he took his daddy's place and went to work for Mr. Philip, his dream came true, didn't it?"

"What about him being Flora's father, Desiree?" Mary asked gently, hoping to get the older woman back on track.

"Well, me and Clovis took a real shine to each other, and for a while I thought about marryin' him. Then I found out he was into *Santeria*. Most folks here look down on *Santeria* 'cause it's so cruel and violent." Her gaze moved from one curious pair of eyes to another, settling at last on Charles. "I don't mind tellin' you that some of the things Clovis did scared me half to death."

Charles nodded in understanding and indicated she should go on.

"I tried to tell Clovis it was wrong, but he was too caught up in it all to pay me any mind. I told him I wouldn't marry him. He was really mad at me, especially when I came up expectin'."

Mary pressed her lips together tightly.

"May God forgive me, but I thought about taking some herbs to flush Clovis's baby out of my womb. I didn't want to have his baby. I was scared to. But I couldn't do it, and when Flora came, she was so beautiful and so sweet, I convinced myself that she hadn't inherited any of his badness. I was wrong."

"Flora wasn't really bad," William said. "She was just trying to make her own destiny."

"Maybe so," Desiree said. "Clovis about drove me crazy for a while after Flora was born, with all his threats about takin' her away from me. He did manage to steal her a time or two, and I'd have to have Mr. Hamilton get the law after him. Clovis was always sayin' he was castin' a spell on Flora to make her just like him. There were times I thought he really had."

"Oh, Desiree!" Mary exclaimed. "I had no idea."

"How could you? It was my problem. My mama always said there was no sense airin' your dirty laundry for the world to see."

"When did it stop?" Charles asked. "Or did it?"

"I spent most of my days worryin' about Clovis until I met Reggie." It might have been a trick of the light, but the old woman's eyes seemed to glaze over with tears. "I met Reggie Guidry when Flora was three. He was the love of my life. I was gonna marry him, but Clovis killed him."

"Dear God!" Mary said, her eyes filled with horror. "How do you know that's what happened?"

"Clovis told me. Smiled all the time he did the tellin', too."

"Reggie was the man you were meeting the night Camille was killed," Justin said.

"That's right. Do you recollect me sayin' I felt something evil in the woods that night?"

Charles nodded. "Yes."

"It was Clovis. He was followin' me to see if I was

meetin' Reggie. That was the night it happened.'' Desiree's dark eyes were filled with the shadows of reminiscences. "When I didn't show up at the bridge, Clovis and Reggie fought. Reggie gouged out one of Clovis's eyes, but Clovis was faster with the knife. He dumped Reggie's body in the swamp for the gators.''

"Why didn't you call the police?''

Desiree's smile was bittersweet. "For what? There's no murder without a body. It would have just been my word against Clovis's, and to tell the truth, Miz Mary, I didn't say anything because I was scared of that man. People disappear all the time. Besides, don't no one care much what happened to a nigger man just passin' through.''

"But when you were on the stand, you implied Uncle Philip was the evil presence,'' Shelby said.

"I know I did, but they were both there. I figured it out after Reggie died. It wouldn't have made any difference had I said who else was in the woods, except that Mr. Philip's lawyer would have asked a whole lot of questions and tried to make the jury believe Clovis could have been the one who killed Miss Camille, and that just ain't so.'' Her twisted smile was bittersweet. "Maybe I should have spoken up. Maybe if Clovis had been arrested, Reggie would still be alive. As it was, I was scared and almost crazy with grief.''

"Well,'' Charles said, "it doesn't matter now, does it?''

"No, sir.''

"Why did Clovis want to kill Dad?'' Drew asked, clearly baffled. "He's worked for him for years. He must have been happy at Belle Terre.''

"He's worked there a long time, all right, but happy? No. Content?'' She shrugged. "Maybe. He always liked lordin' it over everybody that he was in Mr. Philip's employ. Truth was, Clovis despised Mr. Philip for the way he was treated. Mr. Philip liked to belittle Clovis. Liked to make him feel like less than a man. It ate on him real bad.''

''It must have been Clovis who was leaving all those voodoo dolls around there,'' Joanna said, fitting another piece of the puzzle into place. ''Dad kept wondering how Flora was getting inside, and then when she was in the hospital and they still kept showing up, he figured it was you, Desiree. When Dad had Flora shut up in the vault, it probably really set Clovis off.''

''It must have been Clovis who let Mom out of the crypt,'' Jackson interjected suddenly. His eyes were filled with understanding. ''When I got to the cemetery, I thought I heard something in the brush, but I figured it was just some kind of animal. I'd brought a crowbar, but the vault was already open. All I did was open the door and let Mom out.''

''Makes sense,'' Drew said.

For long moments, no one spoke. Like so many other things that had happened to the family the past year or so, this would require time and distance to fully understand and accept.

Finally, Desiree said, ''Jackson, I'd appreciate it if you'd take me home now. I'm real tired all of a sudden.''

''Sure thing, *Grand-mère*.''

Jackson helped Desiree to her feet, and Justin and Charles rose to escort them to the front door.

Shelby was about to comment on Jackson's solicitous behavior toward his grandmother when the phone rang. She answered it and handed it to Annabelle. ''It's Ty. He sounds a little upset.''

Annabelle groaned. ''What now?'' she said, taking the receiver. ''Hello?''

She could hardly get a word in edgeways for listening to Ty's panicked tale.

''Okay,'' Annabelle said at last. ''Tell them I'm on my

way. Now. Yes. Right now. Fifteen minutes, tops." She shook her head and rolled her eyes. "Ty, honey, if you'll hang up, I'll head home immediately. Okay. Goodbye."

With a sigh, she recradled the receiver and went to pick up her purse. "That was Ty—obviously. Come on, Cade. We're outta here."

"Is everything all right?" Charles asked, concern in his voice.

"Everything is fine, Uncle Charles. But since the trial is over there's not a whole lot of reason to stay in Bayou Beltane. Ty says people are wanting to check out of the B and B in droves. His words, not mine. He's all in a twit because he doesn't have the slightest idea how to figure their bills or use the credit card gizmo. He doesn't have the key to the petty cash box to make change and he doesn't know if he should take a personal check or not." She waved her hand in a circle, and mimicking Yul Brynner in *The King and I,* added, "Et-cet-era, et-cet-era, et-cet-era."

The impersonation and the idea of the usually composed Ty Trahan bordering on the hysterical brought a round of laughter. Even Desiree and Jackson smiled. It was just the sort of moment of comic relief everyone needed to help shake off the aftermath of the shock they'd received earlier.

When Annabelle and Cade had followed Desiree and Jackson from the room, William said, "The Lord giveth and he taketh away. But life still goes on, doesn't it?

CHAPTER TWELVE

CLOVIS WAS DENIED BAIL and remanded to the parish jail to await trial. The news of his murdering Philip Delacroix during his testimony at his own trial was fodder for the media mill for days. As per their modus operandi, the various media went into overkill and did pieces not only on Philip, Clovis, Desiree and Flora, but on voodoo and its long-standing roots in the state.

Gator Guzman hounded the family for days, but finally gave up the morning of Philip's funeral, when Drew took him by the collar, forcibly stuffed him into his car and mentioned—as casually as one can through gritted teeth—that a few more visits or phone calls and he just might be guilty of a little thing called "harassment." Then he smoothed Gator's shirtfront, showed him his teeth in a reasonable facsimile of a smile and told him to have a nice day. Gator ceased and desisted immediately, as much put off by the cold fury in Drew's face as the threat of a lawsuit.

Gwen decided to stay for the funeral, out of respect for her children and their father. Her plane would leave for California almost as soon as the final prayer was uttered. Joanna hated to see her go, but promised that she, Logan, Nikki and the baby would come out for a visit as soon as their hectic schedules allowed.

In true Southern fashion, friends and neighbors inundated the family with enough cakes and casseroles and pots of gumbo to feed a small army.

Even after his death there was an inordinate amount of interest in Philip Delacroix. To avoid yet another media feeding frenzy, the family decided it best to bury him in the family cemetery at Belle Terre. Philip didn't have many real friends, and it was decreed that only the family, the governor and members of the Louisiana senate would be invited to attend. The service would be held in the small chapel—unused for decades—right there on the grounds.

Though they could have hired in help, Annabelle, with the aid of Gwen, Cade and Ty, saw to it that the old building was as shipshape as possible. Though Annabelle was puzzled by her mother's willingness to work so hard to see buried a man who'd hurt her so badly, she was grateful for Gwen's help. She and her mother didn't speak much as they worked, but Annabelle watched Gwen's capable hands and listened as Gwen kept Cade and Ty enthralled with stories about Belle Terre that had been handed down more than a hundred years.

The day of the funeral was another hot one. Jake had to string up police barriers and bring in reinforcements from Covington to keep the media and curiosity seekers at a respectful distance from the house and grounds.

The small chapel was filled. It was the first time Charles's children had set foot in Belle Terre. At the last minute, in a move that surprised everyone, Drew went to the back row where Jackson sat and asked him to join the rest of the family. Jackson thanked him and refused, adding that he appreciated the gesture but sensed it might cause friction none of them needed at the moment. Drew said he understood.

As the priest went through the requisite rites that accompanied a burial, Philip's children and grandchildren sat stony-faced and dry eyed. There were no tears cried for Philip Delacroix. Not by his children, grandchildren, political allies or so-called friends. Not by his ex-wife.

Even Mary, who sat near the front with Charles and William, and who understood Philip better than anyone else, felt more of a sense of relief than one of sorrow at his passing. Growing up, she'd always thought he was misunderstood, always believed there was a kernel of goodness beneath his ruthlessness. She still believed it. The sad thing was that that grain of decency had been buried in the rocky soil of self-doubt, self-indulgence and selfishness, where it had little chance to survive. As much as she had loved him, she could not condone the things he'd done. Or the life he'd lived. She could not cry for him.

Because of the heat and humidity, the graveside ceremony was blessedly brief. By mutual consent, the mourners, if they could be called that, convened inside Belle Terre's cool interior to partake of the bounty left by well-meaning neighbors.

Gwen's suitcases were already loaded in the trunk of Joanna's car. She was standing off by herself indulging in a slice of Italian cream cake, waiting until it was time to start for the airport, when she looked up and saw Cade heading toward her. A rush of love so strong it was painful gripped her heart. Her grandson was a fine-looking young man, she thought proudly. He was almost grown, and because of Philip's heartlessness and her own stupidity and weakness, she'd missed out on the first sixteen years of his life. Just as she'd missed the greatest part of Drew's and Annabelle's lives.

Cade smiled at her, and her guilt and melancholy vanished beneath his shy, crooked grin. Now wasn't the time to think about that, Gwen thought, squaring her shoulders and returning his smile. She didn't know what the future held for any of them, but for now, she was going to enjoy this unexpected encounter with her grandson.

He held out his hand. Longing for a hug, not a handshake, but not too proud to take what was offered, Gwen clasped it warmly.

"I wanted to tell you it was nice meeting you," he said. "And I really enjoyed hearing about Belle Terre's history."

"Thank you, Cade," Gwen said. "I enjoyed meeting you, too. Maybe your mom will let you fly out to California for a visit sometime."

"I'd like that," he said, answering as diplomatically as possible. He grinned again and shook his head. "It's been a crazy year."

"How's that?"

Neither of them noticed that Drew and Annabelle had come up behind them.

"I've found a father, a half brother and a grandmother I never knew. Not to mention a half uncle."

"Jackson?"

"Yeah. I think he sorta had a bum life, you know? Granddad didn't treat him right. It's no wonder Jackson turned out the way he did."

"That's a very mature attitude, Cade," Gwen said, genuinely impressed with her grandson.

Cade's face turned red at the words of praise. He shrugged. "My brother, Ty, almost died. The way I see it, everyone makes mistakes and life is just too short to waste any time holding grudges."

"As well you should," Gwen said. "Philip was many things, and not all of them good, but he loved his children and his grandchildren. I think he proved that when Nikki got into all that trouble over Steven Boudreaux's death."

Cade nodded in agreement.

"Is this a private party, or can anyone join you?" Annabelle asked, making her and Drew's presence known.

Gwen turned, her surprise obvious. Her daughter and son stood before her, looking as uncomfortable as she felt.

"Joanna said you were leaving in a few minutes," Annabelle said. "I wanted to tell you goodbye and thank you for helping me clean the chapel."

"You're quite welcome." Gwen looked from her daughter to her son. "I want you to know that it was wonderful seeing you again. I'm just sorry it had to be under these circumstances."

They stood there awkwardly for a few seconds, then, used to smoothing waters Philip's actions had troubled, Gwen reached for Annabelle's hand, but included Drew in what she was saying by holding his inscrutable gaze with hers.

"There's no use beating around the bush. No use pretending the past twenty-odd years never happened. I may be repeating myself, but I want you both to understand that I take my share of the blame for the past, and I want you to know that if you ever want to talk about it, or about anything else, I'm here for you. I pray that you'll be able to forgive me one day and that we can have some kind of relationship."

Her gaze moved to Annabelle. "But if the hurt goes too deep and that isn't possible, I'd at least like to have the opportunity to get to know my grandson." She flashed Drew a smile. "And future grandchildren."

"I'll be honest with you," Annabelle said.

"Please do," Gwen said, her heart quaking with apprehension.

"I hated you for more years than I can remember. I didn't know how you could do what you did. Then, when I came back here and met Jake again, I realized that I'd done something just as bad by denying him his son." Annabelle drew a deep breath. "This family has been through a lot, and Ty's illness taught us all some powerful lessons. Cade's right. Life is too short to hold grudges against someone when we make so many bad judgment calls ourselves. I've learned—maybe we all have—that the only thing worth hanging on to is love and family.''

''Annabelle and I agree that you were as much a victim of Dad's machinations as we were,'' Drew said. ''We both know too well how he was able to manipulate people and incidents.''

Annabelle looked relieved at her brother's words. ''We were wondering if you and Emerson might want to come back to Bayou Beltane for a sort of family reunion some time this summer,'' she added simply.

Gwen's heart felt full to overflowing. Joy rose up, thickening her throat with happy tears. All she could do was smile and nod and say, ''I'd like that.''

SOON AFTER JOANNA, LOGAN, Nikki and the baby left to take Gwen to the New Orleans airport, Mary asked Justin to drive her home for some much needed rest. Soon most of Charles's side of the family was headed back to Riverwood. The media watched them, an occasional camera flashing, recording their impassive faces for posterity.

As the *Times-Picayune* would proclaim the next day, Philip Delacroix's death marked the end of an era.

Later that evening, after joining her brothers, Justin, Shelby and Travis for more of the food the neighbors had brought, Mary took a blanket, crossed the bridge and went to sit beneath the old magnolia tree while William watered the thirsty gardens surrounding both houses.

Mary was tired. Mentally. Emotionally. The past year and a half had been hard for all of them. They'd learned so much—about their parents, their pasts, themselves. What they'd found out wasn't always good, but it was the truth. Her brother Philip had been a killer, albeit not intentionally. He'd kept quiet, deliberately letting Rafe take the blame for his own actions. His silence had even put Charles at risk. She and Charles had kept their own secrets,

and even the sterling Hamilton and Marguerite had lied to
their children and the world about William's parentage.

Mary sighed. The lies and secrecy had hurt those she
loved and those who loved her. None of them could escape
blame. She had lost her idealistic perceptions of her parents and been forced to revise her opinions about many
things. Her peace of mind, something she'd worked hard
for sixty years at finding, lay in shambles beneath the
crushing weight of the truth. Yet somehow there was a
new and different kind of inner peace gathering inside her,
along with a certainty that the gulf separating the two sides
of her family would finally be healed.

The sound of voices pulled her attention back to her
surroundings. Smiling his gentle smile, William stuck his
head inside Mary's sanctuary. A tall, attractive woman
who'd already passed middle age did the same. Even without her glasses, Mary thought the woman looked familiar.
It was only when, at William's insistence, she pushed
through the branches and looked directly at her that Mary
realized who she was.

Almost simultaneously with Mary's startled, indrawn
breath the woman took her own fortifying breath and
blurted, "I'm Claire. Your daughter."

Claire. A beautiful name, Mary thought, her eyes filling
with tears of happiness, her heart filled with thanksgiving.
A beautiful name for a beautiful woman. If the good Lord
took Mary while she slept this night, she could die happy,
having been granted this brief moment with the daughter
she and Rafe had created through their love. Claire looked
like Rafe, Mary thought—all but her Barbra Streisand
nose, which Mary herself had passed along from Hamilton.
On Claire it wasn't unattractive at all.

"You look like your father," Mary said, blinking rap-
idly. Some part of her noted that William had left them
alone.

"Except for the nose," Claire added with a brief, almost shy smile. "I must have gotten that from you."

Returning the smile in kind, Mary reached up and touched her own nose. "Yes. A gift from my father. Your grandfather Hamilton." Mary started to get up. "Let's go inside. I'll give you a glass of my spiced tea."

Claire put out a restraining hand. "No. Sit. Please. I won't take much of your time, and this is a lovely spot."

Mary settled back. "Then have a seat," she offered, patting the blanket next to her. "Your father and I spent a lot of time here. It was a special place for us."

"It is a special place," Claire said, looking up at the leafy canopy above them. "I can feel it."

Not knowing why Claire had come, but sensing intuitively that the visit was conciliatory, Mary said the next thing that sprang into her mind. "I'm glad you came. I've wished so often I could see you, that I knew you."

Claire turned her head to look at her mother. "I was too angry with you to want anything to do with you. It was only recently that Katherine showed me I was behaving childishly. And it was only after I heard your testimony at the trial that I really understood everything you'd gone through and how impossible it would have been for you to keep me."

"Single parenting is hard even now, but girls were more under their fathers' thumbs in those days and even less able to fend for themselves and a child. Still, it wouldn't have been impossible," Mary said. "Difficult, perhaps, but not impossible."

"I understand. And I understand why you did what you did—why you didn't stand up for my father."

"If you understand, then I'm grateful," Mary said. "I'm still not sure I do."

"It was a difficult choice—to side with your brother,

whom you'd known all your life, or the lover you'd known only a short time. I'd probably have done the same thing.''

"You're very kind, Claire. Thank you."

Claire's smile was brief, embarrassed. "You should thank Katherine. She insisted I needed to see you to find out about my past so I could come to terms with being adopted."

"I do thank her," Mary said. They sat awkwardly for a moment, and then Mary said simply, "Tell me about yourself. Are you married? Do you have children?"

"No," Claire said. "I never married. I stay busy, though. I'm a librarian, and on my days off I dabble with watercolors. Actually, I've sold a few."

"That's wonderful!" Mary said. "I paint some, too. Watercolors and charcoal." She gave a small smile. "Or I did. I'll show you the drawings I did of your father sometime."

"I'd like that," Claire said. She sighed. "There's not much to tell. I read a lot and I play piano some."

"You do?"

Claire nodded. "Jazz and blues. But not very well."

Again Mary's eyes lit up with surprise and pleasure. "Your father loved blues, and he played the piano, too. I remember one time when I sneaked off and he took me to this little place called Boogie's...."

Mary spent the next hour telling Claire about her brief time with Rafe and asking questions about Claire's life. When it was nearly dark, Mary let Claire help her to her feet. They stood awkwardly for a moment, Mary wanting to gather her daughter into a longed-for embrace, Claire wanting the same, both afraid to make the move.

Finally Mary stepped forward, her arms open. With a small sob, Claire went into her mother's arms. They stood locked in a tight embrace, swaying slightly, crying tears of sorrow for all the lost years and tears of joy that they'd been granted this opportunity to come together. Later, when their tears were spent and their hearts lighter, Claire gathered up the quilt, and together they crossed the bridge to Mary's house. They both knew it was Claire's first visit, but it wouldn't be her last.

THE LONGER THE SHADOWS grew, the quieter Shelby became—not that anyone had much to say after the funeral. Though he hadn't said so, Shelby knew that Travis would soon pack up his things and head back to Comfort. She didn't think she could bear to see him go, but then, she didn't have any choice. Their marriage hadn't changed certain things. He had a ranch to run, just as she had work here that had to be concluded before she could join him in Texas and they could start a new life together.

After picking up Travis's clothes from Annabelle's, they arrived back at Riverwood at dusk, passing Claire Beaufort, who was leaving.

"Wonder who that was?" Travis asked.

"I don't know."

Travis cut the engine before they made the final curve that would bring Riverwood into view.

"Why'd you stop?" she asked.

"Seemed like a good idea," he said, laying his arm over the back of the seat and turning to face her. "What is it, darlin'?"

Shelby propped her elbow on the armrest and her chin on her fist, staring out the window disconsolately. "Nothing."

"Nothing doesn't make you stop talking." He laughed, a soft, husky sound that sent a frisson of desire scampering through her body. "Matter of fact, I can't think of much that does make you stop talking."

The pitiful attempt to lighten her mood worked. Barely. She turned to him, her mouth turned up at the corners in a halfhearted smile. "That's what I like about you, Hardin. There's a certain charm about your total, sometimes brutal honesty."

"That's me," he said, reaching out and twining a lock of her hair around his index finger. "Charm personified."

They stared at each other in the gathering shadows under the ancient live oaks. Always in control, Shelby didn't like this feeling of vulnerability that went along with being in love and knowing that at least part of her happiness depended on the man sitting next to her.

With a little cry of anguish, she flung herself against him. "I don't want you to go." It was a harsh, angry admission.

Travis's arms closed around her, holding her tight. "I don't want to go, either, Shelby, but we both know I have to."

"I love you. I don't ever want to be without you."

"The feeling's mutual, darlin'," he said. "And I don't ever plan to be out of your life for more than a week at a time."

"Promise?"

"Promise. How long will it take you to get things wrapped up here?"

"I don't know," she said, shrugging. "A month. Six weeks tops."

"Have you told your family you'll be moving to Texas with your new husband?"

She nodded. "They understand. And it isn't like I'm moving out of the country or anything."

"Glad you realize that. I thought you'd like to know that I talked to my dad again this morning, and he's coming around to the fact that I'm married to a Delacroix. T. C. Hardin is a hard case, but he's a fair man. Once he sees all sides, he makes the right decisions."

"Thank goodness!" Shelby said. "I'd never want to

come between you and your father." Her gaze probed his, as if she might find an answer in the deep pools of blue. "It's all over, isn't it, Travis? We can finally put the ugly past behind us and move on? All of us?"

He nodded. "Yes, darlin', I truly believe we can. It might take a little time to get over some of the hurts and accept some of the things you've heard, but knowing what I do about the Delacroix family, I'm positive you'll all come out of this okay."

"Thanks." With that worry eased, her mind turned to another, more bothersome concern. "When are you leaving?"

"First thing tomorrow morning."

Her disappointment was clear. "When were you going to tell me?"

"After I'd softened you up with about an hour of hot and heavy lovemaking."

She smiled. "Why then?"

He smiled back. "I figured you'd be too satisfied to argue, too weak to scratch out my eyes."

She laughed in disbelief. "Pretty confident, aren't you, cowboy?"

His eyes twinkled with little-boy mischief, big-boy confidence. "Yep."

Her fingers began to work his buttons free. "All right then, hot stuff. Let's see if your ability is anywhere near your high opinion of yourself."

Travis drew her close. With his mouth a heartbeat away from hers, he whispered, "I haven't heard any complaints so far."

EPILOGUE

AS THEY HAD FOR HER eightieth, the whole family gathered at Riverwood to celebrate Aunt Mary's eighty-second birthday. Almost four months had passed since the trial and Philip's death, and, as Travis predicted, the Delacroix family was dealing with the last troublesome details of those unhappy events with a strong cohesiveness.

Drew and Katherine bought out Annabelle and Joanna's portion of Belle Terre and planned to raise lots of babies in the old house. Lots of happy babies. The bottom floor would become an antique store, and the second floor, a living area. They hoped that when Claire retired, she'd join them as part of their family.

The swampland adjoining Belle Terre, including the forty acres belonging to Desiree, were turned over to the state and designated as protected wetlands. Desiree could live there as long as she was able to fend for herself. Both plans of action went a long way toward healing the old wounds left by Philip's machinations.

During his statement to Jake, Clovis had admitted to hating his employer for the condescending way he'd been treated, just as Desiree had said. Clovis had stayed because he had his own little power trip going. It was a sort of status symbol to live like a king in the Delacroix mansion.

Clovis had corroborated Desiree's statement that he'd been in the woods the night of Camille's death and that Philip had killed her. As Desiree claimed, Clovis had been following her to see if she was meeting Reggie, whom he also admitted to killing.

In a new and stunning development, Clovis told Jake that Philip was the cause of the heart attack that had taken Hamilton Delacroix's life the day after Rafe Perdido died in prison.

Clovis claimed Philip had gone into the library to talk to his father, who was grieving over Perdido's death and his inability to get him off. Philip told Hamilton the loss of Rafe Perdido was no great thing, no more important than the loss of Camille and her bastard child. Philip had gone on to say there was no way he'd have let Camille talk Charles into marriage so she could worm her way into the Delacroix family.

Mr. Hamilton had gotten real quiet, Clovis had said. Peeking through a crack in the door, he'd watched the horror grow on the older man's face as he put the pieces of the tale together. Finally, Hamilton had spoken, telling Philip he knew it was he who'd killed Camille.

Philip concurred, but claimed it was an accident.

They had argued bitterly, Clovis said. Hamilton urged Philip to turn himself in; Philip refused. Why should he? Someone had already paid for killing Camille. There was no reason for him to come forward now.

The older Delacroix had told his son that his selfishness and cowardice had undermined his own ability to provide Rafe Perdido with an effective defense. He charged that Philip was as responsible for Rafe's death as if he'd used the knife himself. Philip had left in a rage, and Clovis had slunk back to the kitchen. When he'd gone to check on his employer thirty minutes later, he'd found him dead on the floor.

Both sides of the family were stunned when Jake explained in confidence what Clovis had told him. But no one was really surprised to learn that an argument between

Philip and his father had brought on the deadly heart attack, making Philip responsible for two deaths.

But that was in the past, a past none of them could change. The future looked as bright as the eighty-two candles adorning the top of Mary's cake. As she looked around at the happy, smiling faces of her family, Mary knew she hadn't been so happy since she'd lost Rafe.

There was no tension at this gathering the way there had been at her eightieth birthday party. With the truth out and the past behind them, there was nothing but hope and happiness in the air.

Claire had come to the celebration, and Mary could honestly say they were drawing closer day by day.

Desiree and Jackson had been invited, but Jackson hadn't come to the family gathering. He was in therapy—Holly had referred him to a colleague in New Orleans—to come to grips with his gambling and the years of abuse he'd gone through at Philip's hand. With Jackson's career in law enforcement finished, Drew, acting as a silent partner, had lent him some money to buy into a new-car dealership. So far, the arrangement was working out well.

Shelby and Travis had driven over from Comfort, where she'd opened up a small law practice. A flute of champagne in his hand, Travis announced that he and his bride were expecting a baby around Christmastime. Not to be outdone, Remy announced that he and Kendall were expecting, too.

Toni and Brody were there, their brand-new baby son in tow, and Lori looked adorable in a smocked dress with tiny rosebud embroidery and a bow in her hair. Maddi, who was just walking, stole the show as she toddled from one beaming relative to another.

The rest of the clan was adjusting happily to various stages of matrimony. Nikki was dating a boy at school her mother approved of, and Ty and Cade—known to all the girls in town as the Blues Brothers—were breaking feminine hearts all over Bayou Beltane and as far away as Covington.

Even Gwen and her husband had come to the party. Mary was glad. Looking at Gwen was like seeing an older, kinder Camille. Gwen, Drew and Annabelle were working hard at putting the old hurts aside. Joanna had told Mary before the others arrived that Gwen's husband was retiring from the bank at the first of the year. Now that Philip was gone, they were thinking of moving back to Bayou Beltane, where Emerson's children lived, so they could be close to their kids and grandkids.

Mary's heart ached when she thought of Philip. She wondered how and why he had turned out so differently from the rest of them. William said everyone was a free moral agent, and that Philip had made bad choices. All Mary knew was that his actions had split the family apart, had caused two deaths...and ultimately his own.

His lies and ruthlessness were responsible for so much pain...in Gwen, Annabelle, Drew. Jackson. Flora. His selfishness had kept him from being punished for Camille's death, but he'd paid in other ways. Separation from his twin. Loss of his children's love and respect. Death at the hands of a man he'd thought was his faithful companion, his loyal servant.

Mary recalled her father telling her one day about why he'd become a lawyer. He'd talked about the statue of Justice, explaining about the scales she held and the cloth tied around her eyes. He'd believed in the law. Believed that the scales of justice were balanced, not fixed. Believed that justice was blind to all but the truth.

Mary had learned better. But she still believed in justice. Justin had a favorite saying: What goes around, comes around.

Philip had almost escaped the justice of the law. But he hadn't escaped the revenge of a father mourning the loss of his daughter's sanity and his grandson's life. For all his money, power, political connections, lies and machinations, Philip Delacroix had not been able to escape delta justice.

But there was an up side, Mary thought. Putting an end to the lies and secrecy had helped a family breach the chasm Camille's death had brought to them. At odds for so long, they seemed to draw closer with each day. It was a happier family now, a family who'd fought its dragons and won. She glanced at Madeline and Justin. Katherine and Drew. Travis and Shelby. All the others. They were living proof that growth came through adversity. That forgiveness for even the most heinous sins was possible.

The Delacroix were a testimony to the healing power of love. And that, Mary thought, was the greatest justice of all.

DELTA JUSTICE

MEN at WORK

All work and no play?
Not these men!

July 1998
MACKENZIE'S LADY by Dallas Schulze

Undercover agent Mackenzie Donahue's
lazy smile and deep blue eyes were his best
weapons. But after rescuing—and kissing!—
damsel in distress Holly Reynolds, how could
he betray her by spying on her brother?

August 1998
MISS LIZ'S PASSION by Sherryl Woods

Todd Lewis could put up a building with ease,
but quailed at the sight of a classroom! Still,
Liz Gentry, his son's teacher, was no battle-ax,
and soon Todd started planning some
extracurricular activities of his own....

September 1998
A CLASSIC ENCOUNTER
by Emilie Richards

Doctor Chris Matthews was intelligent, sexy
and *very* good with his hands—which made
him all the more dangerous to single mom
Lizette St. Hilaire. So how long could she
resist Chris's special brand of TLC?

Available at your favorite retail outlet!

MEN AT WORK™

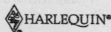 

Take 2 bestselling love stories FREE

Plus get a FREE surprise gift!

HARLEQUIN®

Temptation®

He's strong. He's sexy.
He's up for grabs!

Harlequin Temptation and
Texas Men magazine present:

1998 Mail Order Men

#691 THE LONE WOLF
by Sandy Steen—July 1998

#695 SINGLE IN THE SADDLE
by Vicki Lewis Thompson—August 1998

#699 SINGLE SHERIFF SEEKS...
by Jo Leigh—September 1998

#703 STILL HITCHED, COWBOY
by Leandra Logan—October 1998

#707 TALL, DARK AND RECKLESS
by Lyn Ellis—November 1998

#711 MR. DECEMBER
by Heather MacAllister—December 1998

Mail Order Men—
Satisfaction Guaranteed!

Available wherever Harlequin books are sold.

HARLEQUIN®

Makes any time special ™

Look us up on-line at: http://www.romance.net

HTEMOM

WHEN THINGS START TO HEAT UP
HIRE A BODYGUARD...

YOUR BODY IS OUR BUSINESS

Discreet, professional
protection

1-800-555-HERO

AND THEN IT GETS HOTTER!

There's a bodyguard agency in San Francisco where you can always find a HERO FOR HIRE, and the man of your sexiest fantasies.... Five of your favorite Temptation authors have just been there:

JOANN ROSS *1-800-HERO*
August 1998
KATE HOFFMANN *A BODY TO DIE FOR*
September 1998
PATRICIA RYAN *IN HOT PURSUIT*
October 1998
MARGARET BROWNLEY *BODY LANGUAGE*
November 1998
RUTH JEAN DALE *A PRIVATE EYEFUL*
December 1998

HERO FOR HIRE
A blockbuster miniseries.

Available at your favorite retail outlet.

HARLEQUIN®
Temptation

Look us up on-line at: http://www.romance.net   HTEHFH

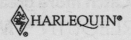

Not The Same Old Story!

 **PRESENTS®**

Exciting, glamorous romance stories that take readers around the world.

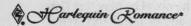 *Harlequin Romance®*

Sparkling, fresh and tender love stories that bring you pure romance.

 HARLEQUIN *Temptation.*

Bold and adventurous—Temptation is strong women, bad boys, great sex!

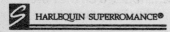 HARLEQUIN SUPERROMANCE®

Provocative and realistic stories that celebrate life and love.

 AMERICAN ROMANCE®

Contemporary fairy tales—where anything is possible and where dreams come true.

 HARLEQUIN® INTRIGUE®

Heart-stopping, suspenseful adventures that combine the best of romance and mystery.

LOVE & LAUGHTER™

Humorous and romantic stories that capture the lighter side of love.